RECKLESS KING

MAYA HUGHES

For my sisters and husband who've taken on so many projects and a to do list a mile long to help me share Heath and Kara with my amazing readers!

1

HEATH

Gritting my teeth, I pushed the dumbbell up over my head finishing my last rep. My muscles burned with that good ache, and I ran a towel over my face. The old gym equipment leeched metal into the air, so strong you could taste it. The weight room was packed with our last team workout session before the winter break.

My phone buzzed in my pocket, I tugged it out.

Colm: We've got five days off just before Christmas. Will everyone else be in town?

Emmett: Maybe...my parents have requested my presence, so I fly in from LAX on the 20th.

Me: Don't sound so happy about it, Em

Colm: Ford, Olivia and I are flying in on the 19th.

Ford: I might have to hang in Boston for an extra day

Colm: Don't even try to get out of it. If I'm stuck with Olivia for that entire trip, I'm going to need some backup.

Ford: Ok

Declan: You two are sitting right next to each other, aren't you?

Colm: Yes.

Ford: No

Ford: I'm sitting across from him

I shook my head. It had been that way with Ford and Colm since freshman year of high school.

Me: One of these days we'll find a doctor who can separate you two

Me: We can squeeze in a couple of friendlies

Me: The Kings reunited finally!

It had been almost three years since all five of us had been on the ice together. Once Ford and Colm had joined a team in Boston, they'd travelled non-stop. And Emmett hated coming back to town. His draft meant it was hard to get everyone into the same city, let alone the same room.

Emmett: I don't know if you'll be able to hold your own against us now.

Declan: Even though you're an NHL player now, I can still kick your ass on the ice

Middle finger emojis exploded from my phone and I laughed.

Readjusting for another set, I whipped around at the harsh sounds from the other side of the gym. The sharp clank of metal on metal wasn't someone dropping weights or screwing around. Bright overhead lights and the heated voices helped me pick out in an instant who was getting into it. It wasn't a hockey only weight session. Some of the football players were also working out, but these guys were definitely one of us.

Dropping my phone, I strode over to the posturing pair of freshmen. Some of the other guys from the team stood by gawking and letting Kaden and John go for each other's throats.

No one seemed ready to step in. I wasn't going to let this

come to blows. The tingling energy shot through my body—fight or flight at its finest. It was the same kind I got whenever people got aggressive off the ice. That, along with the pit in my stomach.

Jumping over the free weights dropped on the padded floor, I stepped between two of the newest members of the team as one raised his fist. Putting my hands on each of their chests, I pushed the two of them apart. John's fist barely missed the side of my head. My flare of anger burned so quickly and so brightly I slammed the lid shut on it.

Taking a breath, I kept myself calm. *Relax.* The anger wouldn't solve anything. It only made things worse and got people hurt.

My palms pressed against their sweat-soaked T-shirts. Their eyes both snapped to me. They were all flared nostrils, bared teeth, aggression mode. My body hummed, and I forced myself to remain calm. Freshmen trying to show off. They'd been digging at each other during practices. Most people didn't notice, but I saw their little attempts to fuck with each other.

"Chill out. What is going on with you two?" I kept my voice low and even. Making this into a big thing and embarrassing them was only going to get them more riled up. The last thing I wanted was someone to throw another punch and screw up our team dynamic.

"Kaden got us both pulled out of the game last week because he couldn't keep his eye on the puck." John jabbed an angry finger toward the other. I used my body to block his advance.

"Maybe if he hadn't been trying to fucking showboat and run the play, it wouldn't have been a problem." Kaden leaned in, shooting his own accusation back at John.

I wrapped my hand around their shirts, so I had two fists

of fabric in my grasp. "Did we win that game?" I glanced between the two of them.

"Yes," they mumbled in unison, dropping their eyes.

"Do you know why you two freshmen were allowed off the bench in the first place?"

They both glared at me.

"It's not because you are both so amazing that we benched the entire starting lineup to give you your chance to shine. It's because we were up by five goals and two of their starters were winded from working their asses off and not coming back out."

Their shoulders slumped as I laid it all out for them. The Kings and I never fought. Never even thought of raising a fist to one another, unless it was a mad dash for the last beer.

"I'm not saying you two aren't good, you wouldn't be on the team if you weren't, but you were out there to get some experience on the ice in a game against another team having a shitty day. You were given the chance to show what you can become with more practice and teamwork. If you two are squaring off against each other because of a play that didn't even matter, then you're not going to cut it on this team."

I let go of their shirts, and they both reached to smooth them out, no longer ready to charge each other.

"This is not how a team behaves. He's your brother when you're on the ice and training together. No fighting." One of them opened his mouth, but I didn't let him cut in.

"That doesn't mean you can't disagree or call him out on his shit, but there's no reason for you to put your hands on him. You save that for the opposing team." My jaw was tight.

They nodded back glumly.

"That's where you funnel that bad juju. Save it for the

game. You two are done. Get out of here. Enjoy your break and don't get in any fights."

"But I—" Kaden tried to jump in.

"You're done. Go home. We have a game in a few days, rest up. Don't fight. Stay safe."

I dismissed the two of them, surprised that they'd listened to me and no one else had contradicted me. I half-expected Preston, our team captain, to show up and tell me off for making the freshman leave, but everyone else kept on going with their workouts like nothing had happened. As my blood pounded in my veins, I glanced down at my hands that were balled up into fists.

With a jolt, I relaxed them and took a breath, calming that flare of anger that tried to peek its ugly head up at their disruption. The gym was where we worked together to be better at what we did, not fight like idiots. I forced myself to relax my jaw. They were cool, everyone was chill. The earlier chill I'd hit working out was gone, edged out by their little fight. I hated it when things like this got to me. I never knew what might set me off and it scared me. I hated it.

I needed to sweat this out and push my muscles to the max. That was always a surefire way to burn up any feelings I didn't want to deal with. Sweat them out through pain and pressure.

Walking back across the gym to the bench press, I sat down as the doors to the gym burst open and Declan strode in, making a beeline straight for me. He'd been getting in some drills on the ice, making up for lost time after being benched in the pre-season. At least he was back and I didn't have to worry about skating without him during the season.

I lay down on the bench and adjusted my grip on the metal bar above me. Declan stepped around the top of the bench and spotted me without me saying a word. Pushing the bar up, I adjusted my grip, the muscles in my arms bunching and tightening to support the weight. Declan's hands hovered just under the bar as I controlled the descent, bending my elbows before pushing it back up.

"How'd it go?" I kept the reps going, pushing myself harder.

"Better than the torture sessions you put me through."

"I'm getting you ready for the draft."

He scoffed.

"Maybe I should add another thirty onto the bar if that's the way you feel." I quirked an eyebrow at him and kept going. Declan and I were the only Kings sticking with college the whole way through.

"How are your grades this semester?" I squirted some water into my mouth and slid down to the floor with my back pressed against the wall.

"Smooth sailing. Do you really think Mak would let me slack off? Plus, if I'm already playing and I flunk anything, I'd fuck over our entire season. Don't worry. I've got senior year locked down. What about you?"

"I've got two requirements left and that's it. Some other fluff classes and I'm good."

"Our winter schedule is brutal. I'm glad I finished all my classes for my major already."

"Did you?"

Sweat poured off his face and drenched his shirt. "I'll be fine. I was cutting it close, but I did like to live on the wild side."

I waggled my eyebrows at him, and he chucked his water bottle at my head. I batted it away and stood. "What the hell was that for?"

Declan shrugged and got up off the floor. Walking over to the leg press, I set up the weights.

"No teachers you're looking to seduce to make sure you pass?"

I rolled my eyes. "You're such a dick."

"What? I'm just saying, maybe you can find a nice hot professor to give you a private class, then it's all taken care of."

Guilt soured my stomach. I'd made that mistake once. Fucked over someone's entire life because I'd been determined to reach an unattainable prize.

"Would you shut up?" I climbed onto the leg press.

"I mean, I'm not saying she wasn't hot. Damn, she was so hot. You never gave us all the details about what happened." Declan stood beside me like he was lost inside a fond memory. Maybe it was for him, had been for me too once, but I'd seen how gossip and innuendo could destroy things.

"Drop it," I bit out, so sharply a few people turned to look.

Declan held up his hands in surrender. "Forget I said anything." We swapped out reps in silence for a while.

"It's been too long since we've seen everyone at once," I said through a sharp exhale I timed to push the weighted platform with my legs. My thighs and calves burned.

"Too long." Declan stood near my head, ready to catch the bar if I dropped it.

My arms shook as I finished the last set of reps. As the weight got harder to push up, my limit came into clear focus. I shot the bar back into the cradle of the bench press and sat up, sweat rolling down my forehead. I wiped my face with my sleeve.

There was a vibrating beside me, and I checked my phone. Declan shoved his hand into his shorts pocket and tugged out his phone.

"Hey." He listened for a moment. "You don't have to do

that. Dude, why do you always do this?" Declan frowned and threw his hands up.

"Fine. We can do a Kings-only game and then another with the Knights. They'll freak if they get to skate with you three. Sound good?"

Declan held up his hand for a high five and ended the call.

"Emmett says he's in. We'll be able to play twice at the stadium—he's arranging it and he also wants to have a big night out with everyone. He said he's paying, and that's the only way he'll come."

I rolled my eyes. Emmett loved to throw his money around. Not in anyone's faces, but it was almost like he didn't think we'd want to hang out with him if he wasn't making it rain 24/7.

"At least he agreed to come back. It's got to be almost a year now since he's been back for more than a day or two." Declan lay down and started his reps.

"I know. He's still letting the Avery-thing get to his head."

The ghosts of relationships past still rode Emmett hard, even after four years.

"I think I know the perfect bar for us to head to after. It opened a few months ago, I've heard good things."

"Perfect. Do you think they'll mind twenty hockey players taking over the place?" Declan sat up, and we both got down on the ground, pushing ourselves out into plank position before shooting up and jumping as high as we could.

"I'm sure having a few NHL athletes with us, we can swing some tables."

We finished our workout and grabbed our bags. Declan wanted to shower there so he could head straight out with Makenna, his official girlfriend now. Still boggled my mind.

Of everyone, I'd have thought Declan would be the last one to get a girlfriend—let alone Makenna Halstead.

They'd been official for a couple months but together longer than that; they hadn't wanted to admit it. She'd gone home for Christmas, and he was going through withdrawal since they'd been separated for more than a couple days. He was also a pain in the ass when we traveled for away games she couldn't come to.

We pushed open the gym doors, and with a puff of frozen air streaking behind him, he was off to see her. Someone was ready to load up on all the Mak loving he could get.

The guys had taken to giving him shit over it, but it was cool. Declan had always been so dead set on not being with someone, he could have missed out on something awesome with her.

I made it home and grabbed a beer out of the fridge. I'd had to hide my craft beers I'd driven up to Connecticut to get from a microbrewery in an empty oversize carton of kale chips I'd found behind one of the sororities.

I'd made that trip after the last home game we lost. I'd spent what seemed like half the game in the sin bin with one penalty after another. It was like the ref had been gunning for me. I'd hopped in the car afterward and driven for hours.

It was that or I was going to take my hockey stick to every breakable surface near me. Those instances scared the shit out of me. The ones where it seemed too easy to let loose and give into the urge to break shit. Getting on the road in the middle of the night and letting the streetlights wash over me, calmed me down when I was ready to lose it.

The ass crack of dawn sunlight had come streaming into the car, and I was in the parking lot of a place I'd read about a while back. I'd grabbed a few six-packs and taken them back to the house, hiding them for safekeeping.

It was the only way to keep Declan from destroying the beer in less than a day. Cracking a bottle open, I sat on the couch and flipped on the TV.

The guys got on me for whoring around, but they never were that observant off the ice. I might have had women flocking to me, but I wasn't falling into bed with whoever. Maybe it was because of the flocking. I needed something different. I needed a challenge, and those had been in short supply.

Letting the muscle fatigue set in and banish the energy vibrating through my body was one of the few times I could sit and relax. I told people to do it all the time, but it seemed impossible for me sometimes. Calm on the outside, but inside the turmoil was always there. Exhaustion took the edge off the constant energy humming through me. I wasn't beat or even that tired, but I wasn't wired like before. The mellow high came when I really pushed myself. When I skated so hard my legs were like Jell-O and I could barely remember my name. That's when shit got weird. Those were the nights I was up on a roof or lying on the grass gazing up at the stars, wondering what the hell this place is and trying to make myself a part of something bigger.

Transported to a place where kids didn't get the shit beaten out of them and moms didn't have to throw themselves in front of a punch or a kick.

I'd stare up into the sky or down at one of my plants, and I'd switch into universe mode. Pondering my own mortality and the meaning of life were a hell of a lot safer than worrying about the person I feared lived inside me. The person I was on the ice where no one got in my way. The man who decided to take out any problem or failing in his life with his fists. The man I never wanted to be and who I feared had been beaten into me over the years.

The cold fingers of dread that crept in when it was too quiet or I was alone sent me looking for a distraction. It was too cold to sit up on the roof. I threw my jacket on and walked the short distance to the greenhouse on campus.

Swiping my ID card, I swung open the door. The earthy scent mixed with fragrant flowers and a watery spray filled my lungs. The tightness in my muscles ebbed away.

One of the other seniors stood beside the potting bench.

"Hey, Heath," Felix called out and pushed his glasses up with the back of his gloved hands.

"Hey. What's up?" I walked along a row of flowering plants.

"Nothing much, planting some new foxglove before the semester starts. What about you?"

"Needed to check on my newest growth." I grabbed my gloves and notebook from my shelf in the back.

"They were looking good last I looked." Felix dropped some more soil into a terracotta pot.

My ears perked up. Working over the summer, I'd had a slew of unsuccessful attempts at a flowering plant cross-breed. Declan thought I was crazy to even go for this major, but I'd always loved watching things grow. Helping them along on their journey to something that could feed you, help or heal you, or give someone a smile with a flower; and if you were really good, it could do more than one of those things.

"Why are you here so late? I figured you'd be out on a hot date or something?"

"Nah, I'm not into dating during the season. Too much of a distraction." I stepped in front of my plants. They were doing exactly as he'd said. The purples and pinks melded together with some sunset yellows. Unusual for sure, but no less stunning.

After checking on some of the other pots, I took off my gloves and jotted down some notes.

"I'm heading out, Heath. Have a good one, and I'm glad to see you guys killing it this season." Felix tugged on his hat with flaps covering his ears.

"Thanks, man. That's what happens when you have the most kick-ass captain in the division cracking the whip." I let out a chuckle. "Where are you off to?"

"Hot date!" Felix shrugged with his hands wrapped around his messenger bag strap. "What can I say? The ladies can't keep their hands off me." He backed away, tugging at his multicolored wool sweater.

"Have fun! Not too much fun!" I called out as he walked past the rows of other plants. Felix was a good guy. We'd been in the program together since we'd declared our majors back at the end of sophomore year, and he'd never treated me like a dumb jock.

"You know me, man. I'm a wild animal!" he yelled. The door closed behind him, and I laughed, finishing up with my notes and putting everything back in its place.

Leaving the greenhouse, I was still restless, which meant TV time. Nothing like some mind-numbingly familiar scenes to push uneasy thoughts aside.

In a few months, I'd probably be playing in the NHL after years of hard work and dedication, but right now I needed a little '80s movie therapy. I flicked the channel, and like the universe knew exactly what I needed, the movie I'd watched a hundred times filled the screen. Saturday detention. A library. Judd Nelson and Molly Ringwald. Hell yeah, *The Breakfast Club*.

2

KARA

Like a twenty-pound weight had been lifted off my chest, I walked down the street to the house after my exam. The freezing December air whipped around me, and I stared up at the sky. It smelled like snow. The icy patches on the ground were dotted with slushy brown piles of no-longer snow. We were supposed to get another dusting soon. I hoped it would cover the sad piles.

Some people were putting their decorations up outside even though the holiday was almost upon us. Christmas time was always so magical, and I loved it when everything stayed up at least until New Years.

Every single question on the exam had been a piece of cake. It should have been after how long I'd studied. I'd missed out on our annual family baking extravaganza to lock myself away in my room and make sure I did well on the exam that determined whether I'd be eligible for the fellowship to fund my PhD.

The exam gods had smiled down on me. There was a small part of me that worried I'd made a mistake. *Was it really that easy? Had Stevenson gotten sloppy and lobbed us a meatball?* I whipped out my phone and sent a group text.

Me: Was it me or was that exam kind of easy?

Charles: You.

Anne: You!

Sam: YOU!

I cringed. I'd left a little early, so I hadn't gotten to do the post-exam recap with everyone else.

Me: Okay, sorry!

Sam: If you didn't have such a kind heart and I didn't know for a fact that you studied about twenty-five hours a day, I'd really hate you right now.

Me: Sorry. It wasn't easy, it really sucked, and I hope I passed.

Sam: Don't worry, we'll drink away our sorrows in the bar car of the train.

Wincing, I opened the front door to the house. Asking if an exam was too easy wasn't how to make and keep friends. Note to self, don't bring up ease of an exam until you've polled at least two other people who've taken it. At least I could finally relax. My exam in the spring semester wouldn't be too much harder, and I had months before that one. The fellowship committee would have made their decision by then. Maybe, just maybe, I could take my foot off the gas a little.

I headed upstairs to my room. My footsteps were nearly silent, sinking into the plush carpet.

"How'd it go?"

The booming, happy voice made me jump.

I stopped short and backtracked to the office doorway. Dad sat in his ergonomic chair with the big computer screens in front of him. I wrapped my hands around the strap of my bag and bounced on the balls of my feet.

"It went really well. I knew every answer she was looking for, and I finished a little early. But I'm worried I might have screwed up and missed something. It seemed too easy."

Dad stood and leaned against the other side of the doorway.

"When are you going to have a little confidence in yourself? I have no doubt in my mind that you did a great job, Kara." He tapped me on the tip of my nose like he'd done since the first day I'd arrived. The little *boop* when he crouched down in front of me when I stood in the doorway with my death grip on my bag of clothes had been the first thing to make me smile in a long time. Still worked now.

I glanced down at my shoes and picked at my thumbnail. "You're right. I'm sure I did a great job." I smiled, and Dad wrapped his arms around me for a big, warm hug.

"One of these days you'll say it like you mean it. There was some mail for you, and I put it on your desk." He let me go, and the front door banged open.

"Looks like your mom and sister are home. Better go run and hide or they'll catch you." He grinned, and I laughed before snapping my lips shut and glancing at the two of them bringing in mountains of empty cookie tins. Dad and I exchanged looks.

"Run for your life," he whispered. I tiptoed down the hallway and made it to my room right at the soft *click* of his office door closing. Gently closing mine behind me, I rested my head against the white wood. Hiding out in here wouldn't work for long. Once Mom and Lauren knew I was home and my big exam over with, they'd be all over me to help. Last year I was finding bits of cookie dough and sprinkles in my bed until January.

It was times like these I wished I'd gotten an apartment close to campus like most twenty-three-year-old college graduates. But standing at my door and taking stock of my room, I knew it was mostly a lie. I loved being home. Loved my room and my family. It was my chance to soak up everything I'd missed out on for most of my childhood.

Sometimes they coddled me and wanted to do silly family things, and while some people chafed at that, I reveled in it. The protective parent shtick was a hell of a lot better than *I don't give a shit about you*. I dropped my bag and spotted the envelopes on my desk.

Grabbing the stack, I plopped down on my bed and riffled through them. My brain had finally stopped swimming now that my exam was over, and I itched to pick up my pen and grab the composition book I'd stashed in my nightstand. Those nights when I was so restless I couldn't concentrate, I'd grab it and pour my thoughts out on page after page. There were over a hundred of those stashed away in my closet.

Somehow, writing in a notebook was different than on the computer. The words I wrote in the black and white speckled books weren't real. Doodles, certainly not me pouring my heart and soul out onto the page. Becoming a writer wasn't something I could do. I'd seen what happened when people went down that path, and it wasn't for me.

I turned the last envelope over and gasped at the handwriting scrawled across the front. *Kara Ellis* with our address underneath. Return address confirmed exactly what I'd known the second I saw the familiar scrawl handwriting all over the front. *Angie Ellis*. My mom. My biological mother. I shot up, my feet landing hard on the floor with a *thud* as the letter floated to the soft carpet.

I stood at the edge of my bed, staring down at the envelope for who knows how long. My hand shook as I picked it up. The outside was a little damp like it had gotten wet and dried out again. I slid my finger under the flap, tearing through the paper.

I hadn't heard from my biological mom in almost five years. It had been my high school graduation, and she'd showed up bombed out of her mind. The shame and embarrassment that dug its claws into my stomach on that day had been something I'd never forget. I'd been there with Carla, Mike, and Lauren, taking pictures with my honor roll sashes draped around my shoulders, when I'd seen her from the corner of my eye.

Like everything had been plunged underwater, I'd watched her approach us. It was my nightmare come to life, but I hadn't known what to do about it. The other kids and their parents had snapped shots, and their joyful, non-slurred words of congratulations had swirled like a tornado around me, sucking the air from my lungs.

Her steps had faltered as she strode toward us. With her arms spread wide, nearly spilling out of her too tight and too short dress, she'd laid a wet kiss on my cheek. The stench of booze had wafted over me and made my eyes water. I'd stood stock straight, not hugging her back but frozen as I'd warred between bursting into tears, shoving her off, and running away.

Other kids and their parents had tried not to stare, but her voice carried across the pristinely manicured field. The smell of freshly mowed grass, balloons, and expensive perfume had hung in the air before she'd arrived, then it had only smelled like vodka. Cheap vodka that might make you blind. Blinking back my tears as she let me go, I'd staggered back into the safety of my mom and dad.

They had been gracious and so nice, even inviting her to come to the family dinner with us. I'd asked to have a word with her privately and told her in no uncertain terms was she going to go.

I'd told her I didn't want to see her again. She'd stared at me like a stranger, and that's exactly what I wanted to be to her. Someone she remembered knowing a long time ago but never wanted to see again. That's how I felt about her.

It seemed like she'd taken what I'd said to heart. Before that day, she'd pop up every so often to embarrass me. She'd turned up at my science fair and tipped over my booth on solar-powered solutions for providing potable water. With a *sorry* she'd tried to smooth things over like she always did.

But I hadn't seen her since graduation. There'd been a few voicemails on my old phone that she'd cleaned herself up, but that was something I'd heard for my entire childhood. More likely she would tell herself she'd only have one more drink, one more night out, one more party and then she'd stop. Only one more time and then she'd be on the straight and narrow.

With trembling hands I unfolded the four sheets of lined paper.

Kara,

There are a lot of people I need to make amends to in my life, but none of them more so than you, my wonderful daughter. That's probably why I've left this letter for so long. I've been sober for nearly three years now. It took a lot to get me to this place and I wish I could say I did it because I wanted to be a better mom to you, but that would be a lie.

I had a chance to be a better mother to you. I had so many chances, and I let them slip through my fingers. I let you slip through my fingers. I wanted you to know how proud I am of you. I found someone to get me a program from your graduation, and I saw the pictures of you online. Magna cum laude. Even though I was sober when you graduated, I thought it would be best if I stayed away. I wished I could take some of the credit for how you turned out, but I know that was all you and the family who gave you so much more than I could.

I know I don't have any right to ask, but would you want to——

I couldn't read any farther. The pounding in my chest made my hands shake harder, and the pages flittered to the floor. I sank, leaning against my bed. I was being sucked down a rabbit hole to a past I'd rather forget.

Snatching the letter off the floor, I opened the small drawer in my desk and shoved it in there. It was a cobra ready to strike.

Those few pieces of paper managed to rip apart the happiness I'd had only a few minutes ago. The happy life I'd created here. The fantasy that Mike and Carla had raised me from birth—that someone had set me in their arms when I was a baby, and things were as they'd always been. That I'd had their love and support from day one and had never known what it was like to go to bed afraid my mom might not come home or worse, she'd come home with someone terrible.

A shudder shot through me. It had only happened once, when I was ten. I'd woken up groggy and probably hungover. When my stomach hurt so bad from hunger, sometimes I'd find Angie's stash and hope I'd pass out until school the next day, so I could get something to eat. But that night I'd woken up, and there'd been a guy looming over me in my bed, his hand on my thigh. Screaming so loud my own ears rang, I'd darted around him and locked myself in the bathroom.

Shaking and crying, I'd curled myself up in a ball in the bathtub, scrubbing at the spot on my leg where he'd touched me. There was a lot of yelling and screaming on the other side of the door. Loud thumps made me bury my face in my knees. And then there was silence. Somehow the silence had been scarier than the yelling. There was a soft knock on the door, and my mom's voice on the other side.

Reluctantly, I'd climbed out of the bath and unlocked the door, cracking it open only a little bit. My mom had sported a nice shiner under her eye. She let me know she'd kicked him out and that she was sorry. Coaxing me out of the bathroom, she sat beside my bed with her hand wrapped around mine.

Her words of reassurance and apologies had lulled me to sleep. I'd thought maybe things would change. Maybe she'd seen how bad things could be when she did what she did, but I woke up the next morning, and she wasn't there. And she hadn't turned up for nearly a week. So much for that.

There was a gentle knock at my door, and I slammed the desk drawer shut and whipped around.

"Hey, Kara. I heard your test went well?" Mom poked her head in my room.

"It went really well." I plastered on a smile.

Mom opened the door all the way. She already had her apron on, and the Christmas music drifted up the stairs from the kitchen. She didn't let up on Christmas mode until after the first. These are the memories I should have had all my life. This was the life I'd dreamed of having. Bringing Angie into this wasn't what I needed. Bringing her up would only put a damper on the holidays, and I didn't want Mom or Dad to think that I wanted anything to do with my biological mother. After everything they'd done for me, it would be a slap in the face.

Maybe after New Year's I'd bring it up. *Maybe.*

"Are you going to come help with cookies or were you

going out to celebrate your big test finishing?" She raised her fists in the air like she was shaking pom-poms. As much as I enjoyed cutting out cookies until it felt like my hands would fall off, I needed to get out of the house. Gazing back at the desk, I had to go somewhere and unwind.

"I'm going to head out with friends. We are still trying to decide where we are going."

"Okay, I'm glad." She held her hand to her chest and let out a sigh of relief. "You can't stay cooped up in this house all the time."

"I love being cooped up in this house."

She rolled her eyes. "I was in college, too, once, and living at home was not my idea of fun at all. Not that we don't love that you're here after you were in Boston for undergrad, but I think you need to have some fun."

"I'm plenty fun. Remember over the summer when I was gone for a whole week."

She pursed her lips and shot me a look. "I hardly consider a weeklong trip with Habitat for Humanity to be a wild and adventurous time."

"I learned how to use a nail gun. I'd say anyone who put one of those in my hands is all about living dangerously." I stuck my tongue out at her, and she laughed.

"Have fun and I'm so proud of you." She wrapped her arms around me and squeezed me tight before heading back downstairs.

Grabbing my phone off my bed, I sent a message to the group.

Me: Are you guys still going out tonight?

I really didn't feel like going to New York. Why couldn't they stay local? Philly had tons of awesome bars.

Sam: We are on our way to party town!

Anne: Train pulled away like 15 mins ago.

Damn it, well there went that idea.

Me: Awesome, I hope you guys have fun!

Charles: What's up?

Me: Nothing, I wanted to make sure you guys were on your way and hadn't dropped dead in the parking lot after the exam.

Sam: Nothing can keep me from the party! Not even failing the hardest exam I've ever taken.

I envisioned Sam standing in the middle of the aisle of the train, dancing to her heart's content while she typed that message. Maybe it was for the best I'd missed the train.

Charles: She's being a tad dramatic.

Sam: Am not!

Me: Aren't you all on the train together?

Anne: Yes. I'm sitting between them trying to keep the peace.

Charles: Sam is the most amazing woman I've ever met and she's part of the reason I'm bi. It's all because I really want a chance at her.

Charles: Damn it, Sam! How in the hell do you type so fast? I swear, she got the phone away from me for like 3 seconds.

I laughed and shook my head. At least if I went out on my own, there would be no pressure to stay out forever and keep drinking. A celebratory drink. I didn't drink too much. Being drunk off your ass more times than I could count as a preteen had left a bit of a sour taste in my mouth when it came to most booze. It also meant I could hold my liquor, not that I planned on a wild night out.

Maybe not one drink. Maybe two, some tasty bar snacks and then back home, get into my pajamas, and tomorrow would be a new day.

Throwing on the most passable going-out outfit I had, I checked my hair in the mirror. The best part about the winter was the low humidity. My wavy black locks turned into a poof ball of gigantic proportions during the summer, which meant I usually kept it braided or in a bun, but in the winter, I could let it breathe a little. Plus, my hair was an extra barrier between the frigid temps. Ear protection to boot.

I toyed with the purple and pink strands that had escaped from my careful tuck. This is what I got for trusting Sam and her suspicious whispers last time I was at the hairdresser. The colors weren't too noticeable, but if I had my hair up or the light caught it right, you could see the streaks there. *Semi*-permanent dye, my ass! The color was holding on tighter than Sam to the leg of that Henry Cavill-lookalike.

I zipped up my ankle boots and got my jacket on, giving myself another once-over in the mirror. *You've got this, Kara. A night out on your own is better than sitting at home and wallowing in self-pity.* Today was a day for celebration, and I'd do it on my own terms. Ordering a taxi, I popped into the kitchen to give Mom and Lauren a kiss and a hug and then hopped into the car.

We pulled up in front of The Bramble, a new bar in Fishtown. What had once been a run-down area was now thriving with awesome bars, cool restaurants, and a lot of foot traffic. I'd read an article about the bar a while ago, and I'd been looking for the perfect time to check it out. Apparently their bacon cheeseburger with onion relish was legendary already. This was the third location in the US. LA and NYC got the first two spots.

Shaking the doubts from my head, I stepped out of the taxi. The wind whipped my hair around my head. Maybe I should have put it up. Closing the door, I took a tentative step toward the entrance

I opened the door, and a flood of noise threatened to bowl me over. Second to that was the delicious smell of so much food. My mouth watered and my stomach rumbled. I hadn't had anything to eat since breakfast. Glancing over my shoulder, I was blinded as my hair smacked me in my face. I grabbed the hair tie around my wrist and put my hair up.

The place was packed, as you'd imagine, but half of the bar seemed to be taken over by a rowdy bunch to one side. They sat at the tables, laughing and joking together. I hesitated. Maybe a different place would be a better choice.

My gaze skimmed across the crowd until it stopped on the one guy standing at those tables. My chest hitched as my gaze locked with his bright blue eyes. His tousled blond hair was mussed enough. The kind where you knew he hadn't spent hours in front of the mirror trying to get it right. It was the kind from a guy who'd been out running or, if it weren't freezing out, I'd have said had spent the day at the beach.

The flutters in my stomach made my knees weak. I locked them so I didn't melt into a puddle right there. Why the hell was Mr. Hottie looking at me? *Please don't let there be a freaking booger in my nose or something.*

Breaking the momentary connection, I stepped all the way in, getting out of the way of someone else coming in the door. I grabbed a spot at the bar, and the bartender plopped a menu down in front of me. Not trusting myself to steal a glance over my shoulder, I shrugged off my jacket and laid it across my lap.

A couple drinks and some delicious food. And don't ogle the guy behind you who makes you feel like you've been strapped into a roller coaster.

That's it.

3

HEATH

The bar wasn't too packed yet. It was still early for most people, but Declan and I had come right from our late afternoon workout. It wasn't required, but we needed this season to be perfect. No more missteps.

I checked my phone and opened the email before it even fully loaded. My dean was the least organized and most forgetful one out of the whole university.

"I finally got my schedule," I said to no one in particular.

"Really? I got mine, like, a month ago." Declan craned his neck to look at my phone.

"Lucky you," I grumbled, and the email finally opened.

It was less than a week before the new semester started, and I still hadn't gotten my amended class schedule. Nerves were getting to me. I'd already had to change classes three times because there were some professors who didn't care why you missed class they wouldn't budge on attendance requirements. Like getting our hockey team to the national championships four times in a row wasn't a major accomplishment and good for the school. Maybe I should have stuck with kinesiology like the rest of the team.

A distinctly feminine and scarily familiar voice called out Mak's name.

Mak, sitting beside Declan, whirled around in her seat and hopped up. "Avery!"

Shit! Our early crew all skidded to a halt the second the new arrival showed up at our table. Everyone's heads snapped up, and their eyes got wide, including mine.

Mak rushed over and hugged Avery. Totally forgot those two were friends. I glanced out the door she'd come through and back down at my phone, checking the time. Emmett would be here any minute.

I stared at Declan, and he looked at me like he was watching a car about to get demolished by a train.

"What are you doing here?" Mak dragged Avery over to our table.

"I was leaving the bakery and I saw your car parked in the lot."

I glanced down at her open coat with a thin layer of flour dusted on her clothes.

Mak squeezed her arm. "Stay and have some drinks."

Avery glanced around at the rest of us, and the blood drained out of her face when she spotted me and Declan and the empty chairs at the section of the bar we'd taken over. She quickly checked over her shoulder.

"I don't think that would be a good idea. I'm beat and I have to be back at the ass crack of dawn for the morning rush. I've got to go." Her words were fast and frantic.

"Avery, come on. One drink." Mak held on to her hand and tried to get her to sit down. Avery looked like she was a second from gnawing her own hand off to escape. With what was brewing, I didn't blame her one bit.

"Seriously, Mak, we can do a girls' night some other time. Alyson's at home, and I'm super tired." Avery slipped her hand out of Mak's grip, using her little sister as the perfect out. Peeking over her shoulder, she backed up. "Call me, and I'll make sure I get the day off, but I've got to go. Bye."

I swore there was a trail of fire etched into the bar floor as she beelined it out of there.

"Avery!" Mak called out to her, but she was already gone. Declan and I let out a sigh of relief.

Declan tugged Mak's shirt. "Books, calm down. It's probably for the best anyway."

She frowned and sat. "Because of Emmett?"

"Yeah, because of Emmett. Not many guys want to hang out with the chick who cheated on them." I tipped back my beer, and Mak reached across the table and yanked it out of my mouth. Beer sprayed all over me and the table. She slammed my drink down, spilling even more.

"What the hell?" I grabbed some napkins to mop it up.

"You have no idea what happened between those two, so don't you ever say that about her again." She looked ready to climb over the table and slam my head into it.

I held my hands up in surrender and shot Declan a look. "Fine. I won't say another word."

Declan whispered in her ear, and they had some back and forth in the chairs beside me. With Mak around a lot more, and her friendship with Avery, it was only a matter of time before Emmett and Avery crossed paths.

A couple of minutes later the wave of laughter and loud-ass voices let everyone know the party had arrived. Emmett headed up the mob. Ford and Colm showed up with Grant, Ford's little brother, and Olivia, Colm's little sister.

The group grew minute-by-minute. Some of Emmett's

teammates were there. All the Kings and some of the guys from our team, The Knights, showed up too.

Every eye in the bar was on us, but that wasn't unusual when you hung with a crew like this. There were more than a few wide eyes and autograph requests once word got out there were NHL players here. Even if they were going up against the Flyers, at least no one threw anything at the group.

The drinks flowed and plates of food were on a constant conveyor belt out to our table. For every two wiped-clean plates collected from the table, another five appeared. This was an over-exercised athlete's dream.

The door to the bar swung open, and a sharp December chill flooded in. But it wasn't the cold snap in the bar that caught my attention, it was the vision standing in the door-way. Her weight shifted from foot to foot like she was trying to decide if she should come all the way in or not. I hadn't even realized I was on my feet until I caught the weird looks from the rest of the table. I didn't care. My gaze returned to her. It wasn't just the way she looked. She was gorgeous, a little on the taller side, maybe five-eight, five-nine, which was fine with me. I was almost six-three, so the taller the better. I hated the crick I got in my neck when I kissed a girl who hit me mid-chest. She had a small beauty mark on her left cheek and wavy black hair she'd done one of those messy knot things with that I couldn't wait to unravel.

Her eyes darted around the room in a way that told me she wasn't there with anyone and she probably wasn't waiting on anyone. She was putting on her brave face and going out on her own. I appreciated that. Don't wait for other people to do your own thing; go for it, even if it was all alone.

A steely look of certainty passed over her face. She'd

made the decision. Committed to coming in even if I saw the bubbles of uncertainty under the surface. Taking a determined step through the doorway, she let the door close behind her while her eyes skimmed the crowd. Like she knew I was looking, her gaze locked on to mine. My hand tightened around my beer. The cool glass did nothing to stop the rising heat one look from her gave me.

Her dark brown eyes made me think of a warm cup of hot chocolate on a blistery night. She dropped her eyes, but I couldn't tear my gaze away. Her yellow scarf and the dark pinks and purples in her hair reminded me of my flowers. It was a subtle color, like she wasn't trying to be flashy or showy, maybe doing it for herself.

The door closed behind her, and the tension I'd had in my back released when I knew I wasn't going to have to chase her down the street like a lunatic...any more of a lunatic than I already was, because I knew in a split second she was the one I was taking home tonight.

"Dude, what are you doing?" Declan grabbed onto the sleeve of my shirt and tugged me back down into my seat.

"I thought I saw someone I knew," I said, absently.

"Hmmm, more like someone you want to know." Mak laughed and craned her neck to get a better look.

But there was a time to go for it and there was a time to back off. She was sending out back-off vibes so strong they threatened to shift the tectonic plates of singledom underneath the bar. She needed to relax, and I needed to enjoy my time with my friends while we were all together.

The mini tacos, ribs, everything was so good I think there was a solid ten minutes when no one at our table made a sound other than grunts of appreciation. After the workouts everyone's hunger pangs hit hard and fast. This food had our normally rowdy group nearly silent while they shoveled their mouths full. I wanted to wrap myself up in a tortilla and not leave the place until I'd put on at least a few hundred pounds.

"It looks like you have an admirer," Colm piped up, his gray eyes twinkling with amusement as the server dropped off a drink for me and pointed to a woman who waved from the corner.

"Seriously? Out of everyone here she picks you." Emmett shook his head.

"What's wrong with me?" I lifted my drink, choked down the super-sweet concoction, and slid the empty glass away from me. It was easier to accept the drink rather than try to return it. So much easier. I'd learned that lesson the hard way. I'd rather drink it than have it thrown back in my face. I'd learned in high school that I got a certain type of attention.

"I mean nothing, if you go for that California guy, surfer-dude look. Me, I'm more partial to the dark and curly-haired guys." Mak shook her shoulders and Declan kissed her on the forehead.

I hadn't even been in the ocean since my mom and I had left our house in the middle of night under the cover of darkness and driven nearly five days straight to the East Coast.

"Declan's mad because ever since we won our first State Championship freshman year at Rittenhouse Prep, they had my picture front and center in the paper." I chucked a wad of napkins at Declan's head.

"They cut my face in half!" Declan slammed his beer down.

"Poor baby." Colm laughed and took a sip of his drink. "And all those girls were there to mop up your tears. Not as many as there were lining up for Heath, but still." A fry bounced off Colm's forehead and landed in his glass.

"What can I say? I'm irresistible." I gulped down my beer.

I would never say walking up to a woman and knowing there was an eighty percent chance you could walk out of there with her wasn't a rush, but I preferred a challenge. Or at least someone who wasn't going to tackle her way through three of her friends to get to me. Someone who wasn't a pushover and knew her own mind was exactly the kind of woman I was after.

"Holy shit, can I have your autograph?" Everyone turned to see the beaming woman bouncing on the balls of her feet beside Emmett's chair at the end of the table.

"Sure." Emmett reached for her paper and pen, but she snatched them back.

"I...I didn't mean you. I wanted to get Blanch's." She held out her paper toward an oblivious Ford. Ford's head whipped up.

"Me?" The words were halfway between a croak and a choke as beer sputtered out of his mouth.

"Definitely. I saw the goal you saved in the last game. It was intense, I don't think I've ever seen a goalie get back in the net so fast and make a save like that. It was amazing." She stared at him like he'd hung the stars and his cheeks burned a bright red under the beard. I was surprised he didn't keel over. He was the perfect wingman for Colm because he never said much. Stood there and looked all huggable, which was the senior superlative he'd missed out on in high school. Most Huggable. We'd had a field day with that one. He quickly scrawled his name and ducked his head as she went screaming back to her friends that she'd gotten Ford Blanchard's signature.

"Dude, better get used to it." Colm clamped his hand onto Ford's shoulder as he grumbled something and went back to his food.

The guys were rowdy as ever. Rowdy but not destructive. Burning off some excess energy during the few days off was even better when you had a patron like Emmett bankrolling the whole thing. While everyone had been focusing on Ford, Emmett had slyly slid his credit card to the guy behind the bar and gestured to our motley crew that had taken over half the bar.

Plunking down in the chair across from me, he rolled his eyes when I smirked at him. Ford and Colm had only agreed to the night if they all split the bill.

"Don't say anything." He pursed his lips, knowing I'd spotted him.

"What? I'm not going to say anything." I crossed my finger over my heart and took a slug of my beer.

"Your ability to keep secrets is right up there with a toddler with chocolate smeared all over their face telling you they didn't eat any cookies."

I clutched my chest in mock outrage. "I'll have you know, I have kept secrets for about as long as a six-year-old found surrounded by candy wrappers."

He snorted. "Right. Keep it quiet. They will give me shit if they think I'm throwing my money around."

"Don't worry. I'll make sure to keep quiet for at least the next..." I glanced down at my phone. "Ten minutes."

He laughed. "Here, take this in case I forget later." He slapped a bright and shiny hotel room key card into the palm of my hand. I quirked up an eyebrow at him.

"Rooms for everyone. It's right across the street. I wanted us to play tomorrow, and I figured if everyone was close, then there was less of a chance of losing someone." He had a sad look in his eyes. It was hard for him being away from everyone. Declan and I had each other; and Colm and Ford were up in Boston together, thrusting their way through all the single ladies.

Emmett was the only one flying solo in LA. He'd run away long and hard after the breakup with Avery. So long and hard he hadn't even gone to our high school graduation so he could avoid her. Avery had been a no-go topic of conversation since.

"Of course we will. Nothing is going to keep us from playing tomorrow." The Kings reunited once again.

We were now taking up more than half of the restaurant and bar. A few ladies were still trying to catch my eye, but not the one I wanted.

Colm and Ford flanked Olivia like a couple of body-guards. Grant sat on the other side of Ford and kept trying to get Olivia's attention but generally only managed to piss Colm off. Colm's little sister had blossomed in her senior year of high school, and it seemed Colm was taking no chances with her. Made sense. She was the only family he had left. But from the deep frown on her lips, she was not happy about it.

I hopped up to return a pitcher to the bar, using it as a chance to get a little better look at the woman sitting there. Nearly bumping into our server, I slid it across the counter and ordered another round. My back pressed into the shiny wooden bar as I leaned against it. Despite my best efforts, Miss Purple didn't look over once.

The women on either side of her had no problem checking me out, but suddenly I felt invisible. I didn't mind working harder. The bartender set the full pitcher down. I reached for a stack of napkins at the same time Miss Purple did. Our hands touched before she jerked hers back. Her gaze collided with mine, and I broke out into a smile that probably made me look like a moron.

I opened my mouth.

"Heath, bring the pitcher," someone called out from behind me at the same time the bartender slid a piping hot and massive burger in front of her. Her hands froze, and she peered over at me. I could wait.

Pitcher of beer in hand, I went back to our table and I lowered myself into my seat. She fidgeted at the bar. I wanted to help her smooth out all those nerves and show her that coming out tonight hadn't been a mistake. Like it was broadcasting her innermost thoughts, the tension in her back practically called out for my hands to knead the stress away.

Someone called my name in a way that let me know it wasn't the first time they'd said it. Tearing my eyes away from the beauty at the bar, I joined back in on the conversation at the table. Olivia maintained her spot no more than five feet from Ford the entire time she was there. I couldn't tell if Ford was oblivious to her or ignoring the way she kept trying to get his attention.

Declan was all wrapped up with Makenna. Thank God they'd gotten back together. His shooting had been absolute shit when she'd ghosted him. It had been depressing as hell.

The final call for food came around, and Colm zeroed in on Olivia. He was the opposite of a fairy godmother and spirited her out of there and back to the hotel room so she'd miss out on the partying. Grant's offer to walk her back was summarily and hilariously vetoed by Colm.

"What the hell is he going to do when she's down here for college next year?"

Declan shrugged. "Probably have her implanted with

some kind of tracker. At least we'll be around to keep an eye on her."

"Hey, can I buy you a drink?" A woman flanked by a few of her best girl pals brushed up against me as I switched seats to the end of our table to get a better look at my mystery woman. Most of the guys had dispersed to the dance floor, picking up someone or having someone pick them up along the way there.

I checked on Bar Girl, and she was tucking into the last of her burger. She had a notebook and scribbled away. Tapping the pencil against her lip, she stuck it up in her hair. If I hadn't liked her already, I was dead set now. But it wasn't the best time to go over. She was eating, probably self-conscious, trying to chew and talk at the same time.

I was crazy patient, especially when it was for something I knew would be worth the wait. People thought I acted without thinking; it was probably scarier for them to think I did the things I did by fully thinking them out. I made my patience and calculations look reckless and carefree, but they were nothing like that.

"No, it's cool. I'll get us all a round of drinks." Buying a drink for all meant I wasn't showing favoritism, and they'd be less likely to freak out when I bailed on them. Gently letting someone down had become a specialty of mine.

I watched as no more than three guys approached Miss Purple while she was eating, and she shut them down before they could even sit, pointing at her food and her full mouth and then making a walk away gesture with her fingers. Chuckling, I left the table.

The small dance floor was packed with hockey players and puck bunnies. I kept dodging invites. The first set of ladies left me behind with a few numbers tucked into my pocket. One even tucked hers into the waistband of my jeans before I grabbed her hand and removed it. And people said guys were handsy. I'd had my ass grabbed more times than I could count.

Miss Purple picked at the last of her fries and wiped her mouth. She lifted her straw to her lips and finished her drink. The bartender retrieved her plate, and I slid away from the women approaching me, not wanting to miss my window. Miss Purple could leave, or worse, some guy might try to move in on her now she wasn't crushing her food.

I slid onto the bar stool beside her and drummed my fingers along the smooth wood, channeling my nervous energy. The bartender walked over to me and slung the towel over his shoulder.

"I'll have a Yuengling, and another of whatever she's having." I pointed at her, and she looked over her shoulder, thinking I was talking about someone else before pointing at herself.

"For me?" Her eyebrows were almost at her hairline.

"For you."

"No, that's okay. I...I was going to go. You don't need to do that."

"I know I don't need to, but I'd like to. Technically, it's not even me buying you the drink." I leaned in conspiratorially, and she leaned in too. "It's my friend over there. He's treating us all to a night out, so it's not even like I expect anything. It's not my money. This is a no obligation, I'm-glad-you-came-out-for-a-drink-when-you-didn't-have-to drink."

Her mouth fell open, and she sputtered. "What makes you think I didn't want to come out?"

I leaned back, checking her out, and she did her best to relax.

"No friends with you, which tells me it was a spur-of-the-moment thing. Maybe you needed to get out of the house and no friends meant if you chickened out, there was no one to call you on it."

Her cheeks pinked up a little, and the bartender returned.

"One beer and a vodka on the rocks." He slid the bottle to me and the glass to her.

Damn! "Straight vodka? You trying to get hammered as quickly as possible?"

"Maybe I really like plain vodka and I can hold my liquor." She toyed with the straw of her drink, the ice clinking against the glass.

"Maybe, but you also put your coat on about thirty seconds before I got here."

She glanced down at herself like she'd forgotten she'd done it.

"Maybe I was cold."

"Maybe you were." I grabbed my beer and gulped some down. She sipped her drink. "Do you think you'll be leaving after finishing this drink?"

"I don't know. I guess it would depend on my mood and the company when this one is empty." She shook her glass at me.

"I think I help on both fronts. What were you running from when you came out tonight? Let me guess. Guy problems."

She shook her head vigorously, and I did an internal sigh of relief. I really didn't want to be That Guy cleaning up the pieces of a girl's broken heart, but for her I'd make an exception.

"Work troubles? Or school troubles?"

She smirked and shook her head. Her full, pouty pink

lips shined, coated with her drink. When they wrapped
around that straw, I bit back a groan.

"Family troubles."

She pushed against my shoulder playfully. First contact,
yes! "How did you know? Oh I know, because you went
through every possible area of life someone could have
trouble with." Her laughter was like music to my ears.

"I didn't hit on space exploration or solving world
hunger."

"You can write that on your list."

I reached up and tugged the pencil out of her hair, a
little disappointed it didn't make her curls drop and cascade
down her back. Waving it in front of her face, I dropped my
hand and let it brush against hers. She didn't shrink away
from my touch. I think I'd finally warmed her up.

"Were you studying?"

She grabbed it out of my hand, her fingers sliding across
mine. The smooth softness of her fingers only made me
think about how she'd feel everywhere else. Her eyes darted
away.

"No, I was writing. I'm a writer. I was looking all over for
that." She laughed and shoved it into her bag. "Kara." She
extended her hand, and I wrapped mine around hers.

"Heath."

"Nice to meet you, Heath." Her bright smile was nearly
blinding even in the dim bar lights. *Stunning.*

The music kicked up a bit, and we had to lean in to hear
each other. She smelled like Christmas. Like warm
cinnamon rolls on a cold winter morning.

"What were you writing before?"

"Oh you saw that. Nothing really. Thoughts, worries,
dreams."

"What are some of them?"

"Huh?" She scrunched her eyebrows.

"What are some of your thoughts, worries, and dreams?"

She hand waved them away. "Nothing too important."

"If you're writing it down, it must be kind of important. Lay it on me." I leaned back, giving her a little space.

The cocoon of the bar sounds seemed to give her courage. "Family stuff. Sometimes it's easier for me to write the things down that I have trouble saying out loud. The things I'm sometimes scared to say out loud. Somehow putting it in here." She tapped her bag. "It makes it less scary. Less real and more real all at the same time. Whatever it is, I need to get through it all."

"I totally get needing to work through stuff like that. For me, it's when I skate. When I'm out on the ice, I see everything so much clearer than I do in real life."

"Totally." She echoed. "Sorry I unloaded on you." She grimaced and stared down at her empty drink.

"It's fine. I have that effect on people. I think it's my honest face." I held both my hands under my chin and made me eyes as big and puppy-dog-like as I could.

She burst out laughing and slapped her hand against the bar. "I'd say your face is definitely a few things, but honest wouldn't be in the top five."

I cocked my head to the side. "What? You don't think I'm honest?"

"Not that, but I think there are a few other adjectives I'd use first." She slid her drink away and turned back to me, chuckling. I dropped my hand to her jean-clad thigh and felt her muscles tighten.

"And what would those be?" I stared into her eyes as

they fixed on mine. Her pupils got huge, and the tension between us swelled from playful to something else.

Her lips parted, glistening and full, and she took a shuddering breath. "I don't remember."

"Do you want to dance?" I lifted my hand from her leg and held it out to her. She glanced between me and the dance floor, nibbling that bottom lip.

"I'm not really that good of a dancer." She leaned in, resting her hand on my shoulder as the music got louder. Her words skimmed across my cheek, and a spark of electricity shot down my spine.

"Neither am I. We can go out there and look like idiots together." Another look between me and the dance floor and she nodded, shrugged her coat off. She slung her bag over her shoulder.

We found a spot on the small dance floor. Our bodies moved together in time to the music, my hand drifting down to her ass as she lifted her arms over her head when the thumping beat of an old-school dance song came on. Her eyes got wide as I tugged her toward me.

Watching the tension leave her body was a reward all its own, but going home with her tonight would be the national championship. And I wasn't even thinking with my dick, although he was in full agreement. We stayed out on the dance floor for at least five more songs, each one bringing us a little closer together. Lips so close but never connecting. Fingers and hands taking liberties with each other's bodies but never going too far. All it managed to do was make me a second away from getting a hard-on in front of everyone. The tension was thick between us. It was a game we were playing. The hunger in her eyes had me looking for the nearest exit, and I'm sure the look mirrored my own. Time to put it to the test.

Leaning in, I let my cheek settle against hers. A shudder shot through her as my words skimmed across the shell of her ear.

"I've got two choices for you, Kara. I buy you another drink, say goodbye, and I head out with my buddies...Or we leave this dance floor right now together." I leaned back and held her gaze as she stared up at me. She licked her lips, and her eyes darted away. Maybe it had been a miscalculation on my part. Moving too fast, but I hadn't wanted her to slip away from me.

"What about option three?" Laughter and desire twinkled in her eyes. It made me want to hold her tighter.

"What's option three?" I lifted one eyebrow, trying to figure out how she'd use it to end the evening and tell me to get lost.

"We get one more drink *and then* we leave together." She smiled brightly at me, and I tucked her under my arm, rushing for the bar.

"Done!"

4

KARA

"A shot of vodka!"

"A shot of tequila!"

We both called out to the bartender at the same time. He jerked at our overenthusiastic order, and my cheeks burned as we dissolved into a small fit of laughter. The bass of the music vibrated the floor, but it wasn't so loud you couldn't hear yourself think.

"Looks like we both had the same idea." He slid his hand along the small of my back with the deep timbre of his voice tickling the shell of my ear. A small thrill shot through my body, and I stared into his eyes. The bright blue was so clear and deep I wanted to swim in them for hours.

The bartender slid the glasses across the bar to us. Heath grabbed them and handed me mine, holding his out for a toast.

"To an evening we won't soon forget." He clinked his shot to mine, and my stomach flipped.

I tipped my glass back and let the white-hot burn make its way down my throat. He finished his shot and squeezed me tight to him as his lips skimmed over mine, the sharp tang of his tequila hitting my lips. My hands instinctively went to his chest like I needed to hold him here to satisfy every sense. The strong press of his lips against mine had my lips parting. Not needing an invitation, his tongue danced against mine. It was like he'd remembered our dance on the floor and was recreating it here.

"Are you sure about this?" He stared into my eyes, running his hands along the sides of my face.

"I'm one hundred percent sure." I kissed him again and I wanted to keep doing it. Every touch made me anticipate the next. Tonight I wasn't Kara, graduate student. I was Kara, writer. Maybe I was in town for a story or a conference. We hadn't gone too deep into the details and surprisingly, I was okay with that.

"You've had a couple drinks." There was a hint of worry in his eyes.

"I've had maybe three, and I can hold my liquor. Let's do this." I held his gaze. This wasn't a drunken decision. I'd wolfed down that huge burger and we'd been dancing, and that burned off a good bit of anything I'd been drinking before our shot race. I had a slight buzz, but other than that, it was a bubbly light feeling that made me crave more.

There wasn't an ounce of hesitation in me. Maybe there should have been. Maybe that should have scared me, but I didn't want to be anywhere other than wherever we were going, so I could really get a taste of him.

"Let's do this." He grinned. When he did that, it was like the weight of the world lifted off me a little. The expectations of everyone around me and the fears of my past melted away, and there was nothing but me and him, those eyes, and the way he looked at me like I was a present he couldn't wait to unwrap. Or maybe that was the way I was looking at him...

Slamming our glasses down at the same time, I smiled. It was like Heath and I were racing to see who'd get us out of there first. He checked his phone and tapped out a message before throwing his arm over my shoulder and maneuvering us through the crowd at the front of the place.

I couldn't hold back the laugh as we burst onto the sidewalk outside the bar, but the laugh didn't last long when Heath spun me around and pushed me up against the brick wall of the building. Our puffs and pants, mingling in the air in front of our faces.

The sounds of the bar and everything else around us faded away like the world had been put on mute when he stared into my eyes. That tingling feeling was back, but this time it pounded hard in my chest, and the vibration traveled all over. He stared at my lips like he wanted a taste and he couldn't wait to sample them all night.

Without a second more to overthink it, I pulled his head down, dragging my fingers through his blond strands. He was a shining sun out on a bleak and dreary day, and I wanted his warmth and brightness. Once my hands were on him, it was like all bets were off. It was all he needed, the green light, and the dam of our sexual tension burst.

His lips, tongue, and hands worked in unison to drive me into a frenzy. His hands pushed under my coat and my shirt and ran along the skin on my waist. The freezing-cold air was replaced by his hot touch, bringing up goose bumps all over my body.

A pounding throb overtook me. Mind and body were in total agreement now, Heath was unlike any guy I'd ever been with before. He made me giddy with only a couple kisses. This wasn't the booze talking, but I was sure as well Heath-drunk.

My heart thundered against my ribs, and I was all about

him. The second he'd slid onto the bar stool beside me, I knew I wanted to go home with him. Words had poured into my head, filling it up so much it was hard to think through the curtain of prose my hands itched to write down from the second our eyes connected.

For a few minutes, I'd entertained leaving. Not giving in to the intense burn in my chest that wanted to reach out and climb onto his lap the second he'd opened his mouth. He was the kind of guy I needed on a night like tonight. Hot. Funny. Sexy as sin and ready to lay it all on me in more ways than one.

His soft lips worked me into a frenzy as his tongue danced around my mouth. It was a demanding but gentle kiss, like he was trying to coax me out of my shell. It had been a while since I'd been kissed like that. His lips beat a hasty path from my mouth to my throat, sucking on my neck and giving a sharp nip that made my knees weak.

We needed to get to wherever the hell we were going, like now. Breaking apart, I tried to stop my trembling. He stared into my eyes, and his fingers skimmed along my nape. He toyed with the hair there, his insistent touch making me melt a little bit more. The strong touch of his fingers was a cross between a massage and a promise of what he had in store for me.

"You taste so good. Good enough to eat." He ran his tongue along his bottom lip, savoring my taste. His lips turned up into a smile that should have been outlawed in all fifty states.

"You taste pretty good yourself." I wouldn't have been surprised if steam rose off our bodies as we stood outside, trying to keep up pretenses about where this was heading.

"I've got a hotel room." He lifted a key card for a hotel out of his back pocket.

I stared back at him with my eyes wide. "That confident, huh?"

Somehow it made it better. We hadn't talked much about him. I'd been too busy word vomiting all over him all night, so he hadn't said a lot about his past. From the whispers and craned necks from the other people in the bar, I knew his group were hockey players. NHL players. They all looked so young, I had no idea they started playing that early.

But if he had a hotel and was from out of town, all the better. If I made a complete and total fool of myself, this wouldn't come back to bite me in the ass.

"Having second thoughts?" He shoved his hand back into his pocket with worry in his eyes.

5

HEATH

"No, I want to go. I really do. It's just...this isn't my usual MO."

"What? Going home with a relentless and incredibly handsome man for a night of hot, wild fucking you won't soon forget?" Was I *trying* to blow this?

She barked out a laugh as my fingers traveled higher up her thigh, cupping her ass, and tugging her harder against me.

"If only you were wearing a skirt." I bit my bottom lip. I could feel her heat through her jeans against my leg. Trapped in a jean-clad prison so close yet so far from the prize I'd been waiting for all night.

"Yeah, that, exactly." Her chest rose and fell in shallow bursts. A big swallow like she couldn't believe what she'd gotten herself into. "Usually I end up with relentless, exceedingly handsome men, but I guess you'll do." Her thighs tightened around my leg.

"What the hell are we doing out here in the cold when you have a perfectly good hotel room waiting for us?" She dug her hand into my pocket and retrieved the key card.

Lifting my hand, I let the soft, gentle waves of her hair glide through my touch. Sliding it to the back of her neck, I pulled her forward, smelling her sweet cinnamon smell and recapturing her lips. "You're absolutely right."

We raced across the damp, slick street. Every brush of her hand on me was pure torture. The hotel staff pointed us toward the elevator, and we fell into it. Her teeth grazed my neck, sending a shiver down my spine. It may or may not have been in retribution for the mark I'd left on her neck from nipping her and sucking on the spot to make it all feel better.

Keeping my hands to myself for the most part, I only ran my fingers along her back as she arched it, pushing her breasts out. She had more than a handful hidden under her sweater, and I'd never been happier to open a present in my life. My mouth watered at the thought of getting my hands, mouth, and teeth on her breasts. Teasing those nipples until she couldn't take it anymore.

Fumbling with the key, I opened the door and tugged her inside, closing it behind her. There was a split second where we stood staring at one another, and then, like our clothes were on fire, we stripped them off.

There was no slow, sensual striptease. This was a basic, driving yearning to get naked and pressed against each other as quickly as possible. Her gaze was riveted to me as I whipped my shirt overhead and flung it somewhere behind me. I was proud of my body. I'd worked hard to be in peak physical condition, and I'd use that prowess to turn her into a trembling mess as we both got exactly what we wanted. She licked her lips, kicking off her boots, and I was on her, our bodies banging into the wall as we rushed to get the treat at the end of our lust-fueled rainbow.

Shoving her jeans down over her ass, I palmed her soft,

supple cheeks. Lifting her, I tugged her jeans down her legs. Like we were completely in tune, she wrapped them around my waist as I pushed her bare back against the door. With my jeans open, her hot, wet heat was inches away from my cock, but I wasn't ready for that yet. She nipped at my chin and wrapped her arms around me while making these needy little noises that sent a zing straight to my balls.

I wanted her delirious, and I needed to get my mouth on her nipples. Holding her up with my body and my arms, I ducked my head and wrapped my lips around her dark, tight peak. Using my teeth and my tongue, I licked and sucked and nipped on her as her fingers delved into my hair, nails scraping along my scalp. She arched her back, giving me even better access.

"Fuck!" She moaned as I used my hips to keep her pinned to the wall, and it gave me a chance to use both hands and my mouth on her. The gentle rock of her hips was torture on my dick. Like a taste of a treat before it was taken away, her pussy was molten, spreading her sweet wetness all over me. The smell of her made me even harder, and I needed to get my mouth on her.

I was torn between feasting on her breasts—squeezing and massaging those overflowing mounds that seemed to get her going—and dropping down to my knees and worshipping at her molten center. The head of my dick rubbed against the entrance to her pussy. I bit out a groan and rocked against her harder. Her slick pussy coated my shaft. The temptation was too strong like this. I was a second from sinking into her without a condom, ready to feel that tight, velvety bliss wrapped around my cock.

Looping my arms around her back, I walked us to the couch, keeping her tight against me and increasing my torture. Her lips traced my jaw and down my neck. My pulse jumped under her tongue as she ran it along the pounding vein in my neck.

"You taste really good, and you smell even better." Her breath danced skimmed the wet swath she'd made on my skin.

My fingers sank into her ass as I got down on my knees and slid her to the edge of the couch. Not letting her get her bearings, I lifted her legs and gave her a crooked smile.

"I was thinking the same thing."

She tried to push up on her elbows when I lifted her legs over my shoulders, keeping my eyes on her as I ran my tongue along the seam of her pussy. Her eyes fluttered shut like the pleasure was too strong to even keep them open.

Sinking down onto my haunches, I pulled her even closer to me. Her taste was addictive, and I'd only had a small sample. Her eyes were wide and her mouth fell open as I sucked her clit into my mouth, savoring her sweet flavor.

Pressing two fingers inside, I groaned as her pussy clamped down on me with a silky-smooth tightness. Her fingers dug into the couch, and she made a small noise in the back of her throat. I gritted my teeth as my dick strained for attention.

I wrapped my fingers around her supple thigh to keep her where I wanted her as I pressed my thumb against her clit, giving her the pleasure she needed.

Her thighs clamped around my head, and I knew I'd hit the right spot. She cried out and shook as her orgasm ripped through her. I grinned at the sharp tug on my hair. I couldn't take it anymore and let go of her leg. She slumped back into the couch ready to be good and stay put so I could wring even more out of her.

Reaching down, I stroked my straining, throbbing dick, running my hands over the tip, smearing the pre-cum around. I shuddered. Sweet, sweet Kara. I needed more, but I was holding on, drawing this out even longer.

She screamed as I painted her pussy with my tongue, and all the muscles in her body went tight before she collapsed back onto the couch. Her body shuddered, tremors racking her body. I let her legs down, running my hands along her thighs. Her eyes were closed, and her lips parted as she tried to form words. The glow from the streetlights outside streaked in through the blinds and painted her in light and shadow.

"You're..." She licked her dry lips. "You're really good at that." Her chest rose, pushing those beautiful breasts higher. She opened her eyes with an eyebrow lifted playfully.

"There will be a comment card at the end of the evening for a full review of your evening at Chez Heath."

"I can already tell you right now. It's a five-star experience." She shot me a lazy smile and licked her lips again. "Give me, like, five minutes, and I'll return the favor."

I shook my head and reached into my back pocket, sliding my wallet out and grabbing a condom. "There's only one place I want inside, and it's sure as hell not your mouth. At least, not this time." I rolled the condom on and climbed onto the couch beside her, lifting her and settling her on my lap facing me with my cock nestled between the soft curls covering her pussy. Her hot center was so close as my condom-covered dick glided through her wetness.

I laid my lips on her collarbone, and she wrapped her fingers around my hair, holding my head to her body and trying to move her hips to get me inside. I chuckled against her skin, nipping her.

She tugged my head away and looped her arms around my neck, bringing our mouths an inch apart. "What makes you think there'll be a next time?"

"Do you still need convincing?" I sank my fingers into her soft skin, squeezing her ass and massaging her body. My hands itched in anticipation of getting her ready for the second phase of our night together. She tasted sweeter than any woman I'd ever tasted before. The feel of her wrapped around me would be unparalleled.

"I think I might."

If she needed convincing, then I was ready, willing and able to give her every bit I had to give. From the second she'd walked into the bar, talking to her had been the only thing I'd focused on. After talking came touching. It still wasn't enough, and tasting had only managed to ratchet up the thumping, pounding desire. Lifting her, I looked down between us, mesmerized by the sight of me poised at her entrance. If she needed convincing, I was prepared to convince her all night long.

6

KARA

He tilted his head to the side and dragged me to him with his hand along the back of my neck, toying with my hair while he feasted on another part of me. I could taste myself on his lips, mixed with him, and it was addictive. My head was still swimming from the way he'd dragged every moan and scream out of me.

I'd had my fair share of guys go down on me, but none had ever been as enthusiastic or committed as Heath. There was no sense that he was half-assing it. If he were half-assing it, then I'd probably die next time he did it because my lips were still half numb from how hard I'd bit them when I came. There were those words again. *Next time.* Explosive wasn't even the word. And now I was getting even more.

Shifting my hips, I lifted and slowly lowered myself down onto him. We both shuddered and groaned as the head of his cock pressed against my entrance. He stretched me to my limit, and I gasped and moaned when he was fully inside me, my ass settled on his lap.

"Okay, you're right, there will definitely be a next time."

My words came out all choppy as I sputtered, trying to form a coherent thought. He wrapped his hands around me, keeping me tight against his chest. His muscled arms and legs were a powerful combination. And he used them masterfully.

He lifted his hips, thrusting into me. I held on, doing my best to give him as much pleasure as he gave me. Dropping my hips down, I let the building pleasure roll through me. My toes curled as he changed his angle and dragged his head against the front wall of my pussy, nearly sending me into a pleasure spiral so good it hurt. We were both racing toward the brass ring of an explosive orgasm ready to shoot me into the stratosphere. And I was ready.

"What do you need, Kara?" He nipped my earlobe, and I bucked against him.

My fingers dug into his shoulders and I rocked my hips. There was one thing missing. We were still so new and frantic together. I knew with the angle and the position he couldn't give me that last little bit, and I had no issues doing what I needed to get myself there. The back of my hand brushed against his stomach as my fingers dipped down between us. He watched as I rubbed my fingers when they found my clit.

His eyes were on me, drinking down my moans. One tap was all it took. Blinding lights and toe-curling bliss raced through my body so quickly I thought I'd pulled a muscle.

"I love a woman who knows what she needs," he growled against my neck. His arms tightened even more as my head swam, lightheaded from the intensity. Our bodies were locked together as his cock pulsed inside me, spilling into the condom. I had no doubt he'd committed my movements to memory for next time.

We sat in our frozen embrace, panting against each

other's necks until I had a cramp in my calf and had to get off. Lifting myself, I groaned as he fell free from me, the evidence of my pleasure coating him. My cheeks heated, and I tucked some of the stray hairs plastered to the side of my face behind my ear.

He stood and stalked toward me with a sly smile.

"Perfect. Let's go to bed."

While the feeling had only recently returned to my legs, I didn't really feel like sleeping. The corners of my mouth turned down.

"I didn't say go to sleep." He chuckled and tapped his finger to my nose. "I thought it would be a lot easier to do what I had in mind with a bed versus trying to do it on the coffee table. But if you prefer the table, I can always change things up."

"A bed sounds great." I rubbed my aching calf.

"Awesome." He took my hand in his and led me from the living room area. I had the perfect view of his ass as we made our way across the crazy-huge room. It was muscled and toned, leading down to his powerful thighs. He was built like an athlete, and I was grateful for every training session he'd been through.

"You checking me out?" He glanced over his shoulder as he stepped through the doorway to the bedroom, and my cheeks heated, but I held his gaze.

"I mean, you do have a rocking body. I can't even lie about that."

He threw his head back and laughed, tugging me up against him.

"I love your compliments. Do you happen to have any more for me?" He sat on the bed, leaning back on his arms, letting me drink him in.

I stepped forward between his spread legs.

"As a matter of fact, I do. I really like the shaggy blond surfer-dude vibe you've got going. It's pretty hot." I trailed my finger down his chest. A hard, muscled chest without being too much. Not a big, bulky guy, but still the strong kind who could pin me to the wall and fuck me into next week.

"Go on." He grinned.

"And you've got that awesome cock cleavage thing going on."

He made a sputtering laugh and sat up straighter. "The what?" He glanced down at himself. Resting my hands on his shoulders, I pushed him back until he propped himself up on his elbows again. I sank down on my knees in front of him. The laughter drained out of his eyes as I ran my fingers along his abs, replaced by a fire that made my stomach do little flips.

I skimmed my fingers lower, tracing that awesome outline from his hips leading straight to the part of him that seemed very interested in my new exploration.

"This is what I call cock cleavage. Except way more obscene than regular cleavage. That leads to these." I used one arm to brace my breasts like a shelf, and the flare of his desire burned even brighter. Biting back a smirk, I let my fingers dance lower along his skin. "Whereas cock cleavage heads to something a bit more tempting." Dropping my eyes to the thick mushroom head in front of me, I wrapped my hand around his shaft, and Heath sucked in a sharp breath. I licked my suddenly dry lips.

"How tempted are you?" His words come out in a whisper as I slowly worked my hand up and down, letting my thumb graze the head with each stroke.

"I'm pretty tempted." I brought my mouth less than an inch from his head.

"Is there anything I could do to tempt you even more?" His thigh muscles tightened, and he shifted his hips.

"You could say please."

"Fuck, please." The words were barely out of his mouth when I wrapped my lips around the head of his cock. Working my way down as far as I could, I used my hands to make up the difference as I worked them together. Heath gathered my hair in his hands and piled it on top of my head. His fingers wrapped around the ponytail he created as he helped me find the rhythm he needed.

Running my tongue around his head, I basked in the power from his groans and grunts, which sent a heady thrill through my body. I'd made him as needy as he made me. Unable to help myself, I reached down and rubbed my clit, humming with pleasure while giving it to him.

"Christ, Kara. Are you touching yourself while you blow me?" His words came out strained and choppy. I nodded and kept going, his cock sliding into and out of my mouth. "That's so fucking hot!" He shifted, trying to get a better look, and I struggled to keep from laughing. Never had that problem before. He was like an energetic puppy that was all man, had an impressive weapon and could give me an orgasm in two minutes flat. I let my teeth graze him, and he nearly jumped off the bed.

"I think you're trying to kill me." He lifted me and flipped me around, bending me over the edge of the mattress. My hair fell over my face, and I brushed it aside, glancing over my shoulder.

"I don't think I'm the only one." I smirked and he winked back.

Like a magician, he had a condom on before I could even make a joke and slid back into me. And then there was no joking. There was only the blunt head of his manhood powering its way into me like we hadn't already had sex a little while ago.

His hands wrapped around my hips, using his weight as leverage to hammer into me. Everything in me centered around him filling and emptying me, each thrust so excruciatingly exquisite I struggled to drag air into my lungs. On edge from tasting him, I wasn't far away. When his hand slid up my back to my shoulder and gripped me tighter, the way he possessed my body, using it to drive our pleasure higher, made me light-headed. Light-headed coupled with a throbbing, clenching, clawing-at-the-bed kind of feeling.

"Your body is too good. Too fucking good." He punctuated each word with a thrust, and that was all it took to shoot me over the edge. Burying my face in the blankets, I fisted my hands around them and screamed out my thanks and appreciation.

My arms collapsed, my body collapsed, but Heath kept going, not letting me come down from the place I thought you could only live in for seconds, not minutes on end. And then he grunted behind me, his muscles tight as he expanded even more and filled the latex between us.

We collapsed into a heap on the bed. Our sweat combined and the giddy feeling returned as soon as I could feel all my limbs again. Heath toyed with my nipples, and I didn't even think to stop him. He was on a sexual mission to drive me completely crazy, and it was working. I'd never had someone so into my breasts before. I had a nice rack, one I often tried to hide because big boobs didn't win any awards when it came to academia. But he didn't give them a nice squeeze and move on from there.

"We should take a shower. Come on. Let's go."

I groaned as he took my hand and lifted me off the bed, leading me to the bathroom. The room was generous. It was more of a suite. Pocket doors hid the bedroom area away. And a bathroom had doors into the living room and bedroom. It was the type of crisp, classic clean modern look you'd expect from a hotel like this. He turned on the shower and tugged me inside.

He'd already learned more about me than guys I'd dated before. He was in tune with the line that went straight from my nipples to my pulsing clit, he wrapped his arms around me from behind and pinched them. He was playing my body like an instrument he'd practiced on for years, and we'd met less than two hours ago. I'd normally be freaking the hell out about that, but when he ran his hands over my body, nothing but hot, wet sex flashed through my mind.

Pulling me into the shower he stood behind me. With my back pressed against his hard chest, his hands keeping me right where he wanted me. One of his hands snaked down my body, cupping my pussy. My head lolled against his shoulder as his fingers worked in time together, tapping out a rhythm only he knew on my clit.

"Is this your plan? Kill me with orgasms?"

"I'm doing my best to convince you that a repeat performance will be needed."

"I'm beyond convinced. At this point, I'm looping back around into thinking you're insane."

"Can't have that, now can we? I'm going to have to keep going until we loop back around to 'repeat performance guaranteed'."

His cock pressed against my ass, but every time I tried to shift myself and lean forward, ready for him, he squeezed me tighter against him. It was like he was into the sexual torture that came with giving me all the pleasure I could handle.

"How does it feel, Kara?" His voice was deep and decadent like a nice warm piece of chocolate cake.

"Good."

"Only good?" He grazed my neck with his teeth. "I'll have to fix that." He sank his fingers into my pussy. I don't know if it was two or three, but they were working together, bringing me to the edge of my orgasm.

"I'm dying. I think I'm dying. Your fingers are lethal weapons."

"That's more like it." He pumped his fingers in and out of me until my knees gave way and he had to fully support my weight. He didn't miss a beat, holding me as the jolts of electricity ripped through my body, and I screamed his name. The patter of the water flowing from the showerhead and my panting were the only sounds in the bathroom.

With a washcloth and some soap Heath took his time, washing me down before shutting off the water and wrapping me up in a nice fuzzy towel with another for the ends of my hair. I'd managed to duck and dodge to keep my hair from getting soaked.

He guided me back to the bed, and I plopped down. I nibbled on my lip. It had been a while since I'd done this. We'd done the bed thing, he hadn't said anything about sleep. *Did I get dressed and go? Or maybe leave in the morning?*

He dragged the covers down the bed and patted one side.

"You're staying the night, right?" Running his hand along the side of my face, stared into my eyes. I nodded, not trusting my voice. *Why the hell not?* He was what I needed. The right blend of sexy as hell and funny. Going out had been the best decision I'd made in a long time.

"Climb in so you don't get cold."

I guessed I was staying.

"My hair is still wet." I lifted the ends and wrapped the towel around them. I hoped it wasn't a rat's nest in the morning.

"It's fine. I'll keep you warm."

Suddenly feeling a little self-conscious, I dropped my towel and hurried into the bed. He climbed in beside me and wrapped his arms around me, my back snuggled up against him.

"I had fun tonight." His words tickled the shell of my ear. I tilted my head to gaze up at him.

"I did too." I really had. Like the streaks of light breaking through a day you hadn't even realized was overcast, Heath had made me smile in a way I hadn't known possible.

"I'd like to see you again." He tucked some of my damp hair behind my ear.

My heart fluttered, and I couldn't help the smile that broke out on my face. I nodded. "I'd like that too." This was what I needed more of. Someone like Heath. Someone so open and happy it was hard not to catch even a bit of it, plus the sex was phenomenal. I'd taken a risk, and it hadn't blown up in my face. Being bold, I sat up and threw the blankets off.

"What's up?"

"I need my phone." A burst of courage compelled me to face what I'd been running from.

"Okay..." He lifted an eyebrow at me. "It's probably by the door."

I slid out of the bed and grabbed it. Tapping out a message I probably wouldn't be brave enough to send in the morning, I hit send before I could change my mind.

I put my phone down on the desk and climbed back in beside him.

"Was that an alert for your hit squad that I'm worn out and they can prep the organ removal?"

I laughed and snuggled in beside him as he sank back down in the bed.

"No, it was me doing something I haven't been able to do earlier, but needed to be done. I needed this little push for myself to do it."

"If you say so." He kissed me on the side of my face, right by my beauty mark, and rested his head above mine.

Running my fingers along his skin, I traced some of the words that refused to leave my mind. *Unforgettable. Unrelenting. Undeniable.*

I wouldn't mind doing this again. *What's the worst thing that can happen?*

7

HEATH

I swear there were birds chirping outside my window even though we were eight floors up and it was the dead of winter. There was a temptation to not even open my eyes, stay in bed all day, but we had the pick-up game going on a little later.

Feeling around on the bed beside me, I cracked open an eyelid, snapping them fully open when I saw she wasn't there. Her spot on the bed was still warm. I sat up and spotted the blue sticky note on the pillow beside me.

I stretched my arms overhead, basking in the soreness of my aching muscles. The never-ending night of sexual pleasure and exploration had wrecked me even more than my intense workouts. Probably using all those different muscles. But it was a workout with Kara I couldn't wait to do all over again. She'd been so open and knew what she wanted. There was no worry about doing something she didn't like because I had no doubt in my mind she'd tell me exactly what she thought.

After we'd made it through most of the condoms, we'd had between the two of us, we'd fallen into a heap on the bed. The soft smell of soap and her sweetness had filled the room. Wrapping my arms around her, I'd fallen asleep with Kara lying across my chest. Her damp, wavy hair had fanned out around her.

Her fingers had trailed along my skin from my stomach to my chest, every pass of her hand slower until it had stopped and her chest rose and fell gently. Tugging the blankets up a little higher, I'd let my eyes drift shut, and my dreams had been filled with the woman who'd commanded my attention from the second I'd laid eyes on her.

I cracked a smile as I read over the note and saw her number at the bottom. Tracing her handwriting with my finger, I climbed out of bed and grabbed my phone off the floor by the front door. I leaned over to pick it up with a vivid play-by-play of what we'd done right by and against the front door flashing through my mind.

The piece of paper in hand, I unlocked my phone. This was one number I didn't want to lose. I saved it in my contacts.

There was a part of me that had expected to wake up and find her gone without a word. I'd hoped she'd be there in the morning, but I'd take her number as a second best. I snatched my clothes up off the floor in the living room. *How long was too soon to call?* Less than a day was probably too much. Didn't want to come off as a stalker. I'd give it a day or two after Christmas. But after that, all bets were off, and Kara had better get used to seeing a lot of me around. New Year's Eve was coming up, and I knew who I wanted to ring in the New Year with.

This semester would be insane with the end of our hockey season, finally signing with our hometown team and wrapping up classes. When things were important you made the time no matter what, and I had a feeling making time for her would be the best decision of my life.

"Why is everything so loud?" Colm stood in the center of the ice with his head perched on his hands on top of his stick, sunglasses firmly in place even though we were inside. If he hadn't said anything, it had been fifty-fifty on whether he was sleeping on his feet or not.

"What's the matter, big brother? A little hungover after your big night out?" Olivia shouted across the rink, and Colm and Emmett winced. Mak laughed beside her, holding out a water bottle for Declan, and Preston's girlfriend, Imogen, sat on the bench.

"Liv." It came out like a hushed curse as Colm lifted his sunglasses.

"What's the matter? Were you out late last night past your bedtime?" She cupped her hands around her mouth for extra focused pain infliction.

Colm's hand whipped out as Ford passed by.

"Help me out here and get her to zip it. I'm too hungover to go into dad mode right now." His fingers were tightly wrapped around Ford's jersey.

"I'll go talk to her," Grant, Ford's little brother, offered, turning in that direction. Colm clamped a hand down on Grant's shoulder and shot him a glare.

"*Ford*, go talk to Olivia." Colm kept his hand on Grant.

Ford chuckled and slapped Colm on the back, nearly toppling him over before skating across the ice to Olivia. For some reason, Colm always thought Grant had a shot with Olivia and made sure to always keep them as far apart as possible, but he seemed completely oblivious to the doe-eyed swooning Liv had been doing around Ford since forever. Her smile immediately brightened as he approached. She leaned in as he spoke to her.

Declan shot me a look, and I shrugged my shoulders.

"What's the deal with Ford and Olivia?" Preston skated up beside me, and I whipped my head up to see if Colm had heard, but he was in the Land of Hangovers and Nausea.

"Nothing there. They are friends. Known each other for a long time now."

His lips turned down like they always did when he was deep in thought. "If you say so." He skated off, and Declan stifled a laugh.

We'd all taken taxis to the stadium, arranged by Emmett of course. We'd visited once before with him, but standing inside the pin-drop quiet rink, soaking up the energy of the place nearly knocked me off my feet. Most of our development teamwork was in the practice rink in Jersey. We didn't get to come to the stadium much, but I couldn't wait for all that to change in only a few short months. They'd had an exhibition game the night before, so we'd persuaded them to let us have some rink time.

"Are these the legendary Kings I've heard so much about? What happened to you guys? I thought this wasn't going to be a fair fight, but it looks like we can probably take you guys with one skate on, no problem." Preston knew how to push all the right buttons. His talents included when to coddle, when to shove you out of the nest with both hands, and when to goad someone into rising to the occasion.

The rest of the Knights arrived and got onto the ice. Emmett, Declan, and Ford groaned and slid their helmets on. Grant skated circles around everyone, drawing a few more glares from Colm. Everyone who'd gone out last night was at some stage of being the walking dead.

Olivia skated out onto the ice with a whistle stuck between her lips. The looks of abject horror on everyone's faces as she clenched it between her teeth with the puck in her hand had me bursting out laughing.

She stood in front of her brother. "Ready, Colm?"

"Olive, I swear, I'll buy you that new wardrobe today if you don't blow that whistle." His eyes pleaded with her.

"Totally worth it!" She grinned and lifted her arm high in the air, blew as hard on the whistle as she could and dropped the puck onto the ice.

Preston faced off against Colm and easily got the puck away from him. The Knights were way less hungover than I'd thought. Colm and Emmett were dragging. It was a slower, friendly game, but Preston had no issues slapping the puck into the back of the net.

Emmett skated up to Preston once the period was over. "Preston, who are you playing with next year?"

We all hunched over the bench, sweating more than usual. Mak and Olivia doled out breakfast sandwiches with a hell of a lot of bacon in them like Civil War nurses tending to the wounded.

"I'm not." Preston bit into his sandwich.

"Why the hell not?" Emmett threw his stick down and grabbed a foil-wrapped sandwich.

"Sometimes there are more important things in life other than hockey." He tilted his head, a small smile on his lips for his girlfriend, Imogen, who smiled back. We hadn't been able to beat it out of him over the past four years why the hell he wasn't going pro. He'd said it was because he'd come into our team as a walk-on, but no-talent walk-ons didn't make the team, let alone become captain.

"But that doesn't mean I'm not still going to go out there and wipe the floor with all of you. Let's go, ladies."

The Kings groaned, dropping the sandwich wrappers on the bench.

The Knights were already up and on the ice as Colm slid his gloves back on.

"I know you're all hungover and probably want to puke right now." I leaned in with my hands on their shoulders.

The guys nodded and grumbled.

"But when was the last time we all got to take the ice together? When the hell will we get the chance again? It's been too long and life is only going to get busier once we graduate and we're all pro." The intensity of what this game meant for us burned in my chest. It was like being transported back in time.

It was a friendly game, but I needed them there with me all on the same page, skating together. Whatever happened over the rest of the season, this would be the game we all remembered. We'd finally, after nearly four years apart, gotten back on the ice all at the same time. I only wished Kara could be there sitting in the box like Mak and Imogen.

That thought blindsided me.

She'd looked so peaceful the night before, resting on me, and I was itching to call her. Maybe after the game. I'd stashed my phone deep in my gym bag so I wouldn't be tempted.

"Look at Heath going all Braveheart on us." Declan stood from the bench.

"Today we've got a chance to show a bunch of cocky players exactly why we'll go down as the Rittenhouse Kings until the day we die. Are you guys ready?" I said it in a fierce whisper.

Some pitiful *yeahs* came from the bench.

"I can't hear you guys. I said, are you ready?" I yelled.

A more enthusiastic round of *yeahs* came from the guys.

"Then let's get out there and show them what it's like to go up against a bunch of Kings!"

We burst out of the box and onto the ice. Colm's face no longer the color of moss, he didn't wince when Olivia blew the whistle. He was the first to the puck and took possession, looking like he did when we saw him on TV. He worked with Declan, falling back into our old groove, and scored our first goal.

"Now that's what I'm talking about." I skated past him with my hand up. He high-fived me, and we spent the rest of our game showing my current team exactly why we'd dominated back in high school and all of us would be playing pro.

Each of us had honed and improved over time, but we still fell back into those old places beside each other where we all seemed to know what the others were thinking and reacted before anyone else knew what was going on.

The final score was 6-3. Preston leaned against the boards with his arm around Imogen, who didn't seem to mind being wrapped up with a sweaty, huffing hockey player.

"That was one hell of a game." Preston gulped down some water and finished it off with a gasp.

"Sure as hell was, man." Emmett came up and slapped his hand into Preston's. "Are you sure you don't want to go pro?"

Preston glanced down at Imogen. "I'm sure."

"Well, that's a damn shame." Colm stood and shook his hand.

"Nah, it's all good."

"You guys want to go to Threes for some drinks?" Declan lifted his head from focusing on untying his skates.

Everyone groaned. Mak worked as a server at Three Streets, the sports bar right beside the hockey stadium.

"A little hair of the dog maybe?" Mak offered with a wicked grin.

Ford piped up. "No freaking way. But I could kill a burger right now."

"Threes it is," Preston said, rounding everyone up like a good captain.

The guys headed into the locker room and changed. A quick trip across the parking lot and we piled into a booth at Threes and grabbed an extra table or two. It was deserted since most people had gone home for the break. Loved having the place to ourselves.

I glanced at my phone every so often as the temptation to call Kara crept up. Holding strong, I didn't tap on her name taunting me from the contacts list. It was too soon, bordering on stalker levels how much I wanted to call her. I put my phone away. Relax.

There was time.

8

KARA

The early morning sun blinded me as I rushed out of the hotel. A white puff of air hung in front of my face. It was decidedly less sexy than it had been the night before.

At least the streets were quiet outside the hotel and there was no one around to see me running in place to keep from freezing my ass off. I slapped my hand against my forehead and winced. He could have been a crazy psycho. I didn't do the walk of shame ever, but I was sure as hell doing it now.

The doorman hailed a taxi.

My text alert pinged on my phone.

Jason: Stevenson is going to be giving you some extra work this semester.

Me: Okay, so why are you telling me and not Prof. Stevenson

Jason: I thought I'd be a friend and let you know.

I don't think he knew the definition of the word friend.

Me: Thank you for the information.

Jason: You could be a little grateful.

I rolled my eyes so hard I thought they might permanently face the back of my head. I wasn't even going to reply to that. Never going on a date with him had been the best decision I'd ever made in my life.

By the time the taxi pulled up in front of my house and I tiptoed inside, I'd talked myself out of a mental health evaluation and chalked the evening up to everything that had happened the day before.

Stress was a hell of a thing. Between my exam and that letter from Angie, it was no wonder I was out of sorts. The automatic coffee maker was running and the smell stopped me in my tracks. Straining to hear any movement, I darted into the kitchen and poured myself a huge mug of coffee. I sloshed some onto my hand and cursed under my breath, shaking the scalding coffee off my skin. No time for any milk or sugar. I sipped on it as I crept up the stairs.

Crossing the threshold to my room, I leaned against the door and groaned at the heavenly smell of coffee. Maybe the caffeine would make its way into my veins through inhalation. The second my bedroom door closed, my parents opened. Mom would be headed downstairs for our Saturday morning family breakfast. It was tradition.

"Kara." There was a gentle knock at my door.

"Yeah." I tried to make my voice alert.

"I need to run to the store first to get more eggs for breakfast; we forgot last night. Did you need anything?" Her sweet voice had me cursing myself.

"No, I'm okay."

"I'm going to make cinnamon rolls, so breakfast will be in a couple hours. If you're hungry, there are some biscuits down there."

"Okay, thanks for letting me know."

Her footsteps retreated from the door. The tension in my

body eased up a bit. At least I could pass out for an hour or so. A nap was what I needed. Once the front door closed, I hopped in the shower and threw on my Christmas pajamas. Where Mom found so many matching sets was beyond me, but the soft flannel was what I needed. Reindeer flannels and a big mug of coffee.

I set an alarm on my phone and curled up into a ball, wrapped around my pillow. Letting my eyes close, I groaned into my pillow as images of the night before bombarded me. Heath's eyes locked onto mine. His hands on my body, and his mouth everywhere. I squeezed my thighs together, but it didn't stop the ache there. His arms wrapped around me was the last lucid memory before I sank deeper into the softness of my bed.

My alarm blared way too soon after I'd shut my eyes. Groggily I reached out, trying to find my phone so I could snap it in half. Maybe a nap hadn't been a good idea. I somehow felt worse than I'd felt before sleeping.

My mouth tasted like I'd cleaned the bar floor with my tongue, and the ache between my legs was still there. This was what happened when I went to a hotel room with hot and sexy strangers I'd met at the bar. The smell of cinnamon and sugar wafted under my door, and my stomach grumbled. Black coffee on an empty stomach had been a mistake.

Why had I told him I was a writer? Why hadn't I said, *"Hi, I'm Kara a biochem graduate student on her way to the most boring PhD in the world? Have you ever heard someone's soul being sucked out while they study ten hours a day? No, well you're welcome to listen when I go back into the library in a week."*

My fingers itched to grab my composition book and harness these feelings into words, but I couldn't do that. Not after how many times I'd woken up to Angie's frantic, early morning, still-drunk-from-the-night-before binge writing sessions.

Absolutely no writing today.

But the words wouldn't stop flowing through my brain, like they were torturing me for not letting them out onto paper.

I grabbed my phone off the nightstand and checked the messages. A couple texts from Sam and Anne along with pics of their evening.

There was also one e-mail in my inbox. Things had been slow with the semester break, so I opened it and nearly dropped the phone to the floor when I saw the message. And then it all came rushing back to me. My mom. The e-mail. It was like I'd been trying to hide this from myself.

I'd sent her an e-mail the night before.

Hi Angie,

I hope you really have changed and I'd like to meet you.

Kara

That was it, and her reply had been almost immediate.

Kara!

I was so incredibly happy to hear from you. I've missed you so much. I am available whenever you'd like to meet and wherever you'd like to meet. Name the time and date and I'll be there. I love you so much, and I can't wait to see you again.

My throat closed as the boot of life pressed down so hard on my chest that filling my lungs was a struggle. I couldn't even blame it on the drinks. I'd *wanted* to meet her last night. With Heath, I felt braver than I had before, emboldened to go for it and hash it out. His attitude had rubbed off on me, and I'd sent the message.

But in the light of day, I saw it for the monumentally stupid idea it was. I had a great thing going here. I had a wonderful family, and I wasn't going to tell them they weren't enough by agreeing to see her. It wasn't going to happen. I wasn't ready to open that door to my past when I didn't even know if I could hold things together in the here and now.

What if I invited her back into my life and she dragged me down again like she did before? What if Carla and Mike thought that they weren't enough or I wanted the connection with my birth mom because I'd missed out on something with them? I opened the e-mail again and hit "Reply".

"Kara, are you up?" Mom knocked on my door and opened it.

I tucked my phone under my leg. "Hey, Mom."

Her broad, warm smile made my decision even easier. I wasn't going to mess this up and take a chance on someone who'd burned me more than once and whose presence was likely to throw a grenade into my life again.

"I'm about to take the cinnamon rolls out of the oven. You coming down?"

"Definitely."

My phone pinged on the bed as I got to the door.

"Was that your phone?" Mom stopped. "Do you want to get it?"

"No, I'm sure it's nothing. I would much rather have some delicious cinnamon rolls than worry about my phone. Can I put on my own icing?" I followed her down the stairs.

"Only after Lauren and your dad have had theirs. The last time you poured first, there was barely any left."

I shrugged my shoulder. "What can I say? It's all your fault for making that cream cheese icing so delicious."

"I can always show you how to make it."

"I don't think that would be safe. I'd be about five hundred pounds by summer."

She laughed, and we walked into the kitchen. Dad and

Lauren were already filling their plates. There were cinnamon rolls, fresh berries, French toast, eggs and bacon. The breakfast of champions. My queasy stomach grumbled, ready for some real food to settle things down.

I pecked Dad on the cheek.

"You were out late last night." He smiled at me and took a sip of his coffee.

I filled my plate and pushed aside the small pangs of guilt about staying out all night and not letting them know beforehand.

"I was. We were out late, and I figured it would better to stay at Sam's instead of coming in late and waking everyone up." I managed to keep my cringe to a minimum. We didn't keep secrets, but it seemed like that was all I had lately. It seemed the family ethos of honesty hadn't been completely instilled in me yet.

And that was what I was afraid of. One day of contact with Angie, and I was already more reckless and irresponsible than I'd been in years.

Everything they'd done for me could be wiped away, and all I'd be left with was who I was before.

"I know you're an adult now, but make sure you tell us next time, sweetheart. We don't want to worry about you." Mom took a sip of her coffee.

"I know. I'm sorry." The guilt crater got a little deeper.

"We know you're responsible, but it's always something in the back of a parent's mind." Dad bit into his cinnamon roll, and Lauren stared at me wide-eyed. This was the closest I'd ever come to a talking-to in the house.

"Since Kara's allowed to have unauthorized sleepovers, does this mean I can have a sleepover at Tracey's this weekend?" Lauren piped up with hope shining in her eyes.

Without looking up from their plates, Mom and Dad responded with a resounding, "No."

"Why not?"

"Because Tracey's mom got her a tattoo for her sixteenth birthday and asked if you wanted to get one too." Mom's voice ratcheted up an octave.

"I wasn't going to get one." Lauren poked at her eggs and slumped down in her seat.

"Maybe not, but I don't want to take any chances. Who knows? Maybe you'll come back home with an eyebrow ring or a belly button piercing."

Lauren grumbled for the rest of breakfast until Mom offered to take her to the mall. She perked up immediately, stuck her plate in the dishwasher and raced upstairs.

"Do you want to come too, Kara?" Mom picked up Dad's plate and stuck it in the sink to rinse while he covered the food.

"I'll hang at home. Get jump start on work for next semester." I smiled and hurried out before there were any more questions.

With the morning I'd had, being stuck among the Christmas crush at the mall after driving around for hours looking for a spot wasn't my idea of fun. And there was the cloud over my head, sitting in the center of my bed up in my room. I couldn't meet Angie. The full breakfast I'd had threatened to rocket straight out of my mouth as I envisioned myself walking up to her in a café or somewhere else neutral, and having her slurred words and stumbling movements send me into a tailspin.

My hands were so clammy I kept wiping them on the bedspread to keep my phone from sliding under my fingers. Every time I read it, I'd erase a line and then erase the whole thing, starting over. Squeezing the bridge of my nose, I went with the first thing that poured out of my head as word vomit. It took me ten drafts to get:

Angie,

I'm sorry. I'm not ready. Meeting with you would not be good for me or my family right now. Maybe in the future.

Kara

My mouth went dry like I'd been snacking on sawdust all afternoon. Closing my eyes, I hit send and turned my phone off. I didn't want to hear the notification that she'd replied. I should have set up a filter so her message would skip my inbox. It was too late now. I couldn't go back in.

Maybe I should swear off technology and go back to the old-school paper-and-pen method. Yeah, that sounded like the best way to avoid dealing with this. Staring up at the constellations on the ceiling, I folded my hands over my stomach. Sleep beckoned me.

The constellations Dad had drawn up there for me during tenth grade astronomy sprawled across the entire ceiling. It had taken us nearly a week to get it done. We both left the project at the end of the day covered in paint and laughing uncontrollably. When he tucked me under his arm and wrapped his hand around my shoulder as we looked up at our hard work dotted across my ceiling, I counted that as one of the happiest times in my life.

"I think this will help with your class." He smiled down at me *with flecks of paint all over his skin and closely cropped hair.*

"I think it will, Dad." I'd said it past the golf ball-sized lump in *my throat. It was the first time I'd called him that. His eyes crinkled at the sides, and he squeezed my shoulder, resting his head against mine. "How about we get some ice cream?"*

He hadn't had to ask me twice. We went out to get ice cream and went over the constellations. The smile was permanently on my face. A few people stared a bit at us, a mismatched pair, but neither of us cared. Father and daughter out for some tasty ice cream after a long project had been completed.

From that day on, he was Dad. I'd never even had a dad up until that point. Whoever the sperm donor was, he'd left my mom before I was even born. Mike was the only dad I ever needed. When I'd opened my grades with Mom, Dad, and Lauren standing beside me at the computer, my heart had pounded and my hands had been so sweaty I didn't think I'd be able to move the mouse.

As the page loaded, I'd wiped my sweaty palms on my pants. Eyes wide, I'd barely caught a glimpse of the screen before they cheered behind me, tugging me up into a group embrace. Closing my eyes, I'd sunk into their arms, basking in the glow and energy of their happiness that I'd done it. After all the late nights and struggles, I'd gotten an A- in that course that marking period.

They'd worked so hard to get me to this point. I'd wanted this fellowship to show them how far I'd come. Mom had gotten a prestigious history fellowship when she'd started her PhD program. I wanted them to be proud of me. No matter what I did, I always got that gnawing pit in my stomach that I needed to keep impressing, keep proving and showing them that I was really their daughter. So one day they wouldn't wake up and realize they'd made a mistake taking me in. Some days that overwhelming, chest-crushing anxiety made it hard to breathe, like one day they'd find out I really didn't belong.

I couldn't risk undermining my real family for my unstable birth mother.

My nap earlier hadn't cut it. The effects from the night before had mostly worn off, but I couldn't help wishing I was back in Heath's bed. His bright summer day smell in the middle of winter made me think of days at the pool and bonfires on the beach. I was glad I hadn't gotten his number. If I had, I'd be calling him up, ready to feel everything he'd made me feel the night before and wash away this tiredness in the crashing waves of his body and the riptide of his eyes.

I was ready to dive into the deep end with him. My phone vibrated under my pillow, and I tugged it out. Unknown number. There was a sharp spark of dread that it might be Angie. I hesitantly tapped 'accept' and lifted the phone to my ear.

9

HEATH

I'd only lasted about twelve hours from when I'd last seen her, but it had been worth it. The thoughts of waiting four more days to see her again sucked, but with Christmas over, there hadn't been a time we could find that worked.

She'd said yes and agreed to see me again. I'd been smiling all through opening presents with my mom and our trips to the shelters serving food. I worked hard to figure out how to make mine and Kara's next night together even more memorable.

My hands were practically numb after peeling and mincing nearly fifty bulbs of garlic. I stood in the kitchen chopping onions like I was serving a small battalion in the military. The double ovens were put to good use, crammed full of trays of holiday favorites.

My dreams had been filled with visions of Kara. Every shower was an exercise in how long I could hold out before I wrapped a soapy hand around my cock, closed my eyes, and recalled everything about that night in vivid detail. Her skin, her touch, her moans. I snapped myself out of it. Getting a boner in front of my mom was not on my to-do list today.

Kara: I still can't believe Duckie ended up alone. Totally messed up! Same with Brian. He definitely should have ended up with Molly Ringwald.

Me: There were only two girls in detention! Who else was he supposed to end up with? The janitor? And John Hughes made her end up with Blane after test audiences hated the original ending

Kara: People suck sometimes.

Me: No argument there

Kara: So you're seriously holding out on me about our date?

Me: Not much to tell

She'd been trying to weasel details out of me since I'd asked her out again.

Kara: ...

Me: Seriously. Low key, fun, at my place. That's all you need to know.

Kara: Alrighty. Ok, my mom is calling me to finish helping her wrap up 5000 cookies she didn't give away before Christmas. Talk later?

Me: Of course

My eyes watered against the stinging burn that only got worse with each chop. I ran my sleeve across my face, trying to mop it all up. It only made the sting worse. Squeezing my eyes shut, I contemplated getting some goggles from the garage.

"Please don't drip your bodily fluids into the onions." Mom laughed, kicking the fridge closed and carrying a massive bowl filled with dough.

"You know what happens when I cut onions. Why do you make me do it every year?" I finished the last of the forty onions and dumped them into the huge pot on the stove.

"Because my face feels like it's going to explode when I cut them, so better you than me." She stuck out her tongue. The long scar along the side of her face was barely visible after all these years, nowhere near as angry and puckered as it used to be. She was beautiful and strong. The scar was a testament that.

My love for plants was a weird quirk to most people, but they'd helped us weather a lot of storms. When we'd first moved to the East Coast, the garden my mom and I had worked on kept us in fresh food until we got on our feet. All her money had gone toward a place to stay and fixing our old broken-down car so she could get to work. That didn't leave much for things like food.

We'd been side by side out back planting, and so excited when our first plants sprouted up. Roasted vegetables, stews, and grabbing them straight out of the ground with a rinse had been our preferred ways to eat them. The safety and comfort of working the soil with my hands had never gone away, and that's why botany.

"You're a cruel, cruel woman! How many shelters are you feeding this week?"

"Only the one. This is only about a quarter of what they need most of the time, but I don't have much more space to be able to safely store the food before we take it to them. People always forget about the crowds that are still there after Christmas. I have to make sure people have some treats even after the holiday is over." She turned the giant dough ball out onto the floured counter and got to work kneading it. A timer dinged, and she checked over her shoulder.

"Can you grab those pies out of there and then put in another tray of the stuffing?"

I saluted her, my kitchen captain, and grabbed a couple of oven mitts. The heat blast from the oven cleared away the stinging in my eyes and replaced it with a dry, scratchy-eye feeling. Wonderful.

The brown sugar and cinnamon smell made my stomach grumble and reminded me of Kara. I'd been on sous-chef mode since the crack of dawn. I was delirious. People thought I could skate forever on the ice, well, my mom could cook forever in the kitchen.

An accountant by profession, cooking and baking for others was where her heart was. She'd sacrificed a whole row of cabinets to fit in another oven and the ability to bake six catering trays of food instead of only three.

The hot meals we'd had when we made it to Philly in the shelters had kept us going while she'd waited for her first paycheck.

We had a break when the ovens were full, every surface was covered in some kind of food that needed to be cooled or stuck in the ovens. There was literally no other place to put anything. I collapsed into the nearest chair.

"You want to go out to eat?" I called down the hallway. The mail from before Christmas was sitting at the front door. I flipped through it and my blood ran cold as I plucked one out of the stack.

"There's about nine thousand pounds of food sitting in the kitchen." Her voice got closer and I shoved the envelope into my pocket.

She walked into the living room, undoing her apron.

"Like you're going to let me eat any of it. I know how this song and dance goes. Not until you've filled the car to the brim and there is barely enough room for you to slide into the driver's seat will you let me take the food."

She paused with her finger raised like she was going to

say something and then nodded. "Okay, where do you want to go?"

Yes! "How about some crab fries?" I was already at the front door with my coat on. The letter would have to wait.

Laughing, she grabbed her purse. "You really are an East Coaster, aren't you?" she teased, and I opened the door, zipping my coat against the blistering cold outside. A small flake landed on my nose, and I glanced up at the overcast sky.

"My heart will always belong to California, but it doesn't mean I won't enjoy the food."

We drove to a place not too far from our old high school, Rittenhouse Prep. Cavanaugh's crispy fries smothered in old bay with a legendary cheese sauce had been a staple back in high school. We'd piled in there after practice sometimes to refuel and relax.

I waved to the guy behind the counter, and we grabbed a spot in a booth. The menu hadn't changed in years, and that made it the best. So many things in life changed, but coming back to this place, sliding into a booth and eating some of the most delicious fries ever created meant all was right with the world.

Mom picked up the menu, and I slapped it down on the table. "Why do you even look? You know you're going to pick the same thing I always get."

"Maybe I want to try something different." She thrived on consistency and predictability. Some of that had rubbed off on me too, but in a different way.

It was probably a side effect of living in a house where you never knew what might happen. Walking on eggshells all the time and never knowing if it would be a good day or a bad day. Would it be a day where we watched TV and ate dinner and fell soundly asleep, or would it be a day where she ended up in the hospital and I slept on the beach?

The waiter came over, and I placed my order. Mom spent a solid minute looking over the menu with him standing there before ordering the exact same thing I had. I shot her a look and chuckled.

She rolled her eyes and handed over the menu to the waiter. The blustery, wintery mix swirled outside the window of the restaurant. There had been a few flurries, but it was coming down harder.

A large figure wrenched open the door to the place and blasted everyone with freezing air. He held the door open for another smaller figure and dragged the hat off his head as the door slammed behind him. I smiled wide as Ford stepped into the place with Olivia at his side.

She rubbed her hands together and blew into them. I waved my arm as they scanned the restaurant looking for a place to sit. Ford smiled with relief washing over his face and motioned for Liv to follow him. She didn't look nearly as happy to see us as he did.

Mom craned her neck to see who I waved to.

"Look at you, Ford! I can't believe how much you've grown up." Mom slid out of the booth and squeezed his cheeks. I stifled my laughter behind my fist. "And Olivia." Mom rested her hand along the side of Olivia's face. She stared down into her eyes.

"How are you, sweetheart? How was your Christmas?"

Olivia throat worked up and down, and there was a slight sheen on her eyes before she smiled and nodded. "I'm good, and it was good. Colm got me this bracelet."

"Wow, that's beautiful." My mom oohed and aahed over it. "Come join us." Mom did her flustered-mother-hen thing and ushered them into her side of the booth and scooted in beside me.

Ford unbuttoned his coat and scooted to the far wall while Liv followed him, sliding in a bit closer. I raised my eyebrow at him, and he shook his head.

Mom reached across the table and covered Liv's hands with her own. "How are you holding up? I hear you're graduating from school soon. A boarding school up in Boston?"

"Yes. I'll graduate in June, and then I'll be going to college at UPenn in the fall."

"That's wonderful." She squeezed Liv's hands. "Your parents would be so proud of you."

Olivia ducked her head and nodded again. "I hope so."

Colm and Olivia's parents had died in a car accident our senior year of high school. Since Colm was eighteen, he'd become her guardian. He'd put her in a boarding school up there while he went to college and was drafted.

"Where's Colm?" I leaned against the table, talking to Ford while Mom and Liv had a little gab session.

"He is finishing up the paperwork to sell their parent's house. They found a buyer. Need to get it done before the end of the year." Ford pushed through the words like he was shoving a boulder up a mountain.

The server came back with our drinks and a couple menus for Ford and Olivia, but they waved him off, already knowing their orders.

"Like the good old days." I leaned back in the booth.

"I was so pissed when we moved to Boston and I never got to come here in high school!" Olivia laughed and looked to Ford.

"I'm sure you can make up for it in college." Ford silently drummed his fingers along the table.

"When you're ready to move down for college, let us

know if you need anything. Heath and Declan are here too. And I'm always around. I can take you shopping. I don't know what you plan on bringing down from school." Mom's eyes lit up talking about it.

I could already see the vision of a tricked-out girl's room dancing through my mom's brain. She'd never gotten to do that stuff with me.

"I really appreciate it, and I'll let you know. It will be weird coming back for more than a visit. Will you come visit me, Ford?" She brushed her shoulder against his.

He raised an eyebrow and nodded. "Of course. Colm and I will be down all the time to check in on you. And Grant's going to UPenn too."

Her smile drooped. He'd better hope he never got traded to Philly.

Our food arrived and everyone dug in. Salty-seasoned flavor exploded in my mouth, and it was exactly like I remembered. Somehow, trying to make these at home wasn't the same. We sat talking for a bit longer.

Glancing out the window of the restaurant, Mom checked her watch and turned to me. "I think I need more catering trays for everything we cooked. Can we run to the store and then the mall for a few things?"

I cringed as even more snow came down. At least the Christmas rush was over. "Sure, but we should go now." I put down a couple twenties as Mom reached for her purse. "Move it, Mom."

"But Heath—"

"Mom, I've got it." I dropped my money and looked around for the server.

"It's cool, man. I'll close out the bill." Ford slid the folio away from me.

"It was so wonderful to see you, Olivia." Mom bent to wrap her arms around Olivia and squeezed her tight.

I slapped my hand into Ford's and slid out of the booth. "Bye, Liv." Waving to her, I shrugged my coat on, and Mom and I headed out into the whipping wind.

Only a few days until I saw Kara again. I was going to make it a night she couldn't get out of her head.

10

HEATH

I hadn't thought I'd be returning to the hotel where I'd had my night with Kara so soon. Walking through the door held open by the doorman under the expansive awning sent a sharp spark of electricity right down my spine.

It was like I could still smell her and feel her by being in the same space we'd been together. Shoving my hands deeper into my pockets and wrapping my fingers around my phone, I resisted the urge to call her. She'd said she had a family thing today and wouldn't be able to talk much. *Calm the hell down.*

Felix had already asked what my deal was the second time I broke a pot in the greenhouse. Turns out lunging across the work bench for a message that may or may not have come through was a quick and easy way to crack a few pots and spill soil all over everything. He'd shaken his head and laughed. I couldn't even blame him.

Walking into the hotel bar, I checked for any sign of Emmett. This dude lived like a fifty-year-old bachelor. I expected him to be sitting in a booth in a smoking jacket with a pipe in his mouth.

"Dude, it's about time," he groused when I spotted him in a booth toward the back, sans smoking jacket. Emmett wasn't as smooth and refined as Colm even though they ran in the same circles. He'd had a little bit of a lumberjack vibe before he shaved the beard right after high school. We hung out and had a few beers. I knew most of the other guys were busy and Emmett's parents were absent as usual. He was probably rattling around his penthouse all by himself.

Emmett's default was to cover the bill. For as long as I could remember, his first instinct had always been to put his hand in his pocket first. Whether it was for pizza, kegs for a party, you name it, and he would try to pay for it. Even if we tried to preempt him.

"I'm serious, Em. You don't have to pay for my drinks."

His gaze locked with mine. "I know, but if I don't spend it on you, I'll end up spending it on something else. Might as well be another King."

I let it slide. Once I got my first pro check, he was getting the biggest and most ridiculous bottle of bourbon delivered to him.

We stepped out of the bar, and I dropped my bag to zip up my coat. A large group of people were filing out of one of the ballrooms. I stepped back to let them pass when a glint of purple caught my eye. For a second, I thought I imagined it. That had to be bound to happen when someone occupied about ninety-five percent of your waking thoughts. But it wasn't my imagination. I flapped my arm in the air waving like an idiot.

"Kara!" I called out. Emmett craned his neck to see who I'd shouted for.

She brushed her curls back from her face as her eyes

searched the crowd. Stopping mid-button on her coat, she spotted me. With a quick word to the people beside her, she zigzagged through the crowd straight for me.

"Hi." She stepped in closer, letting the crowd pass.

"Hey, what are you doing here?"

"I could ask you the same thing." The warm twinkle in her eyes had me fisting my hands at my sides. We'd had one night and planned for another date. Was this caress-your-face-in-public-and-kiss-you-breathless territory?

"I had a family event. A dinner my parents were attending."

Oh shit, parents in the vicinity. Normally I'd be racing off into the sunset, but I stayed put.

"Don't worry, they had to leave early. What about you?" She licked her bottom lip. Had there ever been a more perfect one?

"Meeting Emmett for drinks." I nodded in the general area Emmett had been, no idea if he was still there or had been replaced with a fire-breathing dragon. Everything centered on her. The dress she had on showed off her collarbones and shoulders. The purple reminded me of walking into the greenhouse, so vibrant in a place filled with muted, safe colors.

We both stood there staring at each other. I was ninety percent sure I had the dopiest of grins on my face.

Someone called her name behind her, and she glanced over her shoulder.

"One sec, okay?" She hurried away before I could say anything. I tried to keep my eye on her as the sea of people milling around in the lobby grew.

Emmett found his way back to me. "She's the one from the bar that night, right?"

"Yeah." I craned my neck to find her.

"Then you'll probably need this." He slipped a hotel key card into my hand.

I threw my hands up. "What the hell is it with you and needing to spend money on people? I don't need your charity, Em." He was pissing me off with this shit.

"Did I say you did?" He met my glare with one of his own.

"Do you think you need to buy my friendship or something? It's starting to make me feel cheap. Don't think you're climbing into bed with us. Is this some secret sex room? Are there cameras installed in there?" I eyed him suspiciously.

"Dude, you're insane." He laughed. "Think of this as an early graduation present."

I raised an eyebrow at him, still not one hundred percent sure he wasn't up to something.

"Are you running an escort agency on the side?"

"You found me out, man. That's where all this money comes from." He spread his arms wide. "You'd be shocked what this body gets on the open market. I get free rooms from the hotel because I own the penthouse. Better they not go to waste. Don't make me feel like shit for trying to do something nice."

And now I felt like shit. "I want you to know you don't have to spend money like it's water to get me to show up, or any of us for that matter."

A shadow passed over his eyes for a split second. A haunted look and then it was gone. "I know. Have fun." He winked and walked through the lobby.

Kara was over talking to a group of people. One of the guys had his hand on her shoulder. She took a step back, but his hand followed. My hackles were up as I watched her take another step away only to have the guy refuse to break contact.

And in a flash his thumb traced along the bare skin on her shoulder. I don't even remember moving, but I do remember grabbing the guy by the lapels of his black suit and pushing him away from her. He stumbled back with his eyes wide and glassy.

"Back off," I bit out. My hands fisted at my sides.

The heads of everyone around us whipped around.

"Heath, it's okay." She ran her hands down my arms to my fists and only then did I relax.

"It was a wonderful event, I'll definitely think about that biochemistry fellowship for next summer." She turned, smiling over her shoulder. Using her body to corral me away, she managed to push me back a few steps.

"It's okay. He was a bit drunk."

"It's not okay." My jaw was so tight, I thought I might crack a tooth.

She sighed. "You're right, it's not. But I don't want to make waves for my dad at the hospital."

"That's not even something you should have to think about. That asshole shouldn't have put his hands on you."

"I know, but thank you for swooping in." She pressed a gentle kiss against my lips, and her other hand slid down to mine.

"What's that?"

I glanced down at the partially bent key card.

"I have a room."

She raised an eyebrow.

"We can watch a movie or something. We don't have to go up there. Or we can go eat in the restaurant." I rushed out. She'd just eaten. I resisted the urge to smack myself in the head. "Or we could grab a drink."

She peered up at me with a wicked smile. It was the

same one I'd seen that night. Tugging out her phone, she sent a message to someone.

"Who was that to?"

"I needed to make sure no one is worried about me. And to answer your question, how about all of the above?"

I let out a sigh of relief. My outburst hadn't freaked her out. I hated that feeling that had bubbled up. The one where I wanted to destroy that guy for touching her, but I shook it off. *Relax.*

"I knew you were a woman who wanted to have her cake and eat it too."

It was like a re-creation of our first night together, but this time I'd been sure to study up.

I woke in stages and dropped my hand onto the bed beside me. My eyes snapped open when my hand hit empty space. Turning to the side, the tension left my muscles as I spied a sleepy Kara lying on her stomach with a pillow shoved under her hips.

There was a knock at the door, and I slid out of bed, wrapping a sheet around my waist, careful not to wake her. It was probably one of the guys. Opening the door to the room, my eyes bugged out at the overloaded room service cart stationed in the hallway.

"Mr. Cunning put in an order for this for you." The sheepish-looking bellhop and I glanced down at myself, standing there like I was headed to a toga party.

"I can take it from here." I grabbed the linen-covered cart and dragged it inside.

The guy nodded and let me pull it in. I held on to the

door so it wouldn't slam. There were about ten covered dishes on the cart, and the smell made my stomach rumble.

Dropping the sheet, I walked back into the bedroom and slid in beside her. Kara's exposed skin was a beacon. I trailed my fingers down her bare shoulder, and she grumbled, burrowing deeper into the pillow she held on to. I hoped she thought that was me she was wrapped around. Testing my theory, I slid my arm under her head, and her eyes fluttered open. She squinted, barely opening her eyes before a lazy smile spread across her face. Lifting the blankets up, she covered the tempting bits of skin that had been peeking out from under them.

"Morning."

"Morning." She yawned and shifted over fully onto my arm with her head resting there. "What time is it?" Stretching under the covers like a weird starfish dance, she yawned again.

"I think it's eight."

"Too early." She groaned and rolled in closer, lifting her leg over my hip. She sighed and closed her eyes like her shifting hadn't put her molten core less than an inch from my now aching cock. She cracked open her eyes, trying to look innocent.

"What?" She moved her hips, and my dick grazed her wetness.

A tingle crept down my spine, and I gazed at her with what I'm sure was a lecherous smile.

"You do realize that you're not getting out of this bed until you follow through on this tease." I rocked my hips, and the tip of my cock slid through the hot sweetness already building between her legs like it was waiting for me.

"Hold that thought." She pressed her lips to mine and slid out of the bed. Grabbing my shirt off the chair, she threw it on. It shouldn't be legal for a woman to look that good in my clothes.

I'd never gotten the whole wearing-a-guy's-clothes thing until that moment. She was tall—not as tall as me, but a nice height for resting her head on my shoulder and stuff like that. The shirt was longish for a shirt, but on her, as a makeshift dress, it was out of this world.

She opened the door off the bedroom and poked her head inside. As she moved, the shirt that had barely covered her ass rose, exposing the bottom curve of her cheeks. My mouth watered. I wanted to feast on that ass. And then she was gone.

I slid my arms under my head, waiting for her return. Her sweet cinnamon smell clung to my skin and made me smile. The bed smelled like her too.

The bathroom door creaked open, and she rushed back in, closing the door behind her. She grabbed the hem of the shirt, and it was up and over her head in a flash. Smoothing out her hair with her hands, she crawled onto the bed, the stiff peaks of her nipples calling to me like delicious berries ready to be plucked.

"Did you say something about me being a tease?" She dragged the blankets off my chest.

The cool sheets glided across my cock, and I wrapped my hands around my swollen crown, pumping it up and down as I watched her.

"I think I did say something like that."

"I'm sorry to hear that, there must be some way I could make it up to you." She grinned and put her hands on either side of my hips. Her soft fingers skimmed across my skin, her mouth less than an inch from my swollen head. With her eyes on me, she opened her mouth and closed the gap between my dick and her beautifully plump lips.

"I think you're on the right track." I sucked in a breath.

"How about now?" She stuck out her pink tongue, running it around my crown before taking me into her mouth. The hot, wet suction of her mouth made my toes curl. I sank my fingers into the sheets and forgot anything else existed other than Kara and the pounding pleasure that rolled over me.

11

KARA

We had a lazy morning, finally rolling out of bed at eleven or so. My normally frizzy hair was a poof ball of epic proportions that I tried to tame as I stepped into the other room for some food. The only person with stomach grumbles louder than Heath was me.

He gave me his shirt I'd taken off earlier when I went to search for my clothes. It smelled like him.

"Wear this. We'll get your clothes later." He buttoned up his jeans, going commando.

I was going to ask why, but then I saw the way his eyes went molten as I tugged at the hem of the shirt hitting me on my upper thighs. He ushered me out into the living room. How was I supposed to eat when he was looking at me like that?

My stomach rumbled the second the smell of food slammed into me.

"There's a lot here." He gestured to the cart piled with food.

"You ordered all this?" I turned to him with my eyes wide.

"Emmett strikes again. My friend from the bar. It seems his generosity keeps giving."

Must be nice to have friends like that. I had friends who I could bum a couple fries from. That was as far as it went.

"I don't know what I want to have first. It all smells amazing." I sat in the chair he pulled out for me at the small table in the corner of the room.

"How about I get you a little bit of everything? Do you want some coffee?"

My ears perked up. He grabbed two mugs off the cart and poured us both some piping-hot coffee.

Sliding the plate under my nose with a hand towel draped over his arm, Heath presented me with my meal.

"Brunch is served." His French accent could use a little work.

"This smells so good." I plunged my fork into the food, not even caring what I ate first, it all smelled so delicious. Heath sat in the chair beside me when I was on my third forkful. I looked between him and my plate.

"Sorry." I covered my mouth with my hand so I wasn't giving him a special preview of my already chewed food.

"Don't be sorry. It's really good." He grinned and tucked into his plate.

I groaned as I ate my first mouthful of the French Toast. "Why is restaurant food so freaking good?" I bounced in my seat as I ate. This food made me want to break out into song and dance.

"My mom's food is even better than this, and her secret is that she practically has a tanker truck full of butter—we are stocked to the ceiling with butter at all times. So, so much butter. So I'm going to go with the fact that each plate here probably has about three sticks of butter in it."

Normally I'd be horrified, but I didn't even care. When it was this good, I couldn't care.

"Your mom cooks? Is she a chef? Like professionally?"

Heath shook his head, some of his hair falling into his eyes. I really wanted to brush it back from his face, but that would mean I wasn't eating and that wasn't acceptable.

"No, she's an accountant. She loves to cook for people and give it away. When I was growing up, she didn't get to cook very much, so she takes advantage whenever she can."

"Why didn't she get to cook when you were growing up?"

He froze mid-bite, and I shoveled another heaping forkful of food into my mouth.

"My dad only liked specific things. Nothing that gave off any scents that were too strong. She was never allowed to cook what she wanted or bring it to other people."

My chewing slowed at the look on in his eyes. His normally sun-kissed face had paled. We barely knew each other. Had I just stepped into a minefield?

I slid my hand across the table and wrapped it over the top of his.

"Why not?" Why was I prodding? I hated it when people did that to me, thinking I was being cagey about my past to create a sense of mystery and not to shield myself from massive embarrassment.

"My dad said it was a waste of time and money. That and he was an abusive asshole." His jaw was clenched, and his hand was wrapped tightly around his fork.

"I'm sorry. I... It's never an easy thing to deal with. When the people you love turn out to be the people who hurt you most." The pit in my stomach grew. I shouldn't have said anything.

His eyes snapped to mine, and he dropped his fork and ran his fingers over my knuckles.

"You too?"

That spark of connection. Maybe that was what had drawn us to each other on that first night. Somehow we'd sensed our pasts even through the fronts we'd both put up. Me as an uptight, together grad student and him as the carefree hottie.

"Not like that. It wasn't me they hit. Not that I didn't see a fair share of the men who professed to love my mom whaling on her. But she never let anyone touch me after—" I stopped.

He squeezed my hand. "What happened?"

I should stop talking. *Stop talking, Kara. Say it was no big deal. Zip those lips!*

"My mom and Dad aren't my birth parents. They are my foster parents who adopted me. I came to them when I was thirteen and an absolute wreck. My mom is—" My lips turned down as the words in her letters came back to me. "Is an alcoholic." *Was it a was now? Was she still one and sober now?* "She wasn't the best at choosing people who weren't going to hurt her." The carefully worded retelling of my childhood came off stilted and awkward. I'd never talked to anyone about this stuff before.

"After what?" Heath's hand tightened on mine and I winced. He glanced down, and his eyes got wide. Snatching his hand away, his clenched jaw relaxed, and he shoved his hands into his lap.

"It only happened once. It was an accident, but that at least got her to kick the guy out. And for a little while I thought maybe that might be a turning point, but it wasn't.

She disappeared for a long time after that and then things got worse and then I ended up with my family." And now I'd word vomited my entire life story on a guy I'd spent two nights in person with. I tried to shake off those old feelings. That old hurt that never seemed to go away completely.

"I'm glad you ended up with a good family." He traced a path on the back of my hand.

"What about you?" I glanced over at him. I seriously wasn't going to learn. *Stop prodding!* My heart ached for what we'd both been through. He hadn't told me his story yet, but I could see it etched all over his face. The brightness and lightness dimmed. I almost didn't ask, but knowing I wasn't alone in dealing with some of life's harsh realities eased that tightness in my chest. The one where I wondered if I'd ever feel whole again.

"It only happened once to me too. I couldn't take him going after my mom anymore, so I jumped in and got the shit kicked out of me. Apparently that was what my mom needed to leave him. Had I known that, I'd have jumped in a lot sooner and taken the ass kicking. Once we got out of the hospital, we were in the car and moved here."

"Have you ever seen him since?" A knot formed in my stomach. Angie dropping into my life had been embarrassing but never physically harmful.

He hesitated and then shook his head. More strands of his hair fell over his eyes. His shoulders were stiff and straight. I'd taken his carefree attitude for granted. With the way he spoke and moved through the world, I assumed he'd had a charmed kind of life, untouched by the ugliness so many people experienced.

"He went to jail for a while after what he did, but he never came after us. What about you? Have you seen your mom since?" His eyes found mine, searching for more from me.

I stared down at our hands, his warmth soaking into my skin and the rough pads of his fingers tracing a random pattern on the back of my hand.

"I have. A few times. Not since high school graduation though. She sent me a letter recently. She wanted to meet me. Said she was sober and has been for a while."

"Do you want to meet her?"

The very question I'd warred with since the minute I'd opened the letter. Why was I spilling my guts like this? I guess that bright and giddy feeling he brought out made it feel like I could say these words out loud and it wouldn't implode my life. And, knowing he'd been through hard things too made it feel like he'd understand.

It was like spilling your guts to someone you met on a whirlwind trip. In a few days, he'd be gone playing hockey, and I'd be back to classes. Standing up in front of a class, trying not to choke on the general banalities of my life.

"No. Yes. I don't know. I do, but I don't think I can. I don't think I can handle meeting her and finding out it was all a lie."

"What if it's not a lie? Do you think it would help you to see her?"

"I really don't know. A part of me is always so scared that growing up like I did will mean that something like that is around the corner for me."

"I have a feeling the only thing around the corner for you is great things."

I cracked a smile, even with the unanswered questions about Angie floating around my head.

"I'm glad you think so. I'm never really sure. I replied to her e-mail saying I'd like to meet, and then I chickened out.

There are too many ways it could go wrong if I let her back into my life. Things are good with my family. I love my parents and my sister, and letting her back in would be a smack in the face to them."

"Do you really think that?"

I dragged my fingers through my hair, and they caught in the tangles.

"I don't know. I don't even know if it's what I want or something I think I should do. Maybe later this semester. Once I've found out about the fellowship and things don't feel so up in the air. Maybe then." It sounded a lot like I was trying to convince myself and not Heath.

"Don't let your fear hold you back from something that could give you closure on a part of your life you want to forget."

"We can't all be as balls-out brave as you." I chuckled, and my leg bounced up and down.

"I haven't been balls-out brave since junior year of high school. Learned the hard way that the administration did not look kindly upon my balls being featured in the class picture." He chuckled, and the clouds were pushed aside.

"Why am I not surprised?" I laughed. "Do we still get our New Year's date?" I bit my bottom lip. Had I completely messed this up by bringing in the heavy? This was supposed to be a fun fling, but somewhere things had changed.

"Don't think you're getting out of it that easily." He smiled and got up from the table, picking up my plate.

"I wasn't trying to get out of anything. Just asking."

Heath crouched down in front of me. The sharp tingle was back, and I tightened my fingers around the seat of my chair.

His blond strands fell over his forehead.

"We are most definitely on, unless you don't want to be

on." Hesitancy and worry creased his brow, and I dipped my head, resting my forehead against his.

"I can't wait."

His bright smile created the lightness in my chest I'd been chasing like a high since the first second he'd looked at me.

We piled everything back on the cart after we'd eaten so much my stomach was ready to explode. A food coma was right around the corner. As much as I didn't want to, I needed to get home and get some work done.

Leaving our cocoon where I'd been sexed into oblivion, and the world hadn't ceased to spin when I'd spilled my guts, and hot guys like Heath kept staring at my ass like it was the newest and most delicious dessert ever created would suck, but we still had a real date in a couple of days. Unfortunately, for now, the real world beckoned.

12

HEATH

Declan had grumbled about my intensive cleaning of the house over the past two days. I'd wanted everything to be perfect. I finally figured out the perfect place for New Year's Eve. My place. Why go somewhere else filled with tons of people? Rubbing my hands together, I double checked the blankets and telescope at the spot I'd picked out for us. At a knock so light I almost missed it, I rushed downstairs.

Everything looked normal as I quickly glanced around the living room. I flung open the door and stared into the eyes of the woman who'd had me twisted up in knots since our first meeting. Her smiling face drew a smile out of me immediately. It was like staring into the sun. I was tempted to shield my eyes. We stood in the doorway, staring into each other's eyes. *Why does every time we first see each other seem to end up like this?* Like we were both stunned by each other's presence.

"Hey."

She looked beautiful. The deep purple of her dress

peeking out from under her coat matched the shades in her hair.

I was totally outclassed with my lazy smile, bed-head hair, and fitted thermal shirt.

"Hey." She ducked her head. My hand shot out and wrapped around her waist.

Her warmth battled against the freezing December air. Over the past ten days or so our text conversations had slipped into such a familiar place that I'd forgotten we'd only seen each other in person twice.

"This is your place?" Her gaze darted around our small porch and the brick facade of the house.

"Yup." I pulled her inside and closed the door behind her.

She glanced at me out of the corner of her eye and reached for the buttons on her coat.

"Not yet." I covered her hand with mine and walked her upstairs. She eyed me suspiciously, as we stepped into my bedroom. I led her to the open window, and her eyebrows furrowed.

"It's not exactly what I imagined you had in mind for our New Year's Eve."

"Are we going out on the roof?" She took a step backward, and I snagged her wrist. Her pulse pounded against my fingers. "It's freezing out there."

"Don't worry, I've got you." I stepped out the window and held out my hand for her.

She hesitated before sliding her hand into mine.

"Trust me." I pulled her out with me, and she clung to my side as we gingerly took a few steps over to where I'd set everything up.

"What exactly is this?" Her fingers bit into my arm; her

grip was so tight. I smiled and guided her down onto the blanket.

Taking a lighter out of my pocket, I lit the two candles. The light bounced off the glass candleholder. I flipped the blanket back to reveal the spread I'd set up. Cheeses, fresh fruit, some hot chocolate in travel mugs, and the telescope. Propping it up, I handed her a mug and covered her legs with another blanket.

"Damn, you're good." She glanced over at me with hungry eyes, and I was tempted to call the whole thing off, throwing her over my shoulder to get her into my bed at light speed.

"You ain't seen nothing yet." I winked. Her musical laughter carried on the frigid, crisp air.

This was going to be a night we'd never forget.

13

KARA

The telescope slid along the tiles of the roof, clattering as it went. Heath sat up and grabbed it, tugging the blankets off me. The sharp, biting cold whooshed back in, reminding me that I was in a place I had no business being.

"Maybe we should head back in." I ran my hands over my legs. Had I known we'd be stargazing outside, I'd have worn pants. "I can't believe you talked me into coming out here."

He held out his hand and helped me up. "I think maybe you wanted to." His eyes twinkled with mischief. "Maybe do something a little bit out of the ordinary."

"That's one thing I'd never call my time with you." My foot slipped and I yelped.

Heath's arms wrapped around me, and he tugged me to his chest. "Don't worry, I've got you." The puffs of breath gathered between us, and I stared down the slope of the roof from the safety of his arms.

"Thanks." I swallowed the lump that formed in my throat.

He guided me back to the window and wrapped his hands around my waist, settling me on his bedroom floor. I licked my dry lips that had nothing to do with the blustery December temperature.

I wanted nothing more than to wrap my arms around his neck and run my fingers through his hair. He stepped back and peeled his coat off. The way his shirt clung to every inch of him was not even fair. *How were mere mortals supposed to not stare and drool?*

"Let me grab your coat." He closed the window behind him and took my coat, draping it over the chair at his desk. The star gazing was unexpected. It definitely wasn't what I'd expected when he'd sent his address. Never did the equation become I'd be staring up into the stars with my fingers intertwined with Heath's and my heart racing so fast it made me light-headed. It could have also had something to do with being perched up on the roof with only his fingers threaded through mine to keep me from sliding off.

We walked back downstairs, his hands on mine the entire time. His smile made his eyes shine. The light in the bar and back at the hotel hadn't done them justice. They were blue unlike any I'd seen before. So clear and deep, I wanted to race to the nearest pool and dive in. I could lose myself in them for hours.

He headed into the kitchen and reappeared a second later. I'd never have guessed he was in college, but the taxi trip here pretty much confirmed that one. The night out at the bar, his friend who'd looked the same age had been splashing out, covering all the drinks, springing for the hotel rooms. What kind of college student could even do that? I'd figured he was an NHL player.

I hadn't been to off-campus housing before, but this was definitely it. Thank God I'd already gotten my schedule for the semester and I hadn't seen Heath's name anywhere on it. What were the odds? We'd attended the same school for a year and a half and never seen each other. Why would we cross paths now?

Somehow we'd managed to keep the talk of our lives pretty light. Past traumas were open season, but what we currently did and our lives now outside of pop culture had been a topic we hadn't touched on. I'd assumed with all his hotel hopping, he was only in town for a little while. How did this change things? I tilted my head toward him and prayed to the study gods that he wasn't a sophomore.

"How did you end up in Philly?" I tucked my hair behind my ear.

"Moved from California when I was thirteen with my mom. Got a hockey scholarship at a prep school in the area, and I've stayed local ever since." His smile faltered, and he handed me a glass of white wine like he didn't want me to ask any more about that. I certainly understood uncomfortable stories about your past.

"California, that's cool. It certainly fits." He had that carefree air about him that made me think of sitting out on a beach and watching the tide roll in.

"You wouldn't be the first to say that. What about you?"

"Me?" I took a sip of wine.

"Yeah, we're doing the getting to know you, right? How did you end up here?"

I glanced down at my hands with my fingers wrapped around the stem of the glass, trying to work out exactly how to answer that. "I went to undergrad in Boston, but I went to high school in the area. I came back when I got into the master's program here, and I'll start my biochem PhD next year." My stomach knotted. Following in the family footsteps.

"Impressive. I thought you were a writer?" He took a sip of his beer.

"I do write, sometimes. To clear my head and stuff." I ran my finger over the rim of my glass. "Why do you get a beer and I'm stuck with wine?"

"Figured it would be something special for the evening. If you're not good with wine, I can grab you a beer." He stood, and I wrapped my fingers around his wrist. The sinewy muscles tightened under my grip. He sat back down and threw his arm over the back of the couch. The picture of relaxation and unstudied manliness.

"No, I was joking. I'm good. Everything is perfect."

"And I understand about the whole lying about what you really do thing."

My eyes shot to his. "I wasn't lying. I do write, I happen to also be a graduate student."

"Kara, it's fine. Not like you're my teacher or anything. My classes for the semester are already all picked out and there wasn't a Kara in the bunch."

The blood drained out of my face. Talk about a nightmare scenario.

"And it is impressive. Someone so young already knowing what you want to do and going after it." He continued on like I hadn't died a little inside.

He thought I was young. He was younger than me. How much younger? "Oh my God, how old are you?"

"What if I told you I was nineteen?" He sat forward and rested his forearms on his legs.

I yelped, my face was awash with horror.

He laughed. "I'm twenty-two. I'll be twenty-three over the summer."

My hand shot to my chest as relief washed over me. I'd been ready to jump out the window and not stop running until I hit the shore if I'd bedded down with someone who wasn't even twenty. Which was silly—he'd been served at the bar, but it wasn't like fake IDs weren't a thing, and he could have sweet-talked honey from a bear.

"How old are you?" He gulped down some more beer. The playful look twinkled in his eyes.

"Don't you know it's not polite to ask a woman her age?" I shot back.

"Don't you know it's not polite to ask questions you don't want to answer yourself?"

"What if I told you I was twenty-nine?" I crossed my arms over my chest, and his eyes shot down like I was presenting my breasts to him on a silver platter. I let out an exasperated sound and dropped my arms, taking another drink.

"I'd say you're a terrible liar. I think you're twenty-four tops, but if you were twenty-nine, I'm more than okay with that."

The TV was on mute and the opening credits to my favorite '80s movie started.

"Now this is what I'm talking about! This is my favorite John Hughes movie." I pointed to the TV with my glass.

"I recorded it for you."

"You did?" *Some Kind of Wonderful* opened with a scene of Watts banging away on her drums, complete with fringed gloves and take-no-prisoners attitude.

"The guy ends up with his childhood best friend after chasing after the popular girl the whole movie. It's the exact opposite of *Pretty in Pink*. I knew this would be your favorite."

"Watts is a pretty badass drummer who doesn't take any crap from anyone."

"She's also pretty hot." He stared into my eyes, and I

leaned in closer like there were a thread connecting the two of us and it was being shortened by the second.

"She was also incredibly loyal."

He drank down my words, he was so close. Like each one tipped the scale we were balancing on until we came crashing down onto each other.

"She was, even when she should have probably kicked Keith in the nuts a few times." His lips had already become an addiction for me. Soft and firm all at the same time. Lazy and insistent in equal parts to make me forget myself.

My eyes fluttered closed as he lifted his hand to the side of my face. A sharp buzz snapped spell we were under, and my eyes shot open.

He hopped up. "One second. I'll be right back."

He disappeared into the kitchen. His tight ass in those jeans nearly had me biting on my knuckle to hold back a groan. He was the hottest guy I'd ever slept with. Academics weren't exactly known for their rock-hard bodies.

He came back with a beer for me, and we talked a little more. For some reason, I tried to steer the conversation away from school. We obviously went to the same school but had never crossed paths. The less we knew about that, the better. If we hadn't seen each other yet, then the odds were there wouldn't be any issues with what we had going on.

A timer *dinged* in the kitchen, and he took my hand, helping me stand from the couch. I let him lead me into the kitchen, curious about exactly what else he'd planned for tonight. I had never been happier to be wrong. I'd assumed he'd be having a party, but I was wrong. This was better. A lot better.

There was a timer on the counter, and he let go of my hand, grabbed an oven mitt and took a cookie sheet with two small white dishes on it out. I leaned against the counter and watched him move. Man, I loved the way he knew his way around the kitchen. A deep dark chocolate smell hit me and made my mouth water.

He baked? What kind of lab was he created in? I swear if he mopped the floors and folded the laundry, I was going to have to check him for a bar code or electronic wiring.

He grabbed a plate and slid it on top of the two small white dishes. Using the oven mitt, he flipped the cookie sheet and the plate, reversing the position before dumping the cookie sheet in the sink. A small hiss shot up from it as it hit the drops of water in the sink.

"What did you make?"

"You'll see." He gave me a sideways smirk and reached around me. A cold blast hit me from the freezer. A giant tub of vanilla bean ice cream made its way out past my face in the grip of the man who'd pretty much stolen a cheat sheet on how to get me to lose my freaking mind. Hot guy in a tight shirt—check. Chocolate dessert—check. Ice cream—check, check, check.

He grabbed the drawer and took out an ice cream scoop. Running it under the tap, he scooped out two perfect balls of vanilla ice cream. He even had his scooping technique down. Kill me now.

A can of whipped cream finished off his excellent plating, and he pulled out a chair for me at the table. Two spoons sat on top of a napkin.

"This is my favorite dessert. My mom taught me how to cook it." The happiness oozed from his pores.

"How could it not be? It's chocolate."

"It's a chocolate lava cake, so it will be warm in the middle."

I sliced into one of the cakes on the plate. Warm chocolate spilled out of the center, mixing with the ice cream that was melting already. His eyes were on me as I slipped the first spoonful into my mouth.

Bliss. It was a phenomenally delicious, deep dark chocolate and made me want to crawl onto the plate and never leave. My eyes that I hadn't even realized I'd closed snapped open.

"Are you serious?" I covered my full mouth.

"What?" He had a self-satisfied grin on his face and took a bite of the dessert.

"This is so good! That's seriously not even fair." I hummed my appreciation and pretty much devoured the whole thing. My spoon clinked against Heath's, and I glanced up at the laughter in his eyes. So yes, maybe I had almost completely devoured the entire plate of dessert without leaving him much. *Oops.*

"You were hungry, huh?"

"Sorry," I said through a mouthful of ice cream. "I wasn't expecting it to be so good."

"What, did you think I was going to make you some crap?"

He picked up the plate, and I couldn't resist dragging my finger through the last bits of chocolate on it.

"Jesus, woman, I can make you more. No need to try to eat the plate."

"I mean, it's not my fault someone made something so good, I had to shove my face full of it."

He dumped the plates in the sink and laughed. I craned my neck to get a good look at the back of his. That's where they'd put a bar code, right? Or maybe the bottom of his feet?

"I guess that means I'll have to make it for you again."

"I'm sure you say that to all the girls." I licked the last bits of chocolate off my spoon.

He pushed away from the sink and stepped next to my chair. I stared up at him. The laughter was gone from his eyes, and my stomach clenched at the intensity there.

"I've never cooked for another woman." His fingers cupped my chin, and he dragged his thumb across my bottom lip. He tasted like chocolate. My tongue darted out again, and the blue of his eyes gave way to black as his pupils dilated.

Our playful energy evaporated in an instant, and there was nothing but his thumb on my lip, my heart pounding against my ribs and the goose bumps all over my body.

"Never?"

"Never really wanted to until now." He leaned over and blew out the candles on the table. The smoke trailed from the dimming wick and made the kitchen smell like a birthday.

"Oh." Who was the articulate soon-to-be PhD student who'd talked herself out of so many discussions in class? Not me, because every word I'd ever learned fled my brain except for Heath, thumb, and chocolate.

"You've got some chocolate on your face." He ran his thumb over a spot on the side of my mouth.

Before I could reach for a napkin, he bent down and pressed his lips against mine. His fingers were still on my chin, keeping my head where he wanted it.

He was all chocolaty goodness as I opened my mouth to him. A sigh escaped my mouth as he lifted me up out of my chair and settled me on the table.

Stepping between my open legs, he slid his hand along the side of my face. His fingers sank into my hair as he tilted my head up.

"I thought we were supposed to save that for midnight." My words were choppy as I tried to gulp down air.

"I'm not patient when it comes to something I really want." His voice came out rough and gruff, and I was seconds away from dragging him to the nearest flat surface. Hell, I was sitting on the table. That would totally do.

My not so witty reply was cut off when he delved into my mouth. Our tongues intertwined, and his hand skimmed under my shirt. A chill shot through my body as the rough pads of his fingers trailed along my waist.

I broke our connection and ripped my mouth away from his. My fingers wrapped around his bunched biceps.

"I have a feeling we aren't going to make it to midnight."

"We're going to make it to midnight all right, but I'm not going to be kissing these lips." His thumb traced over my parted lips. "I'm going to be worshipping your pussy."

My eyes got wide, and I let out a sharp gasp. He was throwing me off with his no-holds-barred tactics. It was so free with no pretenses. He was an open book, and I was ready to stay up all night flipping the pages.

He tipped me back before shooting his arm under my legs and scooping me up. I wrapped my arms tightly around his neck. Blood rushed to my ears, and I clung to him in case I ended up taking a dive straight to the floor.

"Don't worry, I got you." His words and tight hold turned me liquid in his arms. How in the hell was I supposed to play it cool when he was looking at me like that? Biting his lips with his golden hair skimming above his ears, I mean come on! He was the picture of temptation and decadence, and my clit throbbed in time to his steps.

He climbed the stairs with his eyes making promises my body would need to catch up with once we got back to his room. We crossed the threshold, and he kicked the door closed behind him. The light glow from the hallway peeked through the gaps in the doorframe.

"You're beautiful." He let my feet down, and I slid down the hard planes of his chest. "We're going to have a fun time ringing in the New Year." He growled against the side of my face.

My heart thundered. I bit my bottom lip. The herd of horses that invaded my stomach were working triple time now.

He spun around and sat on his bed. Pulling me down on top of him, his fingers sank into my flesh. The skirt of my dress hitched around my upper thighs, and I was straddling his lap. A small gasp broke free from my throat as the insistent nudge of his cock against my fabric-covered pussy sent me into a frenzy.

Wrapping his hands around my waist, he slid me along his hard length. Sparking electricity traveled down my spine, and I cursed the clothes between me and the instrument of my undoing.

"I think I'm going to like the way you celebrate New Year's." My words were choppy.

"I think I am too." His hand around my waist tightened, and his hips rocked with mine.

He slipped his fingers from my waist to the zipper at the back of my dress. The metallic slide of the zipper was the only sound other than our shuddering breaths. His strong hands sank into my skin from my shoulders to my exposed waist, and I let out a moan.

My rocking was more insistent and urgent as he lifted me. I let out a mewling sound that quickly turned into a happy sigh when he undid the zipper of his jeans and slipped on a condom. In a motion so quick and practiced I almost thanked the hookup gods, he jerked my underwear to the side and sank into me.

"Oh shit," I hissed as his mushroom tip parted me and he plunged into me in one fierce stroke.

Tugging down the front of my dress, he dipped his head and captured one of my nipples in his mouth. It was the only reprieve I got before the sharp cant of his hips dragged a moan from deep inside.

"Damn, Kara." His words reverberated through me as he pressed his lips against my shoulder.

His firm touch and dirty words whispered in my ear set me off in minutes. It was like he'd figured out exactly what I needed after two nights and he was determined to give it to me as many times as I could handle it. Maybe even more than I could handle, but I was happy to let him push all my boundaries.

Like he'd been working through the study guide nonstop, his fingers were there, parting me and strumming my clit in perfect time.

"Oh God." I bit his shoulder, and my fingers sank into his arms as his muscles strained beneath me. One hand massaged my ass. His persistent, expert strumming had my eyes rolling back in my head.

I came apart at the seams on his lap, riding out the waves of my climax as he whispered in my ear.

We tumbled over onto the bed, and our laughter bounced off the walls. This was the most fun I'd had in a long time—well, since the last time. It was exactly what I needed. Sweaty and exhausted, I battled to keep my eyes open, draped over Heath's chest. His energy seemed to know no bounds, and I was happy to be an experiment in how far someone could be sexed into exhaustion.

His fingers traced an intricate line across my back. Each

pass was another part of my body that belonged to him. I lifted my head and stared up at him. He had his eyes closed, but opened them when I moved. The time blinked on the alarm clock on his nightstand.

"Happy New Year." My voice was raspy and rough from voicing my appreciation of the orgasm he'd wrung from me.

He glanced over his shoulder and smiled. "Happy New Year." He cupped my face and pulled me up to his lips. "I think this was an excellent way to start things off, don't you?"

The words caught in my throat, and I nodded. This was the start of something that would change my life, only I had no idea how much.

14

HEATH

I woke up later beside Kara. Her black hair covered the pillow next to her, and my hands itched to tangle my fingers in it. My phone buzzed.

"Your phone's been buzzing a lot." Kara cracked an eye open before yawning and rolling over.

I leaned over the edge of the bed and snatched it up off the floor.

Declan: *WHERE ARE YOU?!*

I shot straight up, and Kara sat up beside me. I scrolled through the rest of the messages. My stomach dropped, and I called him right back.

"Get here now!" He ended the call and texted me the location. My heart leaped into my throat. *University Hospital.*

I don't even know if I said the words, but I threw on my clothes and Kara got dressed right alongside me.

"You don't have to come." I shoved my feet into my sneakers.

"It's okay. I can drive. You don't look like you should be driving."

She was probably right. My head was swimming. All the

lights in the city conspired against us getting there, and if I'd been driving, I'd have been tempted to floor it right through the red lights. It was almost seven on New Year's Day. The streets were deserted.

Everything moved in slow motion as we raced through the doors of the hospital. The old feelings came flooding back. My squeaky shoes on the tile floor as I'd walked into the room where my mom lay in a bed, bruised and beaten. *Please be okay. Please be okay.*

Shaking off those nightmares from the past, I glanced over at Kara. My footsteps echoed in the stairwell. We burst through the door on the fifth floor. My hand was wrapped tightly around Kara's. I stopped at the nurses' station, and they rattled off the room number. The stop hadn't even been needed because I rounded the corner and came face-to-face with the entire team and Colm, Ford, and Emmett.

Drawn faces and red eyes met me as I walked past them.

"Hey, man." Declan reached out and squeezed my shoulder. His green eyes were ringed with red.

"What the hell happened?" My voice sliced through the murmuring voices and the doctors walking past. It took me a second to realize it wasn't Kara's hand that was shaking—it was mine.

"Drunk driver. Preston was taking Imogen home last night, and someone plowed into them." The fire burned in Declan's eyes.

"How is Imo?" My heart leaped into my throat.

"She's okay. A few scrapes and bruises, but she's fine. She's in there with him now. She said he turned the car so his side took the brunt of the impact."

I closed my eyes as the soft thud hit me in the chest. That was exactly the kind of thing he'd do. Without thinking, he'd have done everything he could to protect her. I swallowed past the lump in my throat and asked the question I'd been dreading since I'd seen everyone faces when I turned the corner.

"How is he?"

Kara squeezed her fingers tighter around mine. Her warmth helped drive away some of the cold.

"He's pretty messed up. He's got a broken leg, fractured wrist, his face is a mess and...there might be some spinal damage." Declan had tears in his eyes.

Fuck! I ran my hand over my face. My blood boiled and my head throbbed. I wanted to wrap my hands around the responsible party's throat after I beat them senseless. Kara gasped, and I released my hold on her fingers.

My eyes snapped to hers. She massaged her hand as I pushed those images from my mind.

"Sorry," I mumbled. I didn't act on that kind of anger and rage.

She gave me a weak smile. "It's okay." She slid her hand back into mine, and I held it to my chest, against my pounding heart. I felt sick to my stomach. We stood between Declan and Emmett against the wall outside the room.

"The older we get, the more life likes to throw us curveballs." Colm stared straight ahead at the wall outside Preston's room.

"The lengths he'd go through to get out of a rematch." Emmett's attempt at a joke fell flat, and he ducked his head. The somber mood stretched on as some doctors went in and out of the room. His parents and Imogen stayed inside.

After a while the nurses shooed us into the waiting room where we each took turns pacing, like our movements would somehow repair Preston and get him up and walking again. The door swung open, and two older people stepped inside with Imogen and Preston's little sister, Becca next to them. *His parents.* All the guys stood, waiting to hear.

"We wanted to say thank you all so much for coming. It means the world to us and to Preston." His mom wiped a tear away from the corner of her eye, and she had her hand wrapped around Imogen's.

Imogen's sweater was ripped some at the shoulder like the seatbelt had dug into her. The bandage on her head did nothing to hide her bleary eyes and ashen skin. Her right arm was in a brace. She looked like she'd seen a ghost.

"He's stable. They need to wait a little while for the swelling to go down before they'll know about his legs." Her voice cracked, and his dad squeezed her shoulder. "Your coach is in there with him now, but I know you'd all like to see him. They said if you go in two or three at a time, that would be fine."

I let the other guys go first. Colm, Emmett, and Ford went in for only a minute to say they'd be up for a rematch whenever he was back up and on his feet. Everyone made their visits short. He'd been through a lot and needed rest.

Declan and I went in last. Kara held down the fort in the waiting room. Preston's parents and Becca had gone home to get some clothes and stuff. Imogen was curled up in the seat at Preston's bedside, and Coach sat in a chair on the other side of him.

The mottled bruises on the side of his face sent me straight back to seventh grade. I'd told myself I was giving everyone else a chance to say what they needed to him because they'd been waiting longer than I had, but I'd been putting this off. Seeing him like this, laid up in a hospital bed, brought up so many memories I'd worked hard to forget and let go of... And the building anger that someone had done this to my friend.

The urge to find the driver and make him feel exactly what Preston felt had my hands fisted at my sides. I jerked back, stopping in my tracks. I was not that guy. I was not an angry monster fixated on hurting someone. That wasn't me and it would never be me, but the simmer that threatened to overflow when someone I cared about was hurt made me want to break things. And I hated how much I wanted to follow through.

"Hey, man, all this to get out of us bugging you about going pro," Declan joked with his voice tight as he took Preston's uninjured hand and wrapped his hand around it.

Preston attempted a chuckle before wincing and holding his side.

"You know me. Always looking for the easy way out." His smile came out as a grimace with his split lip and bandage around his head.

"That's exactly who you are, Preston 'Easy Way Out' Elliott."

"Sorry for the scare. And I'm sorry about the season." He stared down at his arm. That feeling of uselessness was one I knew well.

"Are you out of your mind? This is not your fault. Not even close. We're glad you're doing okay. And we're glad you're okay too, Imogen."

Imogen rubbed Preston's hand and stood, resting her forehead against his and murmuring against his skin. Her head whipped up, and she had tears in her eyes. She glanced up at me and gave me a small smile.

I hadn't been able to play for almost two months while my arm healed when we'd left California. The stakes hadn't been as high as they were for Preston, but moving to a new place and not having the beach nearby, hockey had been my respite. Not setting foot on the ice for that long, it was like I was losing my mind.

Coach pushed forward in his seat. "We're glad you two came in together. I've talked it over with Preston, and we think we know the best person to take over in his spot for the rest of the season."

I glanced over at Declan. He was the natural choice. One of the best and the guys rallied around him. I had a big smile on my face as I stared up at Declan, who stared right back at me.

"We want you to be the captain."

Coach's words came out as a jumble. I swore he'd said he wanted *me* to be captain. My head snapped to Preston, lying in the bed, with my eyes wide.

"What?" I tilted my head, still not convinced I hadn't missed a part of the conversation.

"We picked you, Heath," Coach added, not giving me any room to misinterpret what he'd said.

My eyes shot to Declan, and he nodded.

"Me? Why me?"

Preston shifted in the bed. "You're an excellent player. You're almost unstoppable out on the ice, plus the guys all respect you. They're going to need someone who stays cool under pressure and can also kick their asses in the rink."

"But..." The words died in my throat. I was faster on the ice than anyone on the team, but captain?

"You're who we need." Preston's eyes shone with sincerity, but somehow the walls of the hospital room shifted and closed in on me.

"Heath, you've got this." Declan's voice called me back from the bottom of the well I was falling into.

I wrapped my hands around the small rail at the end of

Preston's bed. My white-knuckle grip made it rattle against the side of the bed.

"You might not know it, but you're not only our fastest, you're also one of our most patient and driven players. I know you don't think anyone notices the extra work you put in with the new guys."

"I'm only helping them get adjusted or find their groove."

"Exactly!" Coach's hand landed on my shoulder. He squeezed it, and I glanced back at him.

"That's exactly what we need in a captain."

"I'm nothing like Preston. I couldn't do everything he does." I nodded toward Preston, who had Imogen perched at his side.

"You're right. You can't." He grinned at me. "And you don't need to. We don't want you to. Every captain has their own style, and you've been a leader in the team without even knowing it. Keep doing what you've been doing and step up to the plate. We need you to bring this season home, Heath."

I glanced between all their faces in front of me. They needed me to do this. I needed to do whatever it took for this season to go down the way we all wanted. Finish it off right. Take the team to victory.

"You cool with this?" I locked eyes with Declan.

"You've got this. I'll be there backing you the whole way."

"Looks like I'm the new captain." The words tumbled out of my mouth, and I had a pit in my stomach. Was I really doing this?

I'd never let myself take on that kind of responsibility. Never trusted myself with something like that. Keeping all my intensity on the ice was how I kept myself from ever going overboard. Never letting those things that got to me boil over into a place I'd stayed far away from. With so much on the line, I couldn't screw this up.

Preston's parents showed up, so Declan and I gave them the space they needed. We said our goodbyes and stopped by the waiting room to pick up Kara.

Coach caught up with us in the lobby.

"I know you're worried, Heath, but you've got everything you need to do this. You've got the skill, patience and drive to keep everyone in line. Three months is all we need to clinch another championship, and you've got it, son."

We got outside, and the temperature felt like it had dropped another ten degrees. Kara tightened her hand around mine.

I flinched as Coach's hand landed on my shoulder. I hated it when he called me that. He didn't mean anything by it, but it brought back a flood of memories I'd rather leave buried. Coach got into his car and pulled away.

"You coming home?" Declan zipped up his coat and tugged the collar higher.

I glanced over at Kara. "Do you have anywhere to be? Or are you cool if we drive around for a little bit?"

"I can do whatever you need me to do." She gave me a small smile, and I loved her.

I knew it was too early.

I knew it was in-fucking-sane, but I loved her.

"I'm going to go out for a bit to clear my head."

Declan nodded and shoved his hands into his pockets. "I need to go tell Mak. I didn't want to worry her." He left, and we walked to my car.

"I'm good to drive now." I held out my hand for the keys. She hesitated before putting them in my palm. Her hand rested on top of mine.

"I'm really sorry about your friend." She wrapped her arms around me, and I dropped my head, burying it in her hair. Her touch, smell, and presence warmed me up even in the biting cold.

"Let's go." I walked her around to the other side and opened the door for her before climbing in on my side.

I cranked up the heat, and she rubbed her hands down the side of her dress. I winced. She had to be freezing, but she didn't let on. "Where to?"

"I don't really know yet." I cranked up the heat and threw the car into drive.

15

KARA

We drove in silence for a long time, and at first I thought we were driving with no destination in mind. I chanced a glance at him. He wasn't speeding or anything, but the determined look in his eye had me thinking he knew where he was going. Maybe he did, even if he thought he didn't.

"Heath?"

His head snapped up like he'd forgotten I was there.

"Are you sure you don't want me to drive?"

He dropped a hand off the steering wheel and rested it on my thigh. "I'm good. Thanks for asking. Sorry about this. I needed to get out of there for a bit. My mind clears when the open road is laid out in front of me and I push forward into new territory behind the wheel."

"I get it. Out on the open road. You can focus on that, and it helps your brain work out the stuff you're dealing with."

He peered over at me. "Are you sure you're not a psych major?"

I chuckled. "Definitely not a psych major, but I get needing to zone out sometimes. I'm here for you if you need to talk."

His hand tightened on my thigh. "I know."

I spotted a big green sign for Shore Points. "Are we going down the shore?" That was going to be crazy freaking cold.

His lips pressed together in a thin line, and he took the exit before the sign. "No, let's go get something to eat. Are you hungry?"

My stomach rumbled, and his eyes got wide. "I could eat." We'd been at the hospital since early this morning and other than some vending machine candy, neither of us had had anything. The heat blasted right into me, thawing out the deep freeze from the hospital waiting room and the brisk January morning.

We pulled into a diner parking lot. It was empty. Maybe people were crashing already after their night out. I'd started nodding off once the car warmed up. Heath's hand was clamped over my legs. He gave me a squeeze when it was time to get out.

"Let's get some food." He hopped out, and I opened my door, not waiting for him to come around and do it.

I slid my hand into his, and we walked up the steps to the diner. A woman who looked like she'd been working there for decades showed us to a booth. We slid into opposite sides with our hands still clasped on top of the table.

He ran his thumb over my knuckles. His usual lightness was dimmed. Having someone so close to you get hurt wasn't easy to deal with. He was hurting, and I hated it. I wanted to do anything I could to fix it, but sometimes there's nothing you can do. Sometimes all you can do is make them smile and hope it's enough.

"What did you want to eat? I was thinking to ask if they had some chocolate lava cake."

I dipped my head to try to catch his eye. A hint of a smile turned up the corners of his lips. I reversed the hold he had on my hand and ran my fingertips over his palm.

"It's okay to be sad. The shock is harder to handle. It's always unexpected when someone close to you is hurt like this."

His pulse picked up under my fingers. "Someone nearly killed him." The muscles in his jaw popped.

I climbed out of my side of the booth and slid in beside him. "Life has a way of blindsiding you when you least expect it. He's okay. He's awake and talking—that's a miracle right there. And his girlfriend is fine." I wrapped my arm around his. "I know it doesn't seem like it right now, but things could have been a lot worse. A hell of a lot worse."

He gave me a grim nod and stared down at the menu.

"What can I get you?" Our server stood at the end of the table with her notepad ready.

"I'll have a cheeseburger and fries and a cranberry juice."

The server turned to Heath who was still shell-shocked. The lost look in his eyes broke my heart. It had been a long time since I'd had to deal with someone I loved getting hurt. I'd pushed those memories aside so they didn't haunt me at night.

"I'll have the same," he mumbled.

The waitress gathered our menus, and we sat in silence. I rested my cheek against his shoulder. He dropped his chin on the top of my head.

"I need him to pull through this and be okay." His voice was rough and raw. "He's the kind of guy who'd do anything for anyone, and the thought of him not being okay..." He stopped. "I've got to do this for him and show him how good he's made us."

"You guys have won the championship for the past three years, right?" I'd heard some pretty big celebrations last year when I was studying in the library.

So many emotions welled in his eyes that it made my hands itch to touch him. "Yeah, we have. But he's the glue." He closed his eyes and blinked away the glittering tears that tried to escape. I held him tighter, determined to let him know I'd be there for him. We might not have known each other for long, but this wasn't something I could let go. He wasn't someone I could let go.

"And you'll be the glue too. You can do this, Heath. Your coach wouldn't have made you captain if he didn't believe in you. Preston too. I've seen you be pretty persistent and persuasive about something you want. There's no doubt in my mind you'll get your team where they need to be."

We ate and talked about our lives growing up in the city. His major and what he'd do after graduation. Going to the NHL was intense, but I didn't really doubt he could do it with how well the team had done.

He dropped me off at home, and I went inside, closing the door behind me, feeling more drained than I'd felt in forever. Mom, Dad, and Lauren were watching a movie. I gave them a hug and climbed into bed still in my clothes. Between my night with Heath and our day at the hospital, I felt like I could sleep for a week.

My gaze darted to the desk drawer. The crumpled and creased letter sat in there. I took it out and traced her handwriting with my fingers. I'd set my email to archive anything else that came in from her, but I couldn't bring myself to throw out the letter. I ran my fingers along her sloped, looping words and crushed it to my chest.

What if she really was clean and sober? What if she really did want to make amends and try to have a relationship? What if I couldn't handle it all and everything fell apart?

16

HEATH

My phone exploded off the concrete wall of the dank locker room. A few heads turned my way, and I ran my fingers through my sweat-soaked hair. *Fuck!*

I couldn't stop the shaking. My hands were bouncing all over the place. We'd lost. It was a demoralizing loss: 9-2 against a team we'd destroyed every time we'd played them. Our first away game since Preston had been injured. My first game as the captain, and I was already fucking up.

"Heath, dude! What the hell?" Kaden, one of our freshman fighters, came out of the shower and tightened the towel around his waist.

"It's fine." I waved him off. Like he had any fucking room to talk. He'd only recently pulled his head out of his ass.

"No, it's not fine if you're freaking out like this." He stepped closer, but a hand clamped down on his shoulder.

"He said he's fine, so he's fine." Declan dragged a towel over his head and pushed Kaden back. "Back off and give him some space."

I dropped my head and stared at the remnants of my phone. *Damn it.* I was supposed to call Kara.

"We're all off our game without Preston. Don't let it get to you. Have a shower, and we'll meet you at the bus. Get a good night's sleep, and we'll have a good game tomorrow."

He gave me a slap on the back, and I ripped all my gear off, slamming it to the floor and headed into the shower. The water was freezing cold. I gritted my teeth as the icy spray washed over me. Maybe this would help get things under control or maybe numb me enough that I felt like I could function without ripping this place apart.

The ride to the hotel was so quiet you could hear a pin drop. The team was tired and beaten down. Every call that should have gone our way hadn't. Every whistle blow had been for us before I even heard the ref's call. The streetlights whipped by, shining in my eyes as I stared into the darkness out there.

What if I couldn't do it? What if I fucked this up or worse, lost it on the ice? Or off the ice? I'd never had to deal with this before. So much rested on my shoulders, and all I wanted to do was talk to Kara. Too bad I'd turned my phone into a million little pieces back in the locker room.

I didn't have her number memorized, which meant I couldn't even call from the hotel. This was what happened when you lost your temper. You fucked things up: I'd already had to change my schedule around for the semester.

With the added pressure of being the team captain and everything going on with Preston, I'd changed my classes. Independent study and a few other requirements were all I needed to graduate and to keep my eligibility for the semester. I stared at the ceiling for a long time with nothing but the patter of rain against the windows outside. Even after playing, I still buzzed with energy. Flipping on the tv, the unmistakable bright red Ferrari and the bass of "Oh Yeah" came on screen. Ferris stood beside Cameron trying to talk him into a day of cookie. I switched it off. Even John Hughes wasn't enough to soothe the burning in my chest. All it made me think of was Kara.

I slipped out of my room and used my room key to get into the gym downstairs. Outside the window, the leaves on the trees rustled in the whipping wind, and I pushed my hands against the freezing push bar to the door outside. Wind stung my face. My feet slapped against the concrete and grass as I took off through the corporate park beside the hotel. Numbness settled into my limbs in a way it didn't on the ice, and I ran, pushing my taxed muscles even harder. Exhaustion was the only thing that would knock me out now. If I couldn't hear Kara's voice, the blankness of sheer exertion would have to do. I stared straight ahead at the rain coming down in sheets against the windows overlooking the parking lot. The dreams would have to comfort me for now because that was all I had.

17

KARA

The first week of classes was always hectic, even more so when your department head decided she wanted to extend her Christmas break an extra week and sent out assignments the day before classes started. Everything was a mess. Heath sent an email that his phone was broken. It helped smoothed out those ragged edges of uncertainty that had popped up when I hadn't heard from him in a while. But he was busy and so was I, we'd see each other soon.

Schedules were screwed up and classes were behind before they'd started. The second I rounded the corner to Stevenson's office, I tried to backtrack; but his beady little eyes snapped up and I was caught. Plastering on my best I-hate-your-guts smile, I adjusted the bag on my shoulder and marched toward Jason like I was headed for a Stormtrooper firing squad.

"Kara." His lips were in a grim line as he flipped through the papers in his hand.

"Jason." I spotted the box on the floor filled with envelopes with our names on them. The stack of thesis proposals determined whether we'd have an advisor for the PhD program. I'd worked night and day on mine for months before turning it in, excited about what my research could do. My fingers tingled like I'd fallen asleep on my hands as I got closer to Professor Stevenson's office.

Jason stood practically on top of the box where our final papers from before the break were stacked. I glanced over at him in the telltale are-you-going-to-move way, and he kept paging through his packet like no one else existed in the world, which was probably what he thought. Clearing my throat did absolutely nothing, as he continued to ignore me.

When was she going to join the twenty-first century and put these things online? Crouching down, I snagged my envelope second from the top and ripped it open. I tugged the small stack of papers out.

I should have been elated. I should have been jumping up and down, but I stared at the grade on my paper and could only muster the slightest bit of happiness. *What was I doing?* I glanced up at Jason, and a sharp, cold zap shot through me. He'd craned his neck to check out my paper as I'd stood.

The bright red circled *A* on the front hadn't set well with him from the pursed-lipped, generally unpleasant look on his face. In his snooping haze he'd let the top of his paper flop over, so I saw the upside-down *A-* on his paper.

Ah, there was the happiness. I wondered how much it had to do with the program and how much of it had to do with showing him up. Stifling a smirk, I kept my face neutral. Well, as neutral as I could with a shit-eating grin ready to burst out and smack Jason in the face. It seemed being a brownnose didn't always guarantee the best grades.

I slid the envelope into my bag. I'd go over her comments later, but for now, I could bask in the fact that I hadn't screwed it up and I'd gotten a better grade than Jason. That last bit was a cherry-on-top moment I couldn't resist.

"Are you applying for the Montfort Fellowship?"

He knew I was. Everyone in the program knew. "Of course."

A small sound of disapproval shot out of his mouth, and I was a second away from literally shoving my A in his face.

"Good luck." He bit it out like it was a curse he was trying to put on me to make me lose all my hair and drop twenty IQ points.

"You too." My broad smile and sunny tone made him glower even harder, which made me smile even brighter. *Suck a bag of dicks, Jason!*

The freezing January air made everything worse. I waded through the slushy, slick walkways crisscrossing campus. The beginning of the semester was insane. Not only did I have to deal with my classes and the quantitative exam coming up, but I had to handle my TA duties. Three independent studies and two small group recitations. Since Stevenson was a dinosaur, she didn't email us our assignments, we had to go to her office to pick them up.

This would have been fine if she were ever in her office. The only reason I'd gotten the thesis review was they'd finally opened the main building after the break. Those had been sitting there outside her door since the first day of the break when she'd unhelpfully decided to let us know where they were, but we hadn't been able to get to them.

I'd contemplated a heist-movie type break-in to get my hands on that paper, but had instead settled on eating all the cookie dough I could to help me forget. But not having anything else for my Calc courses meant I wasn't going to find out anything about my students until I hunted her down. All I knew were room numbers and times. The students added and dropped classes so often, the lists wouldn't be up-to-date until after the add/drop period.

My first couple classes weren't too bad. The sophomore recitation session was to check in and go over the guidelines for the semester. There wasn't anything to review, since they hadn't had their first official class yet. Rushing to the bookstore, I requested a new set of textbooks for the class that Stevenson had neglected to order for the start of the semester.

The good vibes quickly wore off as the hunger pangs hit. I stopped off at the coffee shop and got a bacon bagel and a cup of coffee to tide me over until dinner. I needed to unload the books before I snapped in half under the weight of what seemed like a small fortune in textbooks.

I shoved the last of my bagel into my mouth and dusted the crumbs off my shirt. At times like these, my stomach let me know I'd gone too long without eating, it was all about cramming as much food into my mouth as possible before I turned into a fire-breathing monster.

I checked with the departmental admin about my assigned office for the independent study sessions. It was the same from the previous semester. I kind of hated this building. It was so old and dreary, like the land renovations forgot.

Every other building on campus had been updated and buffed to a high shine, but not the Ansel Building, which meant the floors creaked, the windows rattled, and I expected a ghost to come floating down the hall any second. *Why were these old buildings so dark?* While the labs were pristine our biochem offices were less so.

An email sent from Stevenson about twenty minutes ago let me know I'd have an extra independent study student. I wasn't going to tell her I was already over the workload for the semester because it wouldn't do me any good.

I'd worked with one independent study student the semester before, and it was always interesting to see what the students came up with. It would have been great to know at least something about them, but again, Stevenson only cared about her pet projects in the biochem department.

I was already three minutes late. I hated being late. Double-checking the office number, I rushed down the hall. Of course my shared office was the office the farthest away from everything. The most isolated room in the creepiest building on campus. Perfect.

Taking a second to compose myself, I pushed into the classroom and came face-to-face with my new student for the semester. Everything happened in slow motion as he turned around, his blond hair vaguely familiar. And that's when I realized I was in big trouble. Not big trouble, but huge, *holy shit you're in for it* trouble when I stood in front of the student I was supposed to spend a few hours per week tucked away with in this tiny office.

He smiled at me with that lazy, charged smile, and a jolt shot through me, nearly buckling my knees. *Heath.* My cup slid out of my hands, and I prepared myself for the messy, spray of scalding hot coffee to explode at my feet.

S hocked doesn't even begin to describe what shot through me as my independent study TA stepped through the door. Her dark brown eyes and wavy hair had played a prominent part in many of my fantasies over the past couple weeks. With everything happening with Preston, our games, and being the new captain, I hadn't been able to carve out time to see or talk to her, not since our drive after the hospital. We were supposed to see each other tomorrow.

It frustrated me to no end that between traveling, being on the ice, and in the hospital, I hadn't been able to see her; but it looked like the universe had found a way to reward my patience. The door to the musty old office clicked open, and I came face-to-face with the woman I couldn't get out of my mind.

Coffee cup in one hand, a stack of books in the other, and her laptop bag slung across her, she burst into the room like a woman on a mission. Her blue button-down top and black pants were the picture of professionalism, but I knew what was underneath. The slight strain of the buttons on her top had me replaying our three nights together in vivid detail.

Lightning-fast reflexes definitely came in handy when snagging a piping-hot cup of coffee that's about to splatter all over the floor. Grabbing the cup midair, I righted it. Only a couple drops splashed out of the small opening onto my hand. I didn't even feel the burn, but my grin was so wide I felt it in my toes.

"Kara." Her name came out like the first gasp after being sucked under a monster wave. Sucking in the fresh air of possibilities. My phone was still broken from a couple days ago. I'd been on the ice every second I wasn't in class. "You're my independent study advisor."

"Shit." It came out as a whisper, like maybe she didn't even realize she'd said it. With wide eyes she whipped around and closed the door behind her. I sat on the edge of the desk and watched the scarlet flush travel all over her body. I liked the look of that and the closed door behind her. The small frosted-glass window meant there were so many possibilities for our sessions together. The desk seemed sturdy enough.

She took the couple steps to the desk, tucking her hair behind her ear and setting her books down on the desk. Unloading everything, she stared down at her books for a couple seconds, like maybe she thought I'd disappear if she ignored me.

I slid her coffee into her line of sight, and her head snapped up. Her eyes were not the picture of the playful, uninhibited, and ready-to-roll-with-it woman from our times together. These eyes were guarded and wary.

"Would you mind taking a seat?" She gestured to the worn, green leather seat in front of the desk.

"I'm good right here." I leaned into the desk and peered

down her top. The lacy cups of her bra barely contained her breasts, and I couldn't wait to get my hands on them again.

"I think it would be best if you took a seat over there." She fidgeted, stacking and re-stacking a pile of papers in front of her. I pushed off the desk and sat in the chair. It smelled like an old pipe. Running my hands over my jeans, I tugged them down a little. Things had become extremely tight all of a sudden.

"It seems that you're as surprised to see me as I am to see you."

"Pleasantly surprised," I added.

Her lips turned down even farther. "Heath...these sessions are going to be about work. You have a project you need to complete to graduate, and I have requirements I need to fulfill. If we keep things completely professional, we can both accomplish those goals and have a great semester." She plastered on a fake smile that didn't reach her eyes.

"Don't worry about it. I'm totally cool with keeping our sessions one hundred percent professional. Sitting next to you for a couple hours each week and not touching you will be torture." I leaned forward, resting my arms on my legs and staring directly into her eyes. "But that will make it that much hotter when I rip those pants off you, bend you over that desk and eat you from behind when this session is over." I nodded to the desk she sat behind like it had the magical power of not making her the sexiest woman in a twenty-mile radius. Hell, at least fifty.

She bolted straight up, knocking over her coffee cup, which spilled a few drops out on the desk. Was she pissed we hadn't talked in a couple days?

"I'm sorry I didn't get to call you. I screwed up my phone while at the away game, and I only had time to get a new one today after our session."

She cleared her throat and picked up a paper off the desk, clearly trying to ignore what I'd said, but I knew it had gotten to her.

"I'm not upset about that. It's fine."

She didn't look fine. Her chest rose and fell a bit faster as she tried to compose herself. I didn't mind ruffling her feathers. The woman from the bar made so much more sense now. It took me a couple minutes to realize she was talking to me. I'd been too busy running through the various surfaces and pieces of furniture in the office and how exactly I'd take her on each one of them.

Shaking my head, I cleared my throat as she stood behind the desk staring at me expectantly. "Sorry, what was that?"

"We can't do this, Heath."

"Why not? You're not really my teacher. I get my grade from the department head."

This was nothing like what had happened with Miss Juniper, the student teacher back in high school everyone had had the hots for. I'd been relentless during our senior year, pursuing her for a date and after graduation we'd finally had one. But this situation was different. Kara and I were already seeing each other. Both consenting adults. A little extra study time that ended in some seriously hot sex sounded like exactly the thing to keep me in line this semester.

"Based off my recommendations and feedback. I'm responsible for deciding what your grade is even if she's the one actually typing them in. They could nullify your grade."

My face fell. If they nullified my grade, I wouldn't graduate. The season would be voided because I wouldn't be eligible to play.

"Then, I'll find someone else for independent study.

Swap me with someone else." I wasn't going to stop seeing her this whole semester because of this class.

"There's no one else. I'm the only one in the whole department who even had a spot to take someone on."

I raked my hands through my hair, my frustration mounting. "I'll figure something else out. I'll find another class that works."

There was a hint of desperation in my voice. She was the one thing I had been looking forward to this semester—hell, longer than this semester—but the past few days not talking to her had been torture. Being on the same campus, I'd figured once classes started and we settled into our schedules, we'd be able to see a lot more of each other.

"With what we have going on, I shouldn't have any influence over your grade." She squeezed the back of her neck.

"I don't think I've been playing coy at all here. I, one hundred percent, intend for us to continue what we've had going on." I stared into her eyes, pushing past all the hesitancy and doubt, ready to show her this wasn't going to be something she could run away from.

"Heath, we can't. This is my career we're talking about, and your ability to graduate. If anyone finds out about this, about us, it could destroy everything." Her eyes pleaded with me to understand. And I did, all too well. I'd crossed that line before. Let my pursuit get in the way of something that could hurt someone I cared about, and I couldn't do it again. I wouldn't do it again, especially not to Kara.

"So where does that leave us?" A dull ache grew in the center of my chest.

She dropped her eyes, her fingers running along the desktop. "Why don't you give me the full rundown of your project?"

We went over my ideas about the possible medicinal

extractions from a plant species I'd been cultivating over the past couple years. The guys thought I was insane for not going the kinesiology route, which was the default for athletes, but I knew a hockey career only lasted so long.

By going to college, I was already handicapping myself when it came to getting started. Most guys from Europe joined the NHL when they were eighteen, hell, some were even seventeen. I'd be ancient by the time I started, but I didn't want to come back to college later. I wanted to live it now—and I was so close. The hockey would be there, and even if I only got five years out of it if I were lucky, anyone only needed so much money.

I'd make it work, and I'd have my degree to fall back on —move on with when I retired from the game.

"The new blooms of my plants will make for excellent test subjects for this by the end of the semester. I've already written up the experimental guidelines I'll need to have preliminary results."

She nodded along with an inquisitive glint in her eyes. Talking about this stuff got her as interested as it did when I told her what I wanted to do to her. Her questions came back rapid fire. As she spoke, I tried not to look at her lips and remember every place they had been on me. I longed to wrap my hands about her wavy black strands and settle her legs on either side of me while I showed her how good these sessions could really be.

I envisioned the next time I took her, pressed against the door or maybe over the arm of the chair I was sitting in. I sank my fingers into the soft fabric beneath my hand. I'd managed to keep talking like I wasn't envisioning her spread out on that desk ready for me to devour her. Those images flashed through my mind fast and furiously. *Stop it. This is playing with fire.*

After a couple minutes she'd even gotten up and come around the front of the desk, getting into the other leather chair beside me. Her sweet cinnamon smell wrapped itself around me like another taunt of how close she was.

Her initial questions had been simple and easy, like she thought she might break my brain with the hard stuff, but after breezing past those, her wariness fell away as she geeked out over science.

Hell yeah, I knew the way to a woman's heart was through gene expression.

"Wow, Heath. Interesting topic and I think you'll get some great research out of it. Why don't we figure out your schedule? You're going to be traveling for hockey, right? That's why you picked the independent study option."

"Hockey season stretches on for a few more months." I ran my hand over my face, trying not to think of all that responsibility resting on my shoulders. As part of a team, I had no problem doing what I needed to do and helping to keep people in line, but captain... I still wasn't completely sure that hadn't been a huge mistake on Preston and Coach's part. But I was determined not to let them down.

She leaned forward. "How did your games go?"

I'd tried to put the games out of my head. I was psyching myself out. We'd lost both our away games. The first time we'd had a back-to-back loss since freshman year. I squeezed the back of my neck. "They didn't go well."

She reached out to cover my hand with hers, but then she jerked it back at the last minute, and frowned like she'd realized how hard this was going to be. How was I supposed to go an entire semester without touching her? Without holding her and falling asleep in her arms? She'd already carved out a place in my heart, but five months without contact might wreck me when I was already sinking.

19

KARA

I shouldn't have moved. The second I sat in the seat beside him, I'd known it was a mistake. I swear my mind was playing tricks on me. He smelled like a day at the beach and ice. Like a surfer dude and a snowman had a baby and spit him out. All sunshine and cool attitude and now I was screwed.

Get me talking about any kind of biology and I'm done for. Wrap it up in a package like Heath and you might as well bend me over and—no, not going to go there. *Must keep this professional.*

My gaze drifted to his lips as he spoke. His full pink lips had been all over my body. They looked soft, but the memory of the demanding pressure of them against my thighs started a throb between my legs so strong I squeezed them together.

Snapping out of it, I focused on his words, trying to use science to block the biological urges that almost made me jump out of my chair and straight into his lap. He went over the rest of his experimentation reasoning, and I nodded along, making notes.

Keep this professional. If I wanted to be taken seriously as a PhD candidate, I couldn't get involved with a student I was advising. That was a one-way ticket to dismissal from the program and never finding a job in the industry again. Stevenson had a hell of a lot of pull, and it was a risk I wasn't willing to take. She may have been a dinosaur, but she was also a stickler for the rules.

It was like the universe was punishing me for finding him. A reminder that I'd better not fall into old patterns and make the same mistakes as before or there would be consequences. Somehow, going home with a complete stranger after a few drinks did not hold up to the you're-a-responsible-young-woman-who-won't-end-up-screwing-up-everything-good-in-her-life model.

Now I was sitting across from the sexiest man I'd ever been near, and I couldn't touch him. Spending that first night with Heath, a complete stranger, and then the letter from my mom and everything that brought along with it. *I hear you, universe, loud and clear. He's off-limits.*

The easy way he spoke about his flowers made me want to scream. It was unfair for someone as obscenely hot as him to be this dedicated to something most people would think was boring. When he talked about it, I couldn't help the way my mind raced to fill the gaps in his work to help him improve it.

Without noticing, I was sitting on the edge of my seat, and so was he, our knees almost touching. The energy bouncing between us wasn't only chemistry, it was hard science. Maybe this could work. I put his earlier words and the mental images that made my knees weak out of my head.

"If you only knew how long it took me to find the right

154   MAYA HUGHES

manure supplier. You wouldn't want to know. Let's say it was a distinctly unpleasant experience."

I couldn't hold back my laugh. Even with his lips in a frown, the excitement from what he was working on was still there. If there was anyone who could appreciate someone geeking out over science stuff, it was me. He laughed along with me, and the deep, rich sound of it made the hairs on the back of my neck stand up.

"I'm glad you didn't need any help with that part of your experiment, because you'd have been on your own."

He leaned back in his seat. Like a string was tied between us, I shifted forward before I realized what I was doing, not wanting to lose that connection. Biting the inside of my cheek, I leaned back.

"You'd have left me to the manure farms on my own?"

"Manure comparisons are where I draw the line in the 'for science' argument." I laughed, and he stared back at me, sending a shiver down my spine. I'd seen that look before. It was the one he'd given me in the kitchen when he'd wiped the chocolate off my face. Well, kissed it off my face.

Keep it professional and there wouldn't be an issue. I could make it through the semester without touching him. Pass my exams. Get the fellowship. And make it into the PhD program no problem. Exactly what I needed to do to make my parents proud.

The pit in my stomach grew, thinking of the other problem I was trying to avoid. *Angie.* Seeing her was not what I needed. She was a reminder of my life when everything had been an absolute mess. A barely teenager shouldn't know what it feels like to be hungover. They shouldn't know what it feels like to wake up groggy next to a random guy way too old for you and have to find a way home.

Heath was like a test for me to see if I'd fall into those old patterns of mistakes I'd tried to avoid since I'd left my mom behind. He was the tempting fruit dangled in front of me that I couldn't touch no matter how much I wanted to take a bite.

And if we were still interested in each other at the end of the semester, we could reevaluate then, maybe try this again. I peered at him, hoping he'd agree that a few months wouldn't derail whatever it was we'd started. I could deal with whatever fallout might happen of us being together after the semester was over.

He flipped to the last page of his proposal and dropped his hand onto my knee. The warmth of his touch sank in for a split second before I jumped up, walking back behind the desk, glancing down at my phone, checking the time.

"That all sounds great, Heath. It looks like you have everything under control. These sessions will be about checking in on your research and making sure you're documenting everything for the final paper."

I picked up the papers on the desk and grabbed my bag off the floor. Without looking up, I felt and heard him stand. My heart sped up as he closed the gap between his seat and the desk. His hand popped into my vision as he reached for one of the books at the same time I did. I snatched my hand back and let him pick it up.

He sat on the edge of the desk as he flipped through the pages of my study guide. Running a hand along his jaw, he stared down at the book. My eyes locked onto his neck. Onto the spot at the base where it met his shoulder.

"We'll have our next session next week at the same time. Does that work? You don't have a game or anything?"

He smiled at me. His blond locks partially covered the side of his face. The dark and light strands wove themselves together to make it a gold you wanted to reach out and touch.

My mouth suddenly totally dry, I picked up my coffee and took a big gulp. Wincing against the cold coffee taste, I grabbed the rest of my stuff off the desk and shoved it into my bag.

He closed the book and hopped off the desk.

"No, I don't have a game. We only play on the weekends."

He rounded the edge of the desk, and my pulse pounded as he got closer. I couldn't move. My feet were rooted to the tile floor, and my brain filled with static as he got closer. His steps were slow and measured. He was giving me every opportunity to run away like a scared little rabbit, but I wasn't scared. I was fucking terrified of the feelings I'd tried to push away that came rushing back the second he was within three feet of me.

Using his body like he always did, like he was in full control and he knew it, he stood behind me. I didn't even chance a look back, but I could feel his heat and the gentle whisper of his clothes against my back.

"Does this mean our session's over?"

His words skimmed across my neck and sent a shiver down my spine. *Session* came out like the dirtiest word, dripping with the promise of everything I thought he'd forgotten about in the course of an hour. I was stupid to think that because I sure as hell hadn't.

Leaning forward, his chest pressed against my back. Even though our skin wasn't touching, I was back in the hotel in the shower, dripping in anticipation of what he had in store for me. He reached around me and slid my book into my bag, and I gasped as the lips I'd been trying not to stare at since I'd walked in the door landed on my neck. It was like a gunshot going off.

"Did you forget what I said earlier?"

My knees nearly buckled, and I took a shuddering breath. With my heart hammering against my ribs, I tried to think of what to do next, but there was no next. There was only now, and now everything centered around him pressed against me. His smell threatened to burn me up as his teeth skimmed across my skin.

"Did you think I forgot?"

My thighs pressed into the top of the desk as his body crowded against mine. His hand around the front of me wrapped around my waist and slid down my body, focused at the center of my hips, pushing me back against him. My eyes fluttered closed, and my mouth hung open.

All the while, with each pop of a button, his lips were blazing a trail of destruction along my shoulder and back, using every exposed inch of skin against me. A whimper escaped my lips at the insistent nudge of his cock against my ass. Snapping my mouth shut, I bit my lip so I didn't scream out exactly what I wanted him to do.

"Or maybe you wanted me to show you how much I want you?"

He threaded his fingers into my hair, gathering it into a ponytail and turning my head to the side. He stared into my eyes. Even with his rough touch and growly voice, the playful look in his eyes added a stomach flutter to the pounding ache between my legs.

"Here, let me help you with that lip." He ducked his head and captured my lip in his mouth, sucking it from its safe space between my teeth and plummeting us both into dangerous territory.

With my head tilted, he kept me in place with his body

and his hand in my hair, like he knew I'd try to bolt, only I didn't. I should have, but every nerve in my body was on fire and calling out for him. Without thinking, I opened my mouth to him, and he was an all-consuming force, over-taking my mouth and my body one inch at a time.

"Do you know how hard it's been for me not to touch you this whole time? I need one more taste before you're off-limits. Something to tide me over until June." The fierceness of his words made it hard to think straight.

My voice caught in my throat, or I would have said he had to touch me. And the lasting feeling of his fingers on my knee still lingered as he worked with his whole body to replace it with new sensations.

I jumped at the gentle knock at the door and ripped my mouth away from his. My cheeks heated. Had I really let that happen? *How in the hell was I supposed to make it through the whole semester?*

20

HEATH

Kara jumped away from me like she'd been burned when someone knocked on the door. I tried not to let the ache in my chest dig in too deep. She wasn't rejecting me, she was rejecting the situation for our own good. I stepped back, giving her space. The outline of a small lady showed up through the frosted glass door. I shouldn't have kissed her. I'd wanted to so badly I could barely concentrate, but I shouldn't have done it.

Skirting around the other side of the desk, Kara threw the office door open and stood in the doorway, blocking most of the view of the room. I rounded the desk and snagged my bag off the floor and threw it over my shoulder.

"Hi, Mrs. Robson." Kara's sunny voice boomed from her spot at the door.

"I know you were looking for the room schedule for this semester, and I finally tracked it down. I wanted to get it to you before I left for the day." The woman's voice carried into room.

I loomed over Kara, my shadow covering her. She

pressed herself as hard as she could against the doorframe. Any harder and she might become a part of it.

"Thanks for the insights, Kara. I'll be sure to incorporate them into my experiment." I smiled at her, and she stared back, blinking a couple times. Her lips glistened in the dim lighting, and a keen yearning slammed into my chest. A semester. That was all. I could kiss her again once the semester was over. What if she met someone else? What if she realized it wasn't worth the hassle of getting involved with someone who could implode her career before it even started?

I grimaced and slid past her and out into the hallway. The older woman with glasses on a chain around her neck stepped back so I could leave.

"See you soon, Kara." I gave her a two-finger salute and backed away from the two women. Seeing her had been the one thing keeping me going. How did that happen? In a matter of weeks, she'd gone from the woman I couldn't stop staring at in the bar to the person I needed to see to feel like I wasn't unraveling at the seams.

Relax.

The one-word mantra I'd repeated to so many people over the years wasn't helping.

The one person I felt could save me from drowning was now absolutely off-limits. I'd gone down that path before and almost ruined someone's life. I didn't plan on doing that again, especially to Kara who had enough going on with her family life. As much as I wanted to say screw the rules, sometimes it was a risk that would end up killing the thing you wanted most.

The house was quiet when I got home. I grabbed the last beer from my secret stash. With my coat still on, I stood staring into the fridge, waiting for something. I wasn't sure what, but I wasn't going to find it there. The hum of the fridge motor kicking on snapped me out of my daze, and I shoved the beer back inside and snatched my keys off the table.

Slamming the door to the house, I jogged a few blocks to the greenhouse. It was quiet as usual. Standing over my plants, I stared at their vibrant colors and was immediately reminded of Kara. The colorful streaks in her hair was one of the first things I'd noticed about her.

The frustration mounted. I wasn't going to do this again. *How do I fix this?* This independent study had been a last-ditch effort to salvage this semester.

A sharp *pop* broke the peaceful silence of the green-house. I glanced down at my hands and the cracked pieces of the pot they held together that had shattered.

"Heath, you okay?"

My head snapped up and Felix stared back at me. I hadn't even heard him come in. Plastering on a smile, I dropped the pieces into the trash and brushed my hands on my jeans.

"I'm good. My heads not in it tonight. I'll see you later."

I left before Felix could question my sanity like I was right now.

Her lips pressing against mine ran on a loop through my head almost continuously. We hadn't spoken in days, and it was driving me crazy. The antiseptic smell of the hospital ward with the freezing temperatures outside. It brought back memories I'd struggled to leave behind. I didn't want to be here, but I had to. With a gentle knock on the partially opened door, I poked my head in. The soft melody from the doorway stopped.

"Come on in." Imogen's voice came from behind the curtain drawn across the room.

"Hey." I pushed the curtain back and smiled at the two of them. "Do you ever leave?" I walked over to her and gave her a hug.

"What? She gets a hug before me?" Preston pushed himself up higher in the bed.

"I mean, she is prettier," I said over my shoulder and let go of Imogen before giving Preston the best hug I could while he was stuck in that bed.

The bruising had gone down a lot on his face. The stitches looked like they'd mostly dissolved.

"I don't know about that. I've heard I'm pretty pretty." He pinched his fingers around his chin and struck a pose.

"I'm going to go with straight-up hot, if we're casting votes here." Imogen raised her hand and pointed at Preston.

"You don't have to say that because he's your boyfriend," I stage-whispered to her.

Her laugh was the reward itself. I figured she probably didn't get much of that here.

"Was that you singing, Imo? I didn't know you sang."

Her cheeks turned a bright red. "Sometimes," she mumbled.

"She's got a beautiful voice." Preston beamed from the bed.

"Are you going to be here awhile?" She jumped out of her chair.

"Yeah, until Pres kicks me out." I slid into the empty chair beside the bed.

"I'm going to grab some food and a shower. I'll be back before you know it." She kissed him on the forehead and squeezed my shoulder as she passed. Grabbing a bag sitting by the door, she darted out of the room.

"She hasn't gone home for a day since I've been here." He stared at the empty doorway.

"That's not a bad thing, is it? Of course she'd want to be here for you." I leaned back in the chair, trying to get comfortable. What were these things made from? Bricks?

"My parents haven't even stayed here as much as she has. I keep telling her to go home and get a good night's rest not in one of these torture chairs, but she only goes home to pick up new clothes if she can't get someone to bring her some."

"What's she doing about classes?"

He dragged his hands over his face. "She only had two classes during the semester. She didn't even need to take any, but to stay on campus she had to and she wanted to do all the normal college stuff and graduate with all her friends.

"I keep trying to get her to go for a break. There's nothing more boring than sitting in this room all the time. Hopefully I can get out of this bed and start doing some PT soon. Need to get out of this place."

"Hell yeah, you do."

"How bad is it?" He turned his head and pinned me with his stare.

I let out a deep sigh. "We've not been doing the best."

"I know all about that. You think anyone here could keep me from checking the stats? I mean, whatever's going on with you and the girl from the bar—"

My head snapped up. "What the—how in the hell...?"

He gave me a crooked smile. "I have my ways."

"Meaning Declan has a bigger mouth than he thinks."

"What's the deal? And why did you come in here looking like someone killed your cat?"

"I didn't come to saddle you with my issues. You're laid up here in the hospital. I want to talk about you."

"And I don't. I need some fucking gossip! I need something other than these four walls and the crushing feeling of disappointment that I can't get out of this bed and carry my girl out of here to make her feel better."

"No one expects you to do that."

"I do!" His voice boomed in the room, and his eyes got wide like he'd shocked himself. He sank back into the bed. "I do, man. I hate being here. I hate being broken like this. I've let you guys down. I let Imogen down."

"Don't even say that. You saved her. How would you feel if it were her lying in this bed?"

"I'd lose my mind."

"Exactly. You did what you had to do to protect her, and she's safe and can stand by your side. Of course we all wish you weren't here like this, but don't ever feel like you've let anyone down. Not a single fucking person."

The conviction in my voice seemed to placate him. He leaned back in bed. "Come on, man, give me the dirt."

"She's my new TA. The woman from the bar is my new TA."

Pres let out a long, low whistle. "Damn."

"Tell me about it."

"What are you going to do?"

"Stay away from her as much as possible. There are only four months left in the semester. I have to keep my distance so I can graduate and she can keep her job."

"Didn't you do this back in high school?"

I threw my hands up. "How does everyone know about that?"

"You're not the only one with loose lips."

I dragged my fingers through my hair. "She was a student teacher. She was twenty and a junior in college. I was eighteen. I figured it wasn't a big deal. I'd graduated by the time we even hooked up, and that was all it was. Nothing happened while I was still in school, not that I didn't try." I grimaced. I'd been pretty relentless.

"And what happened?" The motors on his bed whirred as he sat up straighter.

"Everyone made jokes, but I figured it was nothing. I wasn't in school anymore. That summer between high school and college, we went out somewhere. It was something stupid like for ice cream or something, and another teacher at the school saw us together. That was it. She left before the next school year started. Went somewhere else to start over because someone thought something could have been going on while I was in school. It sucked."

"Sounds like it did."

"That was infatuation to the nth degree. Kara is different. It's a whole new ball game. I broke my phone and I couldn't talk to her for almost a week and I nearly lost my mind. She gives me something I didn't even know I was missing, and I can't even put a name on it."

"I'm not going to try because it would scare the shit out of you."

My gaze shot to his.

"What do you want to do?" He laid his cast-wrapped arm across his lap.

"I want to call her up and take her out to dinner, bring her back to my place and fall asleep with her in my arms."

"Why don't you?"

"Because it could ruin her. Ruin the career she's building. People don't get a PhD on a whim. Obviously, it means a lot to her, and I'm not going to lose her because I couldn't back off for a while and let this semester end. And if they find out about us, they could void my grade for the semester. It would DQ me for every game I played when I wasn't eligible and wreck our season."

"What do you think you need to do?"

"Stay as far away from her as I can and try to keep things professional."

Preston nodded his head. "That's what you've got to do when you care about someone, her and the team. Protect them. Keep them safe." His gaze drifted to the doorway.

"Is she all healed up? I saw the brace was off her arm."

"Yeah, she is doing some physio for it. She'd been skipping it to stay here with me. I nearly kicked her out and made her go home when I found out. Sleeping on these chairs and stuff, she's going to break her back."

"It makes her feel better being with you."

"My parents are also relying on her a lot since things at the restaurant are a mess and they've been putting out fires left and right."

"I don't think she minds, man."

"I know, but I still don't have to like it."

We talked more about the abysmal season since the New Year and what he thought I could do to get the guys back in shape. Our dynamics were off, and me freaking out wasn't helping.

I hopped up to grab some coffee from the room on the floor for family. Imo was standing at the counter in front of the coffee machine when I stepped inside.

"Hey, Imo."

She jumped and quickly brushed at her face. Dragging her sleeve across her cheeks, she shoved a cup under the coffee dispenser. Her damp hair hung in a loose pony tail.

"Hey." Her voice was rough.

"Are you okay?" I stepped beside her, and she turned her head.

"I'm fine." She turned to me with a wide smile. "The cleaning products in here sometimes get to me and make my eyes water." The coffee in front of her stopped pouring. She dumped in about ten packets of sugar and some creamer. Spinning around, she held the piping-hot cup of coffee up to her lips. Steam poured over her face. Her eyes were red-ringed, and she avoided my gaze.

"How are you holding up?" I slipped my cup into the coffee machine.

"I'm good. Arm's all better." She bent her arm at the elbow and wrist.

"I'm not talking about your arm."

She tried to take a sip of coffee to stall but ended up burning her mouth. "Damn it!" She hissed, and ran her fingers over her lips.

"I—"

"Imogen, delivery called the desk when you didn't answer your phone. The food you ordered is here." A nurse popped her head into the room.

"Thanks, Marcie. I'll go down and get it."

She tried to breeze past me, and I put my hand on her shoulder. "I can go down and get it."

Glancing back over her shoulder, the corners of her mouth turned up a little, but her attempt at a smile didn't reach her eyes.

"It's okay. I'm glad you came. It always makes Preston's day. Hang out with him, I'll go get the food." She left the room, and I walked back into Preston's.

Five minutes later Imo breezed back into the room with her bag on her shoulder and a few take-out trays balanced on one arm. I hopped up and grabbed the bag, setting it down in the chair.

"Thanks, Heath. Sorry I was gone so long, babe. There was a line in the comfort room for the showers."

She set the take-out boxes on the tray beside Preston's bed.

"I ordered a few different things since the cafeteria decided to cancel taco night. I got one for you too, Heath." She grinned and pushed one of the boxes toward me. I didn't miss the grimace on Preston's face.

"I hate that you have a favorite food day in this place."

"I've got to head out. But thanks for grabbing something for me." I'd head to the rink. It was late, I could skate until my legs didn't work anymore and then maybe I'd be able to fall into a dreamless sleep that wasn't haunted by Kara's mouth, body, voice, and mind.

21

KARA

I tapped my pen against the composition book I'd filled in only a week and grabbed my phone out of my bag. Not a reply yet from Stevenson. A whole seven days without a response. Why was I even surprised?

I'd watched Heath stroll down the hall from the darkened corridor of the Ansel Building and fisted my hands at my sides to keep from calling out to him. Mrs. Robson had looked at me funny as my gaze had followed him until he'd turned the corner.

That was when I knew, this was not going to work. We hadn't made it through one session without kissing—and we'd have done more if we hadn't been interrupted. Our session was barely an hour, and my body had been humming from being in the same room with him.

Once I'd smoothed out my clothes in the office and grabbed a hair tie from my bag, I'd thrown my hair up into a messy bun and sat in the chair behind the desk. Tears prickled the backs of my eyes. *Why wasn't I allowed to be happy? Why couldn't I be with him? Why did he have to be my student?*

Opening my e-mail, I tapped out another message to Professor Stevenson. This was the only way I could look at myself in the mirror and still be with him. I'd dropped my forehead to the chipped and nicked wood and banged it there a few times. Thoughts that I could knock something loose had been quickly replaced by the highlight reel of our hot-for-teacher moment. And that was how I'd ended up fanning myself on the walk to the shuttle on the way home in the dead of winter.

Even worse, Heath and I had been in our session, keeping our hands to ourselves when Jason waltzed into the office like it wasn't my time to be there. Even though there was nothing happening between Heath and I, the look Jason gave me made the hairs stand up on the back of my neck. Heath wanted to know who he was and I filled him in on the most sanitized version I could. Fellow master's student. Asked me out. I turned him down, and he had it out for me.

Closing my notebook, I stared out the window of my bedroom. The way my body responded to him wasn't the only issue. I tried to deny it, but I liked him. More than liked and that was scary enough on its own, without the other complications.

He was smart, hot as hell, and the sex was like nothing I'd ever experienced. The tension between us was palpable from the second we walked into a room together, the risk of trying to make it through the whole semester wasn't worth derailing my whole career. Maybe this was how I could stop myself from plunging down the path of destruction I'd witnessed in my past.

Be responsible. Take control of the situation. *Don't mess up.*

The only problem with my request was Jason was the only person left who might be able to take on another student. He'd weaseled out of having as many as everyone else because of the "special" work he did for Stevenson, which probably meant slacking off sipping espressos and shit talking everyone else in the program who did the work.

Once I made it crystal clear more than once during undergrad that I wasn't the slightest bit interested, he'd been an insufferable prick. I could only hope that he would be as professional as possible around Heath, if Stevenson okayed the swap. I bit my thumbnail and stared at my phone, willing a reply to come in.

Heath was an easygoing guy who knew his shit. There wouldn't be a reason for Jason to nitpick him. And I could still help Heath if he needed it, but being in charge of his grade, even in a suggestion capacity, was a one-way ticket to an ethics violation.

Running my hands across my face, I leaned back in my chair. Heath's smell lingered on my skin. I shook my head. He made me laugh, even when I shouldn't. Mom and Dad's words came back to me about not going out and enjoying the fruits of my hard work. I needed more of that because apparently one fun night out—okay, it had been more than one and a hell of a lot more than fun, but maybe it was because I'd let go a little that I felt that connection to him. Maybe it was circumstantial because I'd been deprived.

I kept touching my lips every few minutes, rubbing my fingers over them. It had been the longest we'd gone without seeing each other since that first night. Opening my notebook again, I scribbled down a few more lines that had been floating in my mind. I could still feel the heat of his touch.

I needed a distraction or I was going to drive myself insane. Pacing in my bedroom, I glanced over at my desk and those warm, fuzzy feelings evaporated by the tell-tale heart thumping away in the desk drawer. I hadn't gotten rid of Angie's letter. That first letter that started all of this. I'd read it over more than once and I still didn't know what to do.

Every time I looked at the desk, I thought of the hidden folder in my inbox. I checked the folder. A big shiny *1* stared back at me beside the folder. Clenching my fingers together, they hovered over the folder. I'd asked for a distraction, right?

I sat on the edge of my bed, took a deep breath and opened the email.

My dearest Kara,

I can't begin to explain how sad I was when I got your last email. I know I have no right. I know the expectation that you'd even want to see me again isn't something I deserve, but I'd hoped I could see you.

I'll give you as much time and space as you need before you're ready, and maybe you never will be. It's the hardest thing I've learned about my recovery. Some things can't be fixed, and if me staying away is what you need to live a happy and healthy life, then I'll do that because you deserve that and more.

I love you more than anything, and maybe one day you can forgive me.

A tear dripped down onto the screen, and I brushed it away, wiping away the ones on my face. I couldn't see her. I couldn't face another disappointment when it came to her. And what did I even do about it? Was I supposed to open my arms to her after all these years? After everything she'd done? After every advantage Carla and Mike had given me? All the love they gave me and the home they gave me, how could I invite someone who'd taken so much from me back into my life?

There was a sharp knock on my door, and it swung wide

open as Lauren bounded in. The only one in the family with little to no boundaries. I slid my phone under my pillow, and she stopped short when she saw me.

I slapped a smile on my face, and she crossed the room and stood in front of me.

"What's wrong?"

"It's nothing. I'm fine."

"Why are your eyes all red?" She crossed her arms over her chest.

"I poked myself in my eye." Bringing up my mom was exactly what we didn't need. A reminder that we were both late additions to the family. I didn't want Lauren to worry about anything to do with my life before or even her life before. She was younger than me when she came home, but happy kids didn't get taken away from their parents. I knew her history, and she knew some of mine.

She raised an eyebrow. "Both eyes? Because they are both red."

"Yeah, both eyes." I avoided her gaze and unpacked my bag, stacking my books on my bed.

She stood there with her arms crossed over her chest. Usually we shared most things, but most things in my life up until that point hadn't included my mom and a hot guy I couldn't keep my hands off.

"What? Why did you come in here?"

She was sheltered in some ways, not knowing about running the streets, getting into trouble and finding her way to guys she should probably avoid. Any hint of that wasn't something I needed to introduce to this house.

"It's Wednesday."

I closed my eyes. Wednesday movie night had been a tradition ever since I'd moved back to Philly. We'd make brownies or bake something else, pop some popcorn and hang out together. It was Carla and Mike's date night.

"I can't, Lauren. It's the beginning of the semester, and I have tons of work to do. I can't do movie night tonight." I glanced up at her, and she dropped her arms to her sides, giving me the most pitiful look of teenage disappointment.

"Fine." She stormed out of the room.

I wasn't exactly the best of company, and I certainly wasn't going to load her up with my adult problems. She had the rest of her life for that. I guess this was what happened when you lived a completely boring life up until your twenties—your teenage sister expected you to share everything with her.

Talking to her about a guy asking me out that I wasn't interested in or how much homework I had was one thing. Bringing up my mom wanting to meet, how I was ready to spill my innermost thoughts into a notebook until it was covered in my black ink, or how much I couldn't handle the thought of not seeing Heath outside of our weekly sessions were strictly off-limits.

I flopped back onto my bed. My mind was mush. I wasn't going to get any work done. Writing would only make me think of Angie, and that was the last thing I needed. Maybe I should go downstairs and watch a movie to veg out a bit, but Lauren would ask questions. She'd want to know what upset me, and I wasn't going to tell her.

Rolling over, I picked up my phone and sent a message to the group chat.

Me: Anyone want to grab a drink?

Sam: How much money do you want? We'll pay anything!

Me: What?

Sam: This is obviously a kidnapper who's stolen Kara's

phone. Don't you touch a hair on her head or I swear I'll come after you.

    Anne: She has a particular set of skills.

    Charles: Hell yeah, she does.

    Sam: Shut up, Charlie.

    Charles: Charles.

    Anne: Oh god, not this again. Stop it, children.

    Sam: You know I'm always up for a drink. Tell me when.

    Me: At nine?

Carla and Mike would be back from their dinner by then, and I could pop out.

    Sam: Wooohooo. Let's do this!

Three hours later I'd given up on pretending to study. I stared at the notebook on my bed like a viper ready to strike at any second. My fingers were wrapped so tightly around my pen my knuckles were white.

I couldn't focus, and if I was already off my studying game, might as well go get a couple drinks and make that inability to focus more fun. I checked the time and knocked on Lauren's door. No answer.

Sliding my arms into my coat, I rushed down the steps when the front door opened at quarter to nine. Mom and Dad came in holding hands, laughing and letting in a blast of cold air behind them.

They were everything I'd always wanted. Wanted in a home. In parents. Beautiful, kind, sweet, and fun. I'd always be grateful to them for not only giving me a family, but they showed me what a relationship should look like. The path I was heading down with my mom would have led to disaster in no time.

"You're going out?" Mom turned to me with a smile reaching her eyes.

I buttoned my coat. "A beginning-of-the-semester meet up. I won't be too late."

"Okay, be safe." A hint of worry entered her gaze.

"I'll be completely safe. Nothing crazy. Some snacks and a drink or two."

"Have fun." Dad winked at me.

Pecking her and Dad on their cheeks, I slid between them and out the front door.

My stomach churned. Glancing over my shoulder, the pair stood in the doorway, waving to me. Did they think I was going out too much? That I might be following in Angie's footsteps drinking too often. My shoulders hunched as I gripped the collar of my coat, tugging it higher as a sharp gust of wintry air swirled past me. The slush from the snow bunched under my shoes as I got into the back of the taxi I'd ordered.

The front door closed as I pulled away from the house. I'd come home hungover during the break the first night I'd spent with Heath. My throat thick with emotions I tramped down, I stared at my phone. I'd never done that before, and Mom was worried about me. I'd upset her and made her worry. Wrapping my arms around my stomach, I stared out the window as the leafless trees whipped past the windows.

I tapped my phone against my palm. Closing my eyes, I shoved it into my pocket. The one person I wanted to call most was the one person I couldn't.

22

HEATH

I grabbed my phone off the bench and wiped the sweat off my face.

Emmett: Back in town. Going to The Bramble. You up for it?

My breath came out in pants. I'd been skating for hours, but the gnawing burn in my chest hadn't gone away. I could ignore the pain in my legs, but the yawning chasm of self-doubt was only the beginning.

We'd lost another game. The guys were counting on me, but it was like everyone had forgotten how to function on the ice. One of us was laying in the hospital bed. We'd been invincible on the ice. Not a serious injury on the team for years. Our invincibility had been a foregone conclusion, now everything was in doubt. Preston's presence had pulled us together in a way we didn't even understand until he was gone. He was the glue.

Declan climbed into the box after me and plopped down.

"Want to grab a drink after this?" I shook my phone at him.

"If it means we can cut this torture session short, then hell yeah. As soon as I can feel my legs again, I'm up for it." He closed his eyes and leaned back. His chest rose and fell. "I can text Mak and she'll meet us at Threes."

"I didn't mean Threes. I meant at The Bramble. Emmett's back in town, and he wanted to know."

"Oh." Declan tugged his jersey over his head.

"*Oh*? That's all you have to say?"

"I'm meeting Mak after, and I don't think she'd really be up for hanging with Emmett."

"Why not? She was hanging out with him before New Year's."

"That was a whole group of people. I have a feeling she was also a bit distracted. But he's not exactly one of her favorite people."

"You mean because she's friends with Avery."

He grunted and stood, leaving the box beside the ice. I followed him, not ready to let this go. My anger was punching through as the door to the locker room closed behind him.

"You're not going to hang out with Emmett anymore? Abandon him because Mak doesn't like him."

"Would you stop yelling? What the hell is up with you?"

I dragged my hands through my hair. *Had I been yelling?* I hadn't even heard it. It was getting harder to keep a handle on things. The pressure was mounting. "Things are already screwed up. The last thing I need is you dropping the guys because Mak has a problem being around us."

"She doesn't have a problem being around you." Declan ripped his pads off.

"Only Emmett."

"She wouldn't feel right being there with everything that went down with Emmett and Avery."

"Everything that went down? Emmett caught Avery cheating on him the night he was going to propose. I'd say if there's anyone who should be pissed off, it's him."

"Mak hasn't told me the full story, but she said it wasn't what everyone thought."

My eyes got wide and my mouth hung open. "Dude, everyone in school was talking about it. He found her in that room with Fischer. No one freaks out like he did over nothing."

Declan held his hands out at his side. "All I'm saying is what Mak said. Things can always be more complicated than they look. Hell, Mak and I hated each other's guts for years."

They had. But I'd seen what was simmering under all that animosity. At least they got to figure that out. They got a chance to find out what things could be like between them. I'd been hamstringed by not wanting to derail Kara's life.

"What's going on with you and the chick?" He wrapped a towel around his waist to head into the shower.

I dragged my hands down my face. Why did this have to be so complicated? Why couldn't I pick the uncomplicated route? *Why did I have to give my heart to a woman I'd destroy to have?*

"She's my independent study TA." I stared at him.

His mouth hung open, and his eyes got so wide. I couldn't help but laugh, even though it wasn't remotely funny. A sharp bark of laughter to cover the fact that my head was a mess.

"Again? What the hell is it with you and going after your teachers?"

I grimaced. "She's not my teacher. She's not even giving me a grade, and I didn't know she was going to be my TA when I met her. I only signed up for independent study after Preston got hurt and I became captain. I needed something more flexible. Now I'm trying to switch out into a normal class, but everything to satisfy my graduation requirements is full." I threw my pads down on the bench.

Declan blew out a deep breath. "Damn, that sucks. What does that mean for the two of you?"

The last thing I wanted it to. "I'm going to stay away from her."

"I mean, she showed up to the hospital with you. That seems pretty serious."

I gritted my teeth.

"I know. It was. It is." I shook my head. Things were getting more complicated by the second. "If I don't want to ruin her career before she even starts, then I need to stay away. If anyone finds out we've been together, it could wreck everything for her and nullify my grade so I wouldn't graduate."

"I don't even know why you're still here, man. You could have gone pro straight from high school if you'd wanted."

"I want to get my degree and I needed to graduate if our season was going to count. If I didn't graduate we'd be screwed. I have to stay away from her for the rest of the semester."

There were only two more days until my next session with Kara, and I'd been counting down the minutes until we'd be tucked away in that old, secluded office. At least I'd get to see her, even if I couldn't touch her. Apparently I liked torture. Even more so when I showed up outside Emmett's place. The hotel we'd spent two nights in. Bracing myself, I pushed through the lobby doors, half expecting to see Kara standing there.

We'd exchanged emails back and forth about a few

things. Nothing but professional. I loved it when she talked botany to me.

The guy at the front desk got on the phone to call up to Emmett's penthouse. He hung up after only saying my name into the receiver.

"If you take a left here, you'll find the private elevator—"

"I know the way, thanks."

A couple wheeled their bags up to the counter behind me. Leave it to Emmett to live in one of the best hotels in the city, even though he was barely here. I pressed the PH button once I got inside and shot up to the top floor of the hotel/apartment building. I guess when you had enough money, anything was an apartment.

I stepped out of the elevator and knocked on the only door in the entryway.

Emmett pulled open the door with a grim look on his face.

"Who died?" I winced at my poor choice of words. With everything going on with Preston, I didn't want any news like that coming my way.

"My house, apparently." Emmett rolled his eyes and waved me in.

"What do you mean your house?"

"I broke up with the woman I was seeing before I flew out here."

"Why'd you break up?"

He shrugged. "It seemed like it was time. She didn't exactly take to our parting quite as amicably as I thought."

He lifted his phone from his pocket and pulled up a home security app and turned on the cameras. There was shattered glass and torn clothes everywhere.

"Holy shit, you weren't kidding."

"Nope. I wasn't. Security will be there in a few seconds. I

figured it was better for her to get out her anger and rage now, plus I'll have lots of evidence if this gets messy and I need to get a restraining order against her."

"How many times have you done this?" I stared at him, really looking at him for the first time in a long time. The starry-eyed romantic was long gone. That part of him had died the night of our party senior year. I wished I could have been there. Maybe I could have helped somehow or stopped it or something, anything to have made it not hurt him so much.

"Seems my choices in women have never been great. She freaked out when I told her I wasn't ready to get married." He crossed to the fully stocked bar cart in his living room. The white and glass furniture filled his apartment. Everything was so bright I could have used sunglasses, and it was after nine.

"If you've got all that here, why the hell are we going out?"

"Staying here and drinking with you on our own doesn't exactly seem like a fun night out to me. Plus, when my place is being trashed, I need more of a distraction than looking into your baby blues. You'll see once you're NHL."

"Okay, so why are you fixing drinks?" Emmett didn't make sense sometimes.

"Because, I got this delivered and I needed someone to try it with."

He dropped two ice spheres into two glasses.

"What is it?" I eyed the glasses suspiciously.

"Diamond Jubilee by Johnny Walker."

"Do I even want to know how expensive this is?"

He shook his head and tilted the crystal decanter and poured the amber liquid over both, filling the glasses more than half full.

"This type of life doesn't exactly allow for certain types of relationships. The real kind. Maybe you're using each other to not feel lonely. Someone who understands you. Pretend you've got someone in the world who cares about you. Maybe you're happy to pretend for a while. When you know it's not real, it can really hurt you."

He stared down at our overly full glasses.

He pretended that the things between him and Avery were over, but they'd never really be over if he kept on going like this.

"I thought you had some arrangement thing going where they walked away after twelve weeks."

He shook his head and laughed. "I said I'd never been with someone for more than twelve weeks. It's like a force field around my ability to see beyond that amount of time."

"But you were with Avery for like three years."

He took a deep breath. "I know."

Wow, he hadn't taken off sprinting like he usually did whenever any of us brought her up. Well, I guess that's tricky to do from a penthouse apartment.

"And they sign an NDA. I learned that the hard way after my first girlfriend after I went pro tried to extort me with what she thought was incriminating information that would embarrass my family." He let out a mirthless laugh. "Little did she know, my parents don't give a shit about me."

He gave me a grim look before grabbing both glasses and walking over to me. Clinking his glass to mine, he turned his up and drained it in one gulp.

"Cheers." I downed mine in two, and he took both back, stashing them on the kitchen counter.

"Looks like my house is no longer in danger." He held out his phone, and the woman who'd been trashing his place was being put into the back of a car with the word SECURITY printed across the side.

"These are the things you have to look forward to." He pocketed his phone and grabbed his coat.

"I do not plan on following the Emmett Cunning Have-All-Your-Shit-Destroyed-By-Crazy-Exes Plan."

"You'll see." He opened his front door, and I followed him out, closing it behind us.

"I really don't plan on it. Not that it doesn't sound about as fun as a bat to the head. In a few months, I won't have to worry about that."

He shot me a look and jabbed the elevator button. "What's that mean?"

"I'm kind of with someone." I jammed my hands into my pockets.

"Who someone?"

"The one from the bar that night you had everyone out. We're kind of seeing each other. Well, not really. We were. We're planning on seeing each other."

He lifted his eyebrow at me.

"It's complicated." I shook my head. Of course it would be complicated. I never liked to do anything the easy way.

"And you're giving me shit about my love life." He laughed, and we stepped out into the crisp early February evening air.

"At least no one has created a mountain of my things in my driveway and lit them on fire."

Emmett's head whipped around. "How did you know about that?"

I couldn't hold back my laughter. "Dude, I was joking. Someone seriously did that?"

His shoulders hunched, and he grumbled. The last of the slushy snow crunched under our feet, and weekend warriors were out in full force, yelling and laughing. We jogged across the street as the light flashed a white walk symbol. Dodging a taxi turning right, Emmett slammed his hands into the hood of the car.

"Watch where the hell you're going!" he shouted, stepped up on the curb.

I turned and grabbed his arm. "Keep it on the ice, Em."

He grumbled again, and I chuckled, pushing the door to The Bramble open and stopping short in the entryway. Emmett plowed into me and nearly knocked me over. My smile was immediate before I tramped it down. This wasn't good. I was supposed to stay away, but it seemed the universe had other ideas.

23

KARA

I stabbed the ice in my glass with my straw. The music wasn't so loud we couldn't hear, but the air was filled with pop songs. Songs about love, loss, happiness, and every one of them seemed to be telling me that this whole Heath thing was a mistake. His bright, clear eyes filled my dreams, replaying the time we'd spent together.

But we couldn't be together. Heath seemed to think after graduation it would be fine, but I'd seen how those things went down. The slightest hint of impropriety could follow people for their whole careers. If we started dating after he graduated, there would still be questions. I could only imagine the snide remarks from someone like Jason. Stevenson had turned down my request to have Heath transferred, which meant...I didn't know what it meant. How was I supposed to deal with this? At this point if I said anything, I was screwed, and if I didn't say something, I was screwed.

"What did that ice ever do to you?" Sam rested her elbows on the table and stuck out her tongue at me as she popped another fry into her mouth. She pushed her glasses up the bridge of her nose with the back of her hands, which were covered with fry salt. Her words jolted me out of the daze I was in.

"What?" My head snapped up, and all three of them were staring at me. I'd obviously missed some of the conversation.

"I understand being pissed that your future rests in the hands of Stevenson, but I didn't think you'd resort to ice murder." She nodded toward my glass. Her straight black hair hung down over her shoulders like a curtain.

Staring into it confirmed I had, in fact, turned my ice cubes into crushed ice.

"I'm worried about the fellowship." I drained the last of my soda.

Charles and Anne slid into the empty seats at the table.

"What took you guys so long? Kara was getting restless and she made me order." Sam grinned across the table at me.

"Hey! I did not. I wanted to wait."

"Don't worry, Kara. We know all about Sam over here." Charles rolled his eyes at me and turned back to Sam.

"Is she being a total downer again?" Charles jerked his thumb toward me.

"She is. We thought when you asked if anyone wanted to come out, you'd be in better spirits." Sam jabbed a ketchup-coated fry at me. The server stopped at the end of our table and snagged my glass for a refill.

"And why shouldn't she be? She's a lock for that fellowship even with Jason's head so far up Stevenson's ass that he can probably give her a root canal. And her section got the best grades on the first exam. The only thing missing is a hot guy." Anne shook her shoulders and grinned at me.

I froze with my sandwich halfway up to my mouth.

"What? I'm not dating anyone." The color drained from my face. I wished I was. His hands trailing their way down my body and how easy it was to laugh around him. The temptation to throw caution to the wind was almost unbearable.

"I know. That's why I said it was the only thing missing." Sam laughed and shoved more fries in her mouth.

"There isn't much time for anything like that with everything going on." And the one person could ruin the season his team had worked for. He would be disqualified, and I could never take that away from him. And if anyone found out, it could derail the career I was trying to build. The career I wanted. I definitely wanted it. Follow in Mom and Dad's footsteps. Get my PhD, become a professor. Make them proud.

The server came back with my refill, and I started to tune them out again. A little over almost three months into the semester and the fellowship award date was getting closer. It was a chance some people waited their whole lives for, but the thought of winning slammed a pit into my stomach so hard I could barely catch my breath.

Like I'd conjured him from my absentminded thoughts while Charles, Amy, and Sam chatted away; Heath walked into the bar. My mind froze for a second, trying to figure out if I was hallucinating, but those were the eyes that shot straight through me. Unmistakable.

One of the guys who'd been there the night we met nearly knocked him off his feet when he stopped in the doorway. The tug toward him and our instant connection shot down to my toes. Heads turned their way immediately. Women swiveled around in their chairs to watch the two of them pass by. While Heath was all light and bright, his friend was the definition of brooding. Dark hair, dark eyes, and a killer five o'clock shadow. They were similar height, but Heath was trim and lithe, whereas the man beside him looked like a bruiser. It probably came in handy playing hockey.

The back of my hand knocked into my glass when I reached for it, and it went tumbling over, splashing across the table. I dragged my eyes away from Heath. Warmth spread all over me at his gentle smile. Like we had a secret no one else could know about. And we did.

"Boo! Kara, WTF?" Sam and Amy grabbed a fistful of napkins to mop up my mess.

"Sorry, my hand slipped." I tried to keep my eyes on our table, but I couldn't help it. His gaze was heavy like a warm blanket in a blustery winter storm. I looked up from my glass and locked eyes with him.

He broke the connection first. Shifting his body so I wasn't in his line of sight anymore. The flutters turned into a pit, which was stupid, but what I wanted. I needed to stay away from him so I didn't end up in front of the ethics council.

Five more years of the academic slough dealing with assholes like Jason and completely oblivious advisors like Stevenson. Why did I do it? Why was I even in the program? Because Mom and Dad put in the work and gotten it done. I wasn't a flake.

The rest of the table got their food, and I tried to join in on the conversation but my eyes kept drifting to Heath. More than one woman approached their table. He and his friend had an easy smile for all of them, but he didn't invite them to sit down.

One woman had the nerve to run her fingers through his hair. I lifted my ass off the seat, ready to take her down. Heath jerked his head away with a laugh and scooted his chair back. I didn't have a claim on him. I couldn't claim him, but that didn't stop me from slipping my phone out under the table.

Me: I have a feeling you won't be hard up for someone to take that ticket on Saturday.

Heath: I gave it to one of the other guys. I don't think it would be as fun for you to see us lose.

He turned his head slightly so his profile faced me. His strong jaw, ridiculous cheekbones, and straight nose were capped off by eyelashes no man had business having. I could see them from all the way over here.

"Kara, did you want another drink?" Charles slid out of the booth and leaned over the table. Waiter service had ended a little while ago.

"Sure, get me a vodka cranberry."

"Sam? Anne?"

"You know what I like, Charlie." Sam made a growling sound and clawed at the air.

Charles rolled his eyes. "Anne?"

"A mojito would be awesome." Anne tucked her hair behind her ear.

"One vodka cranberry, old-fashioned, and mojito coming up." Charles left, and Sam and Anne went back to their conversation.

"Next time you call me saying your legs feel like clouds and you're floating away, I'm sending Charles to come get you."

"Traitor," Sam hissed.

"You nearly broke my pinkie!" Anne threw a wad of napkins at her.

My phone buzzed on the table. I flipped it over, and my heart sped up as I unlocked it and read the whole thing. Keeping my head ducked, I peered over at him. He whipped back around, dropping his arm off the back of the chair and sitting fully forward.

Heath: Who was that guy? Are you on a date?

I cracked a smile. At least I wasn't the only one jealous.

Me: Yes, can't you tell? We've got a whole quad date going. Orgy comes next.

Heath: You're a regular barrel of laughs. Thought maybe it was a double date.

Me: That's Charles, my friend. Sam and Anne are also here and definitely not together.

Anne fed Sam one of the cherries from her drink, holding it by the stem. I laughed and shook my head. Okay, now it made sense why he thought it was a double date.

His little texting bubble popped up and disappeared a few times.

Heath: Good. Does this mean texting isn't against the rules?

Me: Technically, it would be. It is. I shouldn't be doing this.

Heath: Can't help yourself, huh?

My gaze darted to his and the way his full lips curled up. He turned a little bit more and caught my eye. Two more months. I'd already made it eight weeks, what was the rest of my life?

Me: It seems I can't

Charles darted in front of me with the drinks balanced in his hands. Some of the mojito sloshed out onto the table as he set them down.

I took a sip of my drink and kept an eye on my phone. The phantom buzz was a bitch. Every time I thought it buzzed, I'd glance down and see no message. I hated how much I wanted a message. How much I wanted him to shove his chair away from the table, stalk over here, and kiss me like he had the last time we were together. I longed for the sizzle that shot through me when his lips were a fraction of an inch away from mine, and the breathless way I felt when we finally broke apart.

We were playing a game of cat and mouse, but I wasn't sure who was who. Our eyes clashed, and the pent-up energy coursing through that connection could have powered a rocket, but we both kept our butts in our seats. This was the right thing to do, wasn't it?

After a couple more drinks and a nice buzz, I lost sight of Heath through the new arrivals. The volume increased and so did the temperature. It certainly didn't feel like a March evening. A trail of sweat dripped down my back. Time to go. The place was really packed now and mainly standing room only. A band had taken up a spot on the small stage at the back of the restaurant.

Sam went to close out our tab. My phone buzzed, and my heart leaped. I glanced down, disappointment cratered in my chest. It was only my app letting me know my taxi was outside.

"I'll see you on Monday. Try to get Sam home without you both getting arrested." I threw my arms around Anne.

"Good luck to that. She already said this is stop number one." She let go of me and rolled her eyes.

"Can I share your cab?" Charles tucked his scarf into his black pea coat.

"Sure." I buttoned my coat and slid my bag onto my shoulder. Charles and I wove our way through the throngs of people. This place had certainly become a hell of a lot more popular in the last few months. The bar was at least three people deep. Sam would be there awhile to pay.

I followed in Charles's wake as he got people to move out of the way. A hand wrapped around my wrist in a gentle but firm grasp. I jerked to a stop, and whipped my head around. My pulse pounded as I stared into the eyes of the man who'd been on my mind for what seemed like every minute of every day.

"In case you didn't already know. You look gorgeous tonight." His hot breath skimmed over the shell of my ear and sent a shiver down my spine. The blue of his eyes was even more pronounced in the dim lighting. I licked my suddenly dry lips. There were no words because every thought ended up with me leaving with him tonight.

He let go and took a step back. I resisted the urge to follow him.

A hand landed on my shoulder. I spun around.

"Kara, you okay?" Charles stared at me with concern in his eyes.

"I'm good." I craned my neck to where Heath had been, but he was gone. Swallowed up by the tipsy crowd. We slid into the back of the taxi, and I pulled out my phone.

Me: Goodnight, Heath.

The response was immediate, coming through almost as soon as I hit send.

Heath: Night, Kara.

24

HEATH

The slick slap of my stick melded perfectly with the slice of my skates on the ice. This was *the* game. The game it had all been building toward. Preston was watching from the hospital. We'd made sure to get him set up with his laptop and a subscription to the streaming service broadcasting the game.

Declan was open, and with a flick of my wrist I sent the puck through the legs of the wing from the other team and fed it straight to him. The loud horn blared and the flashing light on top of the net spun as Declan sank it into the back of the net. Everyone in the stands was on their feet.

They'd come at us hard the second the puck dropped and had scored a goal in the first three minutes. It all happened in slow motion. Watching the puck sail into the net, my stomach had dropped. This wasn't going to happen. Gritting my teeth, I pushed off the boards. Declan and I dug deep. My new position as the center still felt weird. I kept looking to my left expecting Preston to be there.

Once the shock wore off, we'd equalized the score in minutes. The roar of the crowd couldn't even touch the pounding rush of the blood in my ears. I pushed myself to the limit. Sweat filled my gloves as I whipped around the ice.

Declan swapped out and stood in the box with his hands gripped along the edge of the boards. Like my mind pieced together a patchwork of opportunities and ran through them until there was the perfect combo, I spotted another opening.

Taking it for myself this time, I lifted my stick and smacked the puck in a blind shot. It sailed past two defensemen for the other team. I envisioned the straight path to the back of the net. Then the horn blared and everyone went even crazier.

With my lungs burning from staying out on the ice as long as I could, I climbed over the boards, dropping onto the bench and squirting cold water into my mouth. The stadium came alive as the stands were a sea of standing, clapping, cheering fans. I grabbed a towel and wiped away the stinging burn of sweat in my eyes. Glancing over at Declan as the place vibrated around us, I had a shit-eating grin on my face and I didn't even care.

"Hell of a way to close this out." He slapped my hand, brimming with excitement.

"There's no other way, man."

He glanced behind me, and I followed his gaze. Makenna was on her feet with two fingers shoved into her mouth, cheering the guys on.

"Heath!"

My head whipped up at Coach's call. Every muscle tight, I climbed over the boards. My skates hit the ice, and I took off into the play, ready to finish this.

With the precision and timing we'd honed over the past four years, even without Preston at our side, we held them back. Declan and I had been skating together for almost ten years. We fell into the groove we'd laid down long ago, and the team filled in all the missing gaps.

A wing from the other team came out of nowhere, skating full power across the ice, and slammed straight into Declan while his head was turned. Nothing pissed me off more than a cheap shot, and that was beyond cheap. His stick came up and hit Declan straight in the chest.

Unable to brace himself, Declan went flying and slammed into the glass so hard it rattled and splintered. I was frozen in horror as I watched him fall to the ice. A roar of disapproval blasted the walls of the stadium from the crowd.

Gritting my teeth, I got to them first. The other guys on the team were right at my back, and I could tell they were out for blood. Throwing down my stick and my gloves, I skated right up to the guy, my hands fisted at my sides and my blood boiling.

He tried to get away like a coward, but I was faster. I slammed into him so hard his helmet flew off. With my hands wrapped around his jersey, I gave him another shake. My nostrils flared, and he tried to take a shot at me. I dodged it and held him there. My blood pounded even harder than it had in the game. My vision clouded as I wrapped my fingers around his jersey and slammed my fist into the wing's head. Pain exploded in my fist, but he'd sure as hell feel it tomorrow.

His hands came up, taking wild swings at my face, and I hit him again. My knuckles sliced open, and blood poured down my hand. The ref's whistle sliced through the melee, but it didn't get me to stop. I'd already had one teammate end up in the hospital because of someone's shitty decisions, I didn't need that happening to Declan. The wing from the other team dropped to the ice when I let go of his jersey.

Someone wrapped their arm across my chest, and I shook them off, ready to take on whoever was next. I whipped around and came face-to-face with Declan.

"Heath. Calm down. I'm good." He got in front of me and pushed me away.

The curtain of red lifted, and I could see the guy who'd hit Declan. He sat up on the ice, shaking his head. Hope he liked getting his bell rung as much as he liked ringing others'.

"That was uncalled for, son." The ref skated in front of me.

"And what he did was uncalled for. He could have killed him," I shouted at the ref and got into his face. Declan held me back.

"Two wrongs don't make a right."

"Tell that to one of my teammates when someone puts them in the hospital." We'd already been there. We were already dealing with one man down. I didn't need that shit happening again. Declan wrapped his fist around my jersey and jerked me back. I hadn't even realized I'd been advancing on the ref.

I grabbed my stick from Declan and skated past the ref.

His whistle split the air, and he gestured with his thumb. "You're out of here." And he skated away.

"Are you fucking kidding me?" My nostrils flared, and the boiling anger threatened to overtake me. I threw down my stick, ready to go after him, but Declan and the rest of the guys got in front of me. Coach was shouting at me from the bench. I let them push me back and stepped off the ice, going straight for the locker room.

I ripped my helmet off and threw it against the wall.

Grabbing my stick in both hands, I slammed it down over my leg, snapping it in half. Dropping down onto the bench, I ran my hands through my hair, sweat pouring off me. It dripped down into my face, blinding me.

It was all getting to be too much. Everything converging into this mess I didn't know how to fix. Preston was going to be out for a while. There wasn't spinal damage, so thank fuck for that, but that didn't mean he'd be back out on the ice anytime soon. I could not keep this team together like everyone had had faith that I could.

A bellowing horn filled the stadium. God, I hoped that was one for us. I slammed my head against the lockers. The metal rattled, and I took off my jersey, sliding it up over my head. My shoulders pressed against the cool metal, and I tried to inhale through the burning in my throat and lungs. Staring down at my bag, I let out a curse. My phone lit up.

I shoved my clothes aside and grabbed the phone.

Kara: I know you have a game, but I wanted to wish you good luck. You've got this and I know any guy who can spend months splicing the perfect floral specimen has whatever he needs to do anything.

The next message came in a little while later.

Kara: And I miss you. I know the promise we made, but I wanted you to know that. It's not any easier for me.

I dropped my head into my hands and stared at her words. It didn't seem possible that someone could come into your life for such a short time and make such an impact that every day you didn't see them was like agony, but here we were. Here I was doing what I needed to do to protect her and get her away from me when I was losing my cool left and right. Understatement of the year. I was fucking things up—royally. The guy she saw me as wasn't who I was anymore. Had I ever been that guy, or was I really good at putting up a front? That chill laid-back guy had disappeared into the murky surf, and I needed to get my head on straight. Maybe this was for the best. The universe's way of giving her an out. Getting me away from her before I broke something I couldn't fix.

Heath: *I miss you too. Game isn't going well.*

Another stadium-shaking blast from the goal buzzer. I wrenched open the locker room door and spotted one of the screens lining the hallway: 3-5 us. Maybe I was a fucking distraction on the ice. I'd never dealt with this before, the uncontrolled spiraling that threatened to throw everything off track.

I wasn't this guy. I was the fucking laid-back one, damn it. But these outbursts. This anger scared the shit out of me. I hated to think this was what had always been there. Had I been pretending, covering who I really was and only now was the real me coming out? The guy who got kicked out of games and lost his cool.

The other thing I'd shoved in my bag poked out of the side. A plain white envelope. It looked so innocuous and ordinary, but what lurked inside was one of my worst nightmares. California Department of Corrections and Rehabilitation printed along the top left-hand corner. I'd grabbed it from the pile of mail at home when I'd stopped by.

He might get out. My dad's parole hearing was scheduled, and less than a decade after he'd tried to kill us both, he could be out free and roaming the streets. The urge to get in my car and make that trek across the country thudded hard into my chest so hard I swore I'd crack a rib.

My phone buzzed in my hand, only it wasn't a message. It was a call. Her name lit up the screen, and I hesitated before answering. Somehow she'd known I needed to hear her voice. I answered the call and held it up to my ear.

"Heath?"

"Yeah, it's me."

"Are you okay?" The sweet fullness of her voice was like a salve to the burning anger coursing through my veins. I shoved the letter back into my bag and leaned against the locker.

"I'm a lot better now."

"I saw you got kicked out of the game."

I winced and then smiled. "Been checking up on me?"

She let out a small laugh. The kind that was made from happiness tinged with a hint of embarrassment. "I can't even lie and say I wasn't. I have no idea what all these stats and other numbers are on my screen, but I saw the note about you getting ejected."

"I lost my cool. It shouldn't have happened."

Another blare of the horn signaling a goal sounded outside the locker room.

"They scored again. It's three to six."

"Maybe they're better off without me."

Another bellowing horn to signal the end of the game.

"Don't say that. They aren't. Maybe they are digging deep because they know you're not out there with them and they want to make you proud." I could see her now, down-right indignant over it.

"Maybe." I stared up into the locker room lights. "I've missed the sound of your voice."

"Me too. I mean, not the sound of my voice. I hear that all the time. I've missed the sound of your voice."

I couldn't help but laugh. She was probably the only one who could have gotten one out of me at this point.

"Are you in your office?"

"No, I'm home, trying to remember why the hell I chose this department." Pages flipped on the other end of the line.

"Studying?" I could see her now with her hair up, pencil behind her ear, diligently working through problem after problem.

"No. I should be." She let out a deep breath. "I'm writing."

"As in a story?"

"Sometimes. Sometimes it's poetry. Sometimes it's an entire plot arc, someone's journey. It depends on my mood."

"I didn't know you were writing again." It seemed like something I should know. It didn't make sense as to why, but it did.

"I started back up a little while ago, and I kind of haven't been able to turn it off. Heath, I—"

The door to the locker room burst open, and the guys piled in.

"The game's over. I've got to go. It was nice to hear your voice." *Let's do it again soon. Actually screw that; let me drive back to you right now and bury my face in the side of your neck.*

"It was nice to hear yours too. I'll see you at our session." She ended the call, and I put my phone back in my bag. Coach barreled into the locker room, and his eyes blazed. I steeled myself for the chewing out to come because I deserved it. It seemed like I was fucking up left and right. Glancing down at my phone, I wanted to pick it up and call her back. It seemed I wasn't ready to learn my lesson yet.

25

KARA

My texting with Heath was not advisable. It was downright stupid and only the slightest bit better than what we'd been trying to avoid in the first place, but more than a day without hearing from him and I got antsy. The texts poured in at night. When I was alone in my room and thinking of him. Even when I promised myself I'd wait or I wouldn't reply, I couldn't help it.

My notebooks were filling faster than I could buy them. I'd taken to shoving extra pieces of paper, napkin, backs of menus, whatever I could get my hands on to get the words out that wouldn't stop coming until I'd freed them with my pen and paper.

Heath had made me less afraid of the words. Less worried about what it meant that I couldn't stop writing. It was so fast and furious sometimes I'd fall asleep on top of my composition book. Rereading my words and knowing how much he'd brought them to life made the temptation so much worse.

Not a single hand raised in the air as we neared the end

of the recitation session. We'd worked through the questions, but I had to make sure all the material had sunk in. The midterm had gone well, but they'd have to incorporate the new concepts we'd been learning.

My pacing along the front of the classroom at the beginning of the session slowed to a meandering crawl, but my mouth was still drier than a desert. More than once I'd had to ask one of the busybody students a question where they'd ramble on so I could gulp down some water. The humidity from our rainy afternoon had wreaked havoc on my hair. It was most likely a frizzy mess if I was lucky and a giant poufy triangle if I wasn't.

The handouts I'd given the class of sophomores had gone down well. I distilled everything as simply as I could and prayed they'd retain the information. Things had picked up considerably since the exam. I had no idea how Jason's students were coping, because mine were barely hanging in there and they'd performed a hell of a lot better than his. Standing in front of thirty-five students, I felt like any moment they'd know I was an imposter. *You nearly flunked eighth grade! How can you be teaching us this!*

I hadn't exactly been an amazing student before high school. Detentions. Suspensions. And terrible grades were what I associated with school. It was a place to go and hang out with my friends or a truancy officer would be pounding on our apartment door. It had happened more than once before I'd learned to go to school and sneak off to the bathrooms to smoke with my friends.

No one knew about my past and no one probably would have cared, but it was always like someone was waiting in the wings to rip off this mask I'd created for myself over the past ten years. Those were my nightmares in the days leading up to the first sessions.

Someone would stand on top of their chair and pull out my middle school report card, showing everyone how unqualified I was to teach anyone. My insane fears had been unfounded. Instead of standing up on their desks to point and laugh, the students stared at me with fear in their eyes and shaky pencils as they freaked out about understanding everything we would be cramming into their heads over the next semester.

Waking up in a cold sweat had given way to a queasy stomach before classes started. Examining my stack of notes, I made sure I'd hit on every topic we needed to and had a few students work through some methods aloud. I nearly leaped over the desk with joy when almost all of them could work through problems that followed the same patterns but were different enough that it meant they knew the material.

I don't think I was made for standing up in front of a class. Everyone said your first few weeks were rough, but this was my fifth session standing in and it never got easier. Class days were by far my worst days. It usually took me at least another day to recover from the nerves. It wasn't helped by the crossover at the end of the class. Jason taught his session right after mine.

As if I'd conjured him with my thoughts, Jason whipped open the class door and strode into the classroom like he owned the place. I hated it when he did this. All heads turned to him as I wrapped up the session.

Every eye snapped back to me. The urge to crawl under my desk warred with the one to punch him straight in the solar plexus. With my luck, I'd end up breaking my hand and he'd report me to campus security.

"I think we're good for today. The first exam went well, and you're all well on your way to nailing it. I'll have office hours on Tuesdays and Thursdays, so be sure to stop by if you weren't able to answer the questions we went over. Thank you, everyone."

Notebooks and textbooks closed, bags zipped, and feet shuffled across the floor. Everyone glanced between me and Jason as they walked out of the class. I clenched my fists at my sides and shook my head. In seconds, he'd completely thrown my class into disarray, and he sat in the back with a smug smirk on his face as everyone filed out.

The last student left, and the door slammed shut. My blood boiled so hot I wouldn't have been surprised if steam started pouring out of my ears. I kept my head down and packed up my things. I gritted my teeth at the soft squeak of the desk as Jason unfolded himself from it, jamming my supplies into my bag, imagining it was a straight shot at Jason's solar plexus.

His shadow fell over me as he stepped up to the front of the desk. He leaned in and pressed his hands onto the top on either side of my bag.

"Why are you here so early?" My jaw was clenched tight. It wasn't the first time he'd shown up and interrupted my session. It wasn't like saying anything to Prof. Stevenson would matter. He'd give her some excuse that she'd lap up.

"I like to be on time. I can't help it if you're easily distracted." His bag hit the desk with a thump.

"Don't interrupt my class like that again. Wait outside like anyone else in your session." I tried my best to keep the venom out of my voice, but his smirk stayed firmly in place, so it hadn't fazed him.

"Maybe I wanted to see you in action. Since you tried to foist that hockey player onto me earlier this semester, I thought maybe you might be struggling with the sessions

and I could help you out." His voice was like a slime trail
across my eardrums.

"I didn't try to foist anyone off on you. I thought for so
many reasons Heath would be better suited with you for the
semester."

He sat on the edge of the desk. "And what reasons were
those?"

"It doesn't matter now, does it?"

"Let's see what extra information you might be slipping
your students in here." He slid one of my study sheets across
the desk.

I snatched it back from him and shoved it into my bag.
Just what I needed, him ripping off my study materials and
passing them off as his own. I'd give this sheet to Stevenson
after the weekend and let her know the students found it
helpful. But I wasn't going to let him weasel his way into it.

"I'd have thought you'd have had better manners after
all these years, Kara. How long have we known each other?"
He rounded the desk.

"Too fucking long," I grumbled and slipped the strap to
my messenger bag over my shoulder.

The classroom door flew open so loudly that it crashed
against the wall with a *bang*. I jumped, and Jason backed up,
knocking over the chair behind the desk.

Standing in the doorway was a disheveled Heath. His
eyes were ringed with red. Droplets of water fell from his
hair, and his clothes were wet. *What the hell had happened?*

His gaze darted behind me to Jason, and he backed up.

I took a step forward, and Heath took one back.
Glancing behind me, I turned to meet Jason's wide eyes. I
whipped back around to see Heath disappearing around the
corner. The blood surged in my ears so loudly I could barely
hear. If I raced after him, Jason would know something was

up, but the way Heath had looked at me... The way he looked, disheveled and lost. I'd deal with the fallout later. I called out Heath's name. My feet slapped against the tile floor, sliding as I stepped into Heath's wet footsteps. I pumped my legs harder, determined to catch him.

I rounded the corner to the entrance as he hit the metal cross bar for the door. The rain came down fast, but I didn't even think of grabbing my umbrella. Standing at the top of the steps, I shouted out his name as he hit the last step. Droplets clung to my eyelashes as I shielded them.

He stopped like my voice had frozen him solid.

Racing down the steps to the one he was standing on, I stepped around him. Staring up at him, I panted and tried to get him to meet my eyes. Something was way wrong.

"Heath." I reached for him, and he jerked away. A sharp pain sliced through my heart. "Heath, what's going on?"

The rain soaked through my clothes. I shivered in the freezing air and crossed my arms over my chest.

He was pelted with water but stood completely still. "I had to see you." It was so low I could barely hear him.

"We have our session tomorrow."

His gaze shot to mine. "Not like that. Not sitting across from you and not able to touch you. I needed to see you. To touch you, and then I saw you in there with that guy and remembered all the reasons I said I'd stay away. What me showing up like this could do to you."

"Heath. I don't give a shit. Tell me what the hell is wrong." I reached out again, slowly this time. Gingerly, I wrapped my hand around his arm. He was frozen solid like he'd been outside in this weather for hours.

He moved so quickly I didn't even know what was happening. One second I was standing at the bottom of the steps, and the next I was pressed against the tall brick columns that sat at the either end of the staircase. My touch broke him out of his trance.

His body shielded me from the rain that soaked through his clothes. He traced my jaw with the back of his hand. It trembled, and my heart hadn't stopped racing. Something was wrong. So, so wrong. *Was this about hockey?* I knew they hadn't been doing well this season. They still had a chance at the playoffs from what people told me, but it hadn't been like their other seasons.

"Heath, you're scaring me. Tell me what happened. Tell me what's wrong."

"I needed to touch you. And I needed to do this." His lips pressed against mine. They were hungry, greedily drinking down my kisses. I parted my lips, and the freezing rain melted away into nothing but background noise.

He shot his fingers into my hair, dragging his frozen digits along my scalp and wrapping the strands around his hand. He was drinking me down. Gulping so hard and fast it made my head spin.

I hadn't forgotten how he felt, but my memories didn't compare to the real thing. Hard and gentle at the same time, his touch made me light-headed. A shiver that had nothing to do with the rain shot through my body, and I needed to be closer to him. So much closer.

I fisted my hands around his wet shirt. The hard planes of his muscles were tight under my hands. Breaking his hold on my mouth, I stared into his eyes. They were no longer in the shadow of the building, but lit up from the lights from the lampposts. Pain radiated off him.

"Heath." I skimmed my fingers over his cheeks. The freezing temperature of his skin sent my worry into over-drive. My fear ratcheted up. Whatever it was, we could fix it.

"Tell me what's wrong." I closed my hand around his forearm and the other along his jaw.

He leaned down and rested his forehead against mine. Pain radiated off him. We needed to get somewhere warm. His lips were blue, and a tremor shot through his body. I was soaked, but he was shaking from more than the cold. What I needed was for him to tell me what was going on.

"Heath, please." My voice walked the fine line between soothing and panic.

A tear joined the water cresting down his face.

"Preston..." He took a shuddering breath, and his shoulders shook. His arms wrapped tightly around me, so tightly it was hard fill my lungs. "Preston, he's...he died."

26

HEATH

I got the message from Preston that he wanted to see me minutes after the team got onto the bus. I'd shown up at the hospital ready to get my ass chewed out, dragged myself down there with a gnawing in my chest. I was losing it. Losing my grip on things, and I didn't know how to fix it.

Stepping into his hallway, I pressed myself against the wall. A flurry of activity greeted me. Doctors and nurses blew past, pushing carts of medical equipment. Imo stood in the hallway with her hands pressed up against her mouth and her eyes wide.

"What's happening?"

Her gaze darted from the room to me. "He...I don't know. He was having headaches all day. His legs were hurting him. And then his speech got slurred. I called in the doctors, and his eyes rolled back in his head." She'd dissolved into tears by the end. I wrapped my arm around her shoulder, and her whole body trembled.

The team of people rushed him out of the room and into surgery. We were left there, staring after him, and the waiting began. It was almost worse to not know what was going on, but confirmation of our worst nightmares was something we'd gladly put off.

"I need to call his parents. I need to call Becca." Imogen's words were stilted and stunned.

"I'll do it." With trembling fingers, I called and texted everyone.

We stood out there as more people arrived. Preston's parents burst through the doors. Imogen jumped up from her spot on the floor. They wrapped her in their arms as she explained what had happened.

I couldn't stop moving. I couldn't sit down, like the second I did something bad would happen.

The guys showed up. Declan with Mak and everyone else on the team. After more than three hours the doctor came in, dragging the hat from his scrubs off. He opened his mouth, but the look on his face told us everything we needed to know.

He started the we-did-everything-we-could speech, and I stopped. My brain shut off, trying to protect me. Insulate me from the crushing devastation of knowing one of my friends was gone.

The numbness replaced it. Shell-shock. Everyone stood there in silence as the doctor talked. And then there was a sound, a wailing from beside me. I don't know if it came from Imo or Preston's mom, but I couldn't look. I'd break.

Preston's dad and the guys all stood there around them, hugging them tight. Mak and Declan's fingers were tightly woven together. I'd been coming to get chewed out by him, not looking forward to it, but I'd give anything to have heard it now. Have him give me shit about losing my cool at the game and listen to his sage advice on how to handle things going forward. The last memory he'd have of me was getting thrown out of the game and letting the team down. The disappointment dug that hollow spot in my chest even deeper. The crushing disappointment he'd have felt at me losing my shit and now there was nothing.

The sharp shock of freezing rain registered that I was outside, but other than that my brain wasn't working properly. The universe had betrayed me once again. I had one goal. Only one person could keep me from losing my mind. I needed more than a text from her or a stolen glance when we were alone. The thought of another second without her when time could snatch someone away in an instant. It made my palm sweat and my vision tunnel like I was dropped down a well I couldn't escape.

I needed to feel the life pumping through her veins and touch her skin, because I was coming apart. Slowly shattering and becoming nothing. I needed the roaring pounding of blood in my ears to be replaced by her gentle words telling me it would be okay. Someday soon my chest wouldn't be so tight and I'd be able to not feel like someone was slowly plunging a knife in between my ribs.

On autopilot, I went to her class. I had her schedule memorized and I'd been tempted to have our paths cross accidentally, but I'd kept away, trying my best to stick to the plan we'd decided on. The blast of heat when I opened the doors to the building on the far end of campus did nothing but send the shivers even deeper.

I opened the door to her classroom and saw her standing there with the other guy in her program, and it all came rushing back. The warnings I'd repeated over and over in my head. Preston's words to me. *If you care about someone, you protect them.* The guy recovered from his shock and looked at me and then at Kara. I literally couldn't think of an excuse to be there. Selfish asshole, that's what I was. I shouldn't have been there. My muscles ached unlike any workout before, like my body was willing me to stop. Stop and deal with what had happened, but I couldn't.

She turned her head, and I took off back out into the elements. The shock of the freezing rain barely made a dent as my feet pounded against the stone steps.

"Heath!" Her sharp and frantic voice froze me on the spot. Shoving my hands into my soaked pockets like that would protect them against the biting cold, I willed her to leave me with my living nightmare and slicing pain. My throat was tight, and I tried to swallow past the choking pressure. I didn't need to bring her down. I shouldn't have come. *Go back inside, Kara. You don't need to deal with this.*

She didn't, and I couldn't hold back. Rain poured down over the two of us. The faint rolling boom of thunder in the distance snapped me into action. She was there, standing in front of me. Flesh and blood and alive and I needed to feel that.

Her chocolaty eyes were filled with so much worry. I needed to push that away. My lips were demanding on hers. I was drinking her down, letting her warm, full lips soothe and comfort the burning ache in my chest. I needed to feel her. Her touch kept me grounded and from being torn away into the unknown as I tried to make sense of what had happened. It didn't make sense and it would never make sense, but I needed to hold onto the one real thing I'd needed since the day I'd decided I couldn't see her anymore. I'd sworn it would be as long as it took to protect her, but I was a selfish asshole.

She stared up at me trying to figure out what was going on. Her warm fingers trailed against my numb skin, nearly frozen from the pelting rain.

"Tell me what's wrong."

The pleading tone in her voice broke me. I rested my forehead against hers and tried to shield her from the rain with my body. A single trail of warmth cascaded down my cheek. I didn't want to say the words out loud, but I had to.

Her eyes searched mine, and the worry hit me hard.

I wrapped my arms tightly around her and said the words I'd been running from since I'd left the hospital. A shudder shot through me, and her arms crisscrossed my back.

"Come on, we need to get back inside." She tried to drag me back toward the building, but I couldn't go in there.

"There's somewhere we can go." I threaded my fingers through hers and walked even farther into campus. She didn't say a word and kept tight to me. Her fingers interlaced with mine, and her other hand wrapped around my bicep.

The rolling thunder gave way to a streaking bolt of lightning, and she jumped, pulling herself in tighter against me. Some of the lights flickered, and the building that would be our refuge came into view. The large glass panels were covered in condensation from inside.

Pushing the doors open, I seized up even tighter as a blast of heat slammed into us. Warmth and a strong earthy scent hit me as we stepped inside. Some of the rough edges were smoothed down a little as her hands tightened on me. The outlines of pots of plants and flowers in rows on tables and hanging from the posts on the columns were cast in long shadows as the lightning increased. The crack and rumble of the thunder traveled through me.

Kara shivered beside me, the tremors a reminder that I was fucking this up, but the pain inside didn't give a shit. We stood in the humid, glass-enclosed greenhouse.

"Heath?" She touched my chest tentatively as she stood in front of me. My gaze locked onto hers. It was hard to see through the shimmer of tears in my eyes. No longer hidden by the pelting rain, I blinked them back.

"What happened?" She ran her thumb along my cheek, and I held on to her hand, pressed her flesh even tighter against my face and soaked up her warmth.

I shook my head, trying to block out those words I'd heard back in the hospital. My wet hair sprayed droplets of water all around us. Sucking in a shuddering breath, I squeezed my eyes shut.

The words came out stilted and hollow, like someone else was saying them. "They said something about a blood clot. It made it to his brain." A streak of lightning lit up her face.

Her eyes were wide, and she stepped in closer. She held my gaze with eyes full of sorrow and compassion. It was hard to look at her face and into those eyes, knowing in a split-second any of us could be taken. Her other hand came to the side of my face. We could stay in this embrace forever, where her touch soothed the raw ache, and I could pretend that one of my best friends wasn't gone. It was me and Kara in the greenhouse in a thunderstorm.

Blocking out the rest of the world, I stared into her eyes. Her pulse thrummed against the side of my face through her touch.

"I need you, Kara." I slipped my fingers under the strap of her bag and lifted it up and over her head. It hit the floor with a *thud*. My fingers trembled as I skimmed the hem of her shirt. She stepped back and unbuttoned her shirt, exposing her breasts to me, her beating heart under them, pumping hard.

I folded her into my arms and walked her back against the wide white column farther inside. My mouth was pressed against hers. She opened her mouth and whispered against my lips.

"I'm here." Her voice was a balm to the open wounds I'd been living with. Every touch was more than I could have hoped for. Reaching between us, she fumbled with my drenched jeans and unbuttoned them.

I sucked in a sharp breath as the warm air hit my bare flesh.

She peered up at me, and I wrapped my arm around her waist. Shoving my hand under the waistband of her pants, I yanked them down. The power between us and the driving need to feel her everywhere compelled me forward. How much time did we have left? Stolen moments might be all we got, and I couldn't let this get away. She shoved her hands up under my shirt and whipped it off, up and over my head. The hints of color had almost faded completely from her hair now, proof that time was passing too fast while we were apart. I struggled to make the days make sense anymore. There was only a yawning void in her absence. She made quick work of her shoes, toeing them off.

Her wet pants pooled at her feet, and I lifted her. The cool skin of her bare legs wrapped around my waist. The crown of my cock slid against her hot and slick core. She was the salve. She was the light I'd tried to close out of my life to protect her flame. But I needed that light now. I needed her now more than I'd ever need her.

She wrapped her arms around my neck and moved her hips forward.

I braced us against the column and powered into her in one hard, smooth thrust. Her legs tightened around me, and she hissed into my ear as her body curled in on me. Worry prickled the back of my mind that I'd hurt her, but she moved her hips against me.

"Don't stop."

That was all I needed. I unleashed all the pent-up frustration at not being able to touch her into right now. The pleasure coursed through me and pushed away the anger, sadness, and anything else that didn't revolve around her words in my ears, her body pressed against me, and her pussy gripping me so hard I could barely move.

"I missed you so much." My words were clipped and strained.

Life was about choices, and I'd made one that might ruin everything, but there were times when nothing else mattered other than being with the person you loved. I tightened my arms around her and sent up a silent prayer that I hadn't undone us.

27

KARA

Staring into Heath's eyes, I'd seen the pain there. His words took so long to process, it wasn't until we were in the greenhouse that it truly hit me. Not until the warmth of that space brought my numb limbs back to life that I realized what had happened.

His keen need was so sharp and clear, I couldn't stop. My own selfishness at relishing the touch I'd craved since the second his lips left mine nearly more than two months ago didn't escape me. Texting wasn't enough. What if something happened to Heath? If I'd never be able to feel him against me like this. Touch him. Feel him. I held on and give him everything he needed. Everything I didn't want to live without.

"I missed you so much." His hot breath skirted across the curve of my neck. Every word was filled with so much more than the word itself. For all the words we'd held back over the past weeks that separated us, he was making up for them, painting them onto my flesh with his touch and steady strokes.

"I missed you too." My voice trembled.

I hitched my legs higher on his hips, keeping them firmly against his trim waist as he thrust into me. The pulsing pleasure rolled through me so fast and sharp I couldn't move. His lips were on mine, hard and demanding as he drank down the sizzling energy between us.

I clung to him, holding on as his dick stretched and filled me. His short, hard thrusts sent shocks of pleasure through my system. It was like he never wanted to leave me, never pull all the way out, but jerked his hips back enough for the friction of our bodies together to rub my clit. The raw, fierce perfection of it sent me over the edge. Still shaking in the midst of my climax, he lifted me. Moving through the space with him still embedded in me, I was trembling around him, my fingers clawing at his back.

The humid air of the greenhouse sizzled with the energy between us. His arms bracketed mine as he bent me over the potting table along one of the glass walls. My hands slid across the scattered potting soil covering the surface. His hand dipped down between my legs and found the bundle of nerves at the top of my pussy

He rolled and tapped my clit, sending shivers down my spine so hard and fast only his unyielding grip held me up so tightly it was hard to breathe. A crack of lightning lit up the space and my reflection in the glass.

His lips and teeth working together, pressed against my neck as his hips kept up their rolling and grinding. I clawed at the wooden surface as he lifted me higher and pinched my clit, setting off the rocket of sensations that had been building since the second we'd stepped through the doors.

I could barely move. His arms were so tight across my chest there was almost no movement. A gentle rocking and deep thrusts of his already embedded thickness. It was like he didn't want an inch to separate us. I dug my fingers into the sinewy muscles of his arms. His grinding strokes came at a punishing pace. I'd never had anyone take me like this before.

It was all new, like everything else with Heath. My legs shook as the grinding sent me over the edge. He tightened his grip even more. My orgasm crested even higher at the complete and total possession of my body.

His cock expanded inside me, triggering another orgasm as he pumped into me. My thighs were coated with our combined essence. We both groaned at the separation when he slid free from me and held me tight against him. My shaky legs barely held me up.

My back was pressed against his hard chest. I wrapped my hands around his arms still barred across me. Tugging against them, he loosened his hold, so I could spin in his arms.

I pressed my hands against his back and rested my head against his chest, listening to his racing heartbeat. We stood there with the insistent *tink* of the rain off the glass, rolling thunder. The glass enveloped us in its warm embrace.

His arms tightened around me, and his fingers trailed through my hair, playing with the last vestiges of the purple that clung to my strands. "He's gone." His voice cracked.

I squeezed my eyes shut against his skin and wrapped my arms even tighter around him. "I'm so sorry." Words escaped me. Tears glittered and clung to his eyelashes.

"Let's get you home." I took his hand, and we both got dressed in our soaked clothes. By the time we left the greenhouse, the rain had quieted to a gentle spray. The rolling thunder was farther off, and the lightning had stopped. His movements were stilted and robotic, like leaving the cocoon of the greenhouse had been too much for him. My heart ached for his pain.

With our fingers threaded together, we walked to his house. It was quiet and dark.

"I think Declan might still be at the hospital. Or maybe he's at Mak's." His words were far away and hollow.

"Let's get you out of these clothes and into bed." Not even a smirk or a smile. I was at a loss. The devastation hung so heavy that it sucked all the air out of the room. I had only met Preston briefly, but I couldn't imagine what Heath was going through. The guys on the team all seemed so close from the few interactions I'd had with them.

We climbed the stairs together, every creak and groan of the wood beneath our feet highlighted by the silence. Declan's door was open, and his room was empty. I turned on the shower and put it as warm as I thought Heath could take it. Slowly I peeled the wet clothes off his body, exposing every inch of him in a way that felt so much more intimate than any of the other times we'd been naked together. I shoved his sopping wet clothes into the plastic laundry basket. There was a small closet behind the door.

Opening it, I was relieved to find a stack of neatly folded towels. I grabbed a couple and a cloth. He stood outside of the curtain with a thousand-yard stare. Drawing back the curtain, I tested the temperature. The *clink* of the shower rings on the rod broke through the droning patter of the water. I gestured for him to get inside.

His hand shot out. "Don't go." It wrapped around my wrist as I turned to put the towels down on the counter.

"I won't." My words seemed to placate him, and he stepped inside, drawing the curtain back to keep the water from splashing out.

I hadn't been sure the best thing to do, but I nodded and slowly stripped out of my clothes. His eyes followed my every move, and somehow I felt more naked than I had back in the greenhouse. We were both an exposed nerve, raw and aching in so many ways. He stood under the spray completely still and jumped when I ran my hand over his shoulder. Closing his eyes, he leaned against the tile wall and placed his hand over mine.

The water cascaded over us, washing away some of the soaked-through-to-the-bones feeling. He tilted his head to the side and opened his eyes. Staring into mine, he dragged my hand from his shoulder to his chest. The strong thump of his heart pounded under my hand.

"I couldn't stay away." His voice was laced with regret.

I shook my head. My throat tightened, and I hated this helplessness. I hated that I couldn't fix this and make him feel better. That the world might not make sense right now, but there was something...someone he could hold on to. There had been so many times in my life so early on that things had spiraled out of control. Turned my world upside down and there hadn't been anyone there to show me I wasn't alone.

Sometimes the only thing you needed to do for someone was show them that the crashing waves wouldn't last forever and that there would be a time when the pain wasn't so keen and sharp that it brought you to your knees. That there were people who would give up anything to smooth the ragged edges of your heart. I pressed my hand into him. He covered the back of my hand with his.

"Turn around." His words caught me off guard, coming out rough yet calm. I slowly turned.

The spray of the water sent a shiver down my spine, and his hands skimmed across my shoulders. A squeak as a bottle top opened, and then his fingers were in my hair. His touch delved deep to my hair, scraping along scalp. Goose bumps rose on my arms as he worked the shampoo into a gentle lather. I closed my eyes and sank into the moment. This was something I wanted to brand on my brain and never forget. Something so small, but it was something he needed to do. I wasn't going to tell him that my hair would be an epic frizzy poof ball if I didn't use my special curly hair shampoo, or that he'd better be prepared for the tangled mess in the morning. If he needed to take care of me right then, I'd give that to him because I needed to. More than anything I'd ever needed before, I couldn't stop myself, even if I wanted to from giving him that comfort.

A strong spray of water rolled through my hair and crested down my back. Once all the soap was gone, his lips brushed against my shoulder. The slow, gentle way he ran the soap over my body and every second he showed me how much he cared brought tears to my eyes. We didn't make it out of the shower until we were both pruney.

I turned off the water as we were both asleep on our feet. The events of the day—and I'd only experienced them through him—had wiped us both. The mirror was steamed over with streaks of water trailing down the glass. He stepped out and wrapped a towel around his waist before holding one out for me. His arms enveloped me as he blanketed me in the towel and got one for my hair.

Running his fingers through it, he spun me around and folded me into his arms. He rocked me like there was a song playing I couldn't hear. It hit me how much this was like that first night. I stared into his eyes and some of the light had returned. The edges were still tinged with pain, but I didn't nearly double over with it when I looked into them like I had before. He took my hand, and we walked back to his room with the towels wrapped around us.

Declan's door was closed. He must have come in while we were in the shower. Heath closed his door and sat on the bed, pulling me closer so I stood between his open legs. Slipping his arms around my waist, he rested his head against my stomach.

Running my fingers through his damp, golden locks, I stared into his eyes.

"He was too good to go." His words skirted across my skin. "Why is it that horrible people seem to live forever and come back to haunt us, but the best of us get taken away too soon?"

"I don't know." I ran my hands along his back. His muscles strained like he was trying to keep it together.

"I'm letting everyone down. I let him down." His voice cracked.

I leaned back until his arms loosened. Crouching down in front of him, I grabbed his hands and held them in mine. "No one would ever say that. We're all only doing the best we can. That's all anyone can ask. Do the best you can and be true to who you are. That's all you need to be. Let's get some sleep."

He nodded, and I turned off the light. We crawled into bed together and wound tightly around one another. His head rested on my stomach. I ran my fingers through his hair. It slowly dried as his eyelashes fluttered, and his breathing evened out. His arms that had been wrapped tightly around my hips loosened a little as he drifted away into sleep.

I had no idea what tomorrow would bring, but this was a turning point for us. A turning point for me. I'd been fighting this thing between us for so long for a goal I didn't even know if I wanted anymore. It wouldn't end at the end of the semester, it could be something that followed me for the rest of my career. *Was that even what I wanted to be doing?*

Give him up for something I didn't even love? Not like I loved him.

A tingle shot through my fingers, and I wanted to write somewhere, on something, but I wasn't going to move. Instead, I traced the words I hadn't yet been able to say across Heath's corded back, hoping they would give him even more comfort and strength when I couldn't stand beside him.

28

HEATH

Standing in front of the mirror in my room, I adjusted my unknotted tie around my neck, the long black fabric in stark contrast to the white shirt underneath. Suits weren't exactly something I was comfortable in. There were a few times back in high school when we'd had to wear them for board of director's types of events to celebrate our wins. Colm, Mr. *GQ*, would have to round me, Ford, and Declan up and tie our ties for us. Emmett had run in those circles, so it wasn't anything out of the ordinary for him. Declan and I had worn them a couple times for events with the president of the university. Preston had always been there to make sure we weren't late watching our hundredth YouTube video to get the knots right. He'd always been there like a mother hen, trying to keep us all in line.

I glanced behind me and drew in a shuddering breath as her warm touch ran across my shoulders. Our gazes locked in the mirror, and she stepped in beside me in her black knee-length dress, only we weren't going out for a nice meal; we were going to say goodbye to my friend way too early. It had all been arranged in less than a week. Her hands ran along my lapels and up to my tie. Working quickly and efficiently, she twisted the fabric and looped it up and over itself, and gently pushed the knot up higher and fixed my collar.

All I could do was stare down at her as the soft and gentle curls of her hair draped along the side of her face. The days were melding together, but she was my constant. She'd been there since the day I'd found out, only leaving to go to classes. We'd slept wrapped up in each other every night, making slow, gentle love where I poured out my heart into her hands and only expected the quiet comfort of her arms in return.

I could hear his voice saying I needed to protect her. This wasn't protecting her, but sometimes the hurt was so deep and so raw you were clinging to the side of a lifeboat even if you knew it might bring you both down. Where we went from here, I had no idea. Not falling asleep with her hair tickling the side of my face or her leg hitched over the top of mine as she snuggled in tight felt like I might as well ask the sun not to shine. She hadn't said anything about it yet, but the conversation was one we couldn't avoid.

My phone buzzed.

Mom: *I'll be there as quickly as I can for the service. I'm stuck in traffic. I love you, sweetie.*

Mom had wanted me to come home, but I'd decided to stay on campus. Better to be around the guys and with Kara. There wasn't anything she could do. There wasn't anything anyone could do.

Things had been put together quickly. Imogen had worked overtime, handling everything Preston's parents couldn't. There wouldn't be a burial, only a celebration of life on campus. It was the best way to ensure everyone in the campus could be there, and no one wanted to do this twice.

Imogen'd been the picture of strength and resolve, and I had no idea how she was doing it because I could barely walk straight. We'd tried to help out however we could, but she assured everyone that everything was taken care of.

Kara threaded her fingers through mine. We turned around at Declan and Mak's grim reflection in the mirror. They stood in the doorway with the same dour expressions. Mak had her hair up in a bun and wore a dress similar to Kara's. The past few days had been weird. You don't notice how much people talking filled the silence until no one was talking. Until everyone was staring back at you with the same shell-shocked expression and no idea how to form words that made sense in the new world you'd been ushered into.

The looks on our faces were reflected in every face we saw as we walked closer to the center of campus. I held the umbrella over my and Kara's heads as we stepped into the hall they usually used for graduation and other big events. Some people in regular clothes heading to their normal classes glanced at us as we passed.

Preston's parents sat in the front row. Imogen was crouched down beside them, holding on to Preston's mom's hands. An older couple sat beside them. The woman looked like Imo—they must have been her parents. People filed in behind us, and she popped up the second she saw us. Striding down the aisle, she smoothed out the front of her dress.

"I'm so glad you guys are here." Imo's small smile was eclipsed by the tears glittering in her eyes. "You can sit anywhere, and there will be a chance for you to say something if you'd like."

We nodded silently and filed into a row of seats behind his parents. The hardwood creaked as we worked our way down, taking over the entire space. Our team would be here to support them.

Imo walked back down the aisle and up onto the stage. Outright sobbing came from the back of the auditorium. I fisted my hands as the tears built in my eyes. Blinking them back, I glanced over at Kara. She gave me a watery smile. When would there ever be enough tears?

A gentle hand squeezed my shoulder. I glanced back and covered my mom's fingers with mine. They were both here with me. The two most important women in my life.

Kara ran her hand over the back of my other hand. Her fingers traced a pattern, and slowly the tension ebbed out of my muscles. There were hockey jerseys lining the edge of the stage. Large floral wreaths on both sides and one with Preston's picture in the center. It wasn't a long event. Declan got up and spoke. I couldn't do it. It was like my feet were frozen to the ground. Preston's parents got up and thanked everyone for coming, for being so supportive of our team and giving him some of the greatest years of his life on the ice. His dad wrapped his arms around Mrs. Elliott, and they collapsed into their seats.

Our coaches spoke about Preston's determination, overcoming adversity to become our captain, and the way he united the team. It was Becca's turn, and her hands trembled as she tried to read the prepared words she'd brought up onstage with her. Imo stood next to her with her hands on her shoulders. Preston's parents were a wreck, so she'd gone up with her.

Two sentences in, Becca's voice wobbled. Imo whispered something against the side of her face, and Becca cleared her throat and tried again. The papers shook in her hand, and Imo held her close and slid the papers away. Becca clung to her with her arms wrapped around her waist.

"There aren't many people in this world who always look for a way to help, but that was Pres in a nutshell. He would do whatever he could to make sure the people around him succeeded and were protected, even if that left nothing for himself." Imo's voice cracked, and she dropped her arms from around Becca before bolting out the back of the stage.

Preston's mom shot up and chased after her, with Becca only a few steps ahead. Tears streaked down everyone's cheeks. There wasn't a dry eye in the place. Coach got up and said Preston's number would be retired and the season would be dedicated to him.

Everyone poured out of the hall in a daze. Mom wrapped her arms tightly around me and squeezed me so hard. I hugged her back, while still holding onto Kara's hand.

Breaking her hold on me, Mom glanced down at our intertwined fingers.

"Looks like you've been keeping a secret." She pulled Kara to her.

It had been a secret. One we were still in danger of having discovered, but Kara was the only thing that kept me tethered through the fog and haze of despair.

"Kara, this is my mom, Theresa. Mom, this is Kara."

They exchanged their hellos, and I looked back at the jerseys lining the stage as we filed out. One second Preston was here and I'd been ready for him to kick my ass, and then he was gone. No more friendly hungover games together. No more...anything.

There was a reception afterward, but we were drained. Only out of the house for an hour, and I couldn't think of anything other than crawling back into bed with Kara. Declan and I would be gone for a game tomorrow. No fucking clue how we were going to pull that off. The coaches had put it to us for a vote, and everyone chose to play. We needed to go out there and do this for him. We needed to get back into our routine, so it didn't feel like we were members of the walking dead.

Some pizza and *The Breakfast Club* was what we'd decided on. Mom promised to make us even more food than she already had. Old comforts to get us through a time like this. We walked under the budding trees that lined the path that crisscrossed the main campus quad. I tightened my hold on Kara and peered over at her, kissing the top of her head.

"I knew there was a reason you wanted to transfer him." A snide voice came from beside us as we hit the path cutting across campus.

Kara's hand tightened on mine, but she didn't let go.

"Now is not the time, Jason." The hard edge to her voice snapped me out of the haze. I hadn't ever heard her use a tone like that before.

"It seems awfully inappropriate for you to be holding hands with one of your students."

I whipped around. "Why don't you mind your own business?"

"I'd say it's probably university business with what's going on here." He raised his voice, and my hackles were up.

I stepped forward, ready to pound the shit out of this asshole. Kara wrapped her hand around my arm. "Heath, don't."

"Is this what you do now? This is how you get your rocks off? Fucking students."

She tensed beside me, and I shook her hands off, closing the distance between me and this asshole in two steps. His eyes got wide, and he glanced around like he was looking

for someone to help him out. Declan and Mak had been
following behind us but stopped to talk to another
teammate.

"Don't you ever fucking talk to her like that again." I
stood at my full height, which was a few inches taller than
this guy.

"Heath," Kara said my name and put her hand on my
back. I shrugged her off. This was the same guy from the
night in the rain. The one who'd been so close to her. Who'd
been giving her crap since she turned him down for a date.

That this asshole even thought about touching her made
me want to explode. I wasn't going to let him say a single
thing about her. She was the most selfless, warmest, and
most caring person I'd ever known. She'd been my rock for
the past week, and there was no way I'd have made it
through this without her. If this fucker wanted to say something about her, he'd be in for a rude awakening.

"I can say whatever the hell I want." He puffed out his
chest like he thought he could intimidate me.

"You can say it, but you don't say it around me and you
sure as hell don't say it to her," I growled and leaned down
to meet him eye to eye.

His face went white as a sheet, but he kept his feet
planted.

"Do you want to call off your attack dog, Kara? Or is he
only good in bed?"

My hand shot out before I could stop it. His eyes got
wide as my fingers wrapped around his neck and tightened.

There was a commotion beside me, but my tunnel vision
meant I only saw one person. This asshole.

"I'll have you expelled for this," he rasped as his throat
worked against my grip.

My blood pounded in my veins, and I lifted my other

hand ready to take this taunting piece of garbage out. If I was getting expelled, might as well make it worth it. I balled up my fist, lifting it. I was ready for impact when Kara wedged herself between us.

My fist missed her by an inch. She jumped back, and shock reverberated through me. I dropped the asshole. He collapsed to the ground and scurried away on his hands and feet like a crab.

"Heath." She reached for me, but I jerked away. I'd almost hit her. The scene around us came back into focus.

My mom looked back at me with wide eyes. Nausea soured my stomach. He'd pissed me off so much that I'd almost hit Kara. If she hadn't jumped back, or I'd let myself continue to be blinded by the anger, I could have hit her. Intentional or not.

I leaned over, digging my fingers into my thighs. My chest was so tight, I could barely breathe. Everyone around me was in a tunnel, and I was at the far end of it, falling fast.

Kara ran her hand over my back, and I flinched. Snapping up straight, I stepped away from her. She stared back at me with a stricken look in her eyes. I couldn't look at my mom. I couldn't meet her eyes again. What would she think of me? The yawning hole I'd thought I was climbing out of got a hell of a lot bigger.

"Heath, it's okay. He's an asshole. Don't worry about it."

"No." My voice came out harsh and gravelly.

"Heath." She reached for me, and I backed up, banging into Declan. I glanced over my shoulder at him and Mak.

"He doesn't matter. I don't care what Jason says or who he tells. This is more important."

My heart pounded. I couldn't let her throw away her future on me. I didn't even recognize myself at the moment.

"No, it's not. This was a mistake, and it was going to end one way or another."

Her eyes got wide, and her lips parted. The ones I'd lost myself in night after night quivered.

"I'm ending this. You saw what happened with that guy. He's one guy. What about when the rest of your department finds out and your advisor, like you were worried about? What happens five years from now and someone finds out you were with someone you taught? How does that affect you?"

"I don't care. I'm not worrying about anyone else. I'm worrying about you."

She reached out her hand, and I dodged her touch. "You shouldn't. You don't need to be involved in any of this." *Protect her.* That's one of the last things he'd said to me, and I couldn't even do that.

"It's not about needing to. It's about wanting to."

"Maybe I don't want you to." I stared at her and steeled myself around the way her eyes tried to peel away the armor I'd thrown on. Bouncing off Declan and Mak, who stared at us wide-eyed, I turned and stalked off. Turning back wasn't an option. I'd see the look on her face, and I'd crumble.

This was stupid. I should turn around.

Protect her. His words echoed in my head, and I couldn't escape them.

The only thing she needed protecting from was me. I was the train wreck, but she was the one getting derailed. The team would suffer for this too, if Jason said anything. I had to remove myself from the equation. Get my head on straight and hope that I could figure this out. Find a way out of the raging surf and back onto dry land.

My feet slapped against the street on the way to the house. Throwing open the front door, I grabbed my gear and went to the stadium. Maybe skating myself into oblivion, I'd be able to get to sleep without the gentle thrumming of Kara's heart against mine. Maybe I'd forget I'd just cracked my chest open and taken out the only thing that was keeping me going.

29

KARA

I don't know how long I stood there. Mak's soft touch on my arm made me jump. My gaze whipped to hers. The sympathetic look in her eyes told me I hadn't hallucinated what happened. That the disappearing figure in the distance was Heath and he had broken up with me. Not that we'd been together. *We weren't, were we?*

A few days of emotionally wrought comfort after a death didn't exactly signal this was a long-term thing. He'd been on board with us keeping our distance until the semester ended, but this felt different. Final. I sucked in a shuddering breath. Who'd blotted out the sun on the bright barely spring day? Or maybe it was the blindside that made it hard for me to see past the man who'd trailed his fingers along my skin every night for the past week and made my words flow freer than they ever had before walking away from me.

"Kara..." Mak's words trailed off, and she glanced over her shoulder to Declan and Heath's mom. I squeezed my eyes shut. Embarrassment, shame, anger warred for the front and center spot, but despair won out.

They couldn't help this. No one else could. Everyone was

already dealing with so much. I wasn't going to add to everything going on.

I forced the corners of my mouth up the slightest bit.

"I'm okay, Mak. I'll be okay. I'm wiped, and I'm sure you guys are looking forward to that pizza. Going home is probably what I need now. It was nice meeting you, Ms. Taylor."

"Please, call me Theresa. I...he..." Words failed her, but they hadn't failed me. They were fighting, clawing their way out of my chest, and I swallowed them down. With a quick hug, she ran off after Heath.

Mak wrapped her arms around me and squeezed me tight. I hugged her right back. It had been nice having a fellow outsider around while all this was going down, but there wasn't a need for a comrade anymore. I'd be shut out.

"He's upset. His head is a mess. I'm sure he'll figure out what a moron he is being." Mak leaned back with a gentle smile tugging on her lips. "Try not to go too hard on him when he comes crawling back."

How did you make someone crawl when you wanted to run to them and jump into their arms? The tears I'd kept at bay during the service threatened to break free. Only now I wasn't crying for their lost friend, I was crying for my tattered soul.

"I promise." My voice wavered, and I blinked hard.

She nodded and slipped her hand into Declan's. Her head rested on his shoulder as they walked away from me. Seeing their closeness and support of each other was a stinging blow. A breeze rustled the leaves in the trees. I stared up at them and wrapped my arms around my waist. The walk across campus felt a hell of a lot longer than it usually did.

I stepped out of the cab and up to the front door of my house completely numb. It was like I was watching myself from above. My keys jingled in my hand, and I composed myself before opening the front door.

"Hey, stranger." Mom passed by on the way to the kitchen. "Why are you in that dress?" She stopped in front of me.

"I was at a memorial service."

"For who?" Her voice went up an octave.

"It was for a friend of a friend on campus. I went for moral support."

She tugged me close, and I breathed in her soft cocoa-butter scent. "Why didn't you tell me? That was so nice of you. Do you need to go back out?"

I shook my head when she let me go. "No...I think they'll be okay now."

"Did you want something special for dinner?" She held onto my hands and squeezed them. Concern was heavy in her eyes.

"No, I'm not really hungry." My voice was dull and flat. Letting go of her hands, I climbed the steps, ignoring her looks of concern. Each step settled the weight of what I was about to do even heavier on my shoulders.

The soft carpet under my feet wasn't like the hardwood in Heath's. The faint smell of leather and sweat mixed with Heath's scent didn't fill the room. In my room, it's comfortable familiarity filled me, but it felt off. Like walking into a cloned existence where everything was the same, but different.

My composition book peeked out from under my pillow where I'd left it. Digging into my bag, I grabbed a pen, uncapped it with my teeth, and dropped onto the bed. The words I'd been scrawling across his skin when we were wrapped up in each other came pouring out of me. Like a torrential downpour that couldn't be stopped, my fingers flew across the page. My tears joined in with the words, melding them together and making them one as I filled each piece of paper with every emotion I'd held back until I hit the last one.

There weren't any other books. No scraps of paper. My gaze darted to my laptop sitting nestled in the bag I'd barely touched over the past week. I slipped my hand inside and took out it out.

This wasn't something I could hide from anymore. The words in these books were real. As real as anything else in my life, and locking them away wasn't going to help. Baring my soul and writing until this well of turmoil was drained dry was the only thing that could help me now.

It wasn't until the sun set that I slowed down. The words were still there in the background, but they weren't so loud and unavoidable that I couldn't even think straight until they were out in the world.

Mom wrestled me away from the computer for a little bit to eat dinner with the rest of the family. The darting looks of concern made me want to fold in on myself. After shoveling the minimum appropriate amount of food into my mouth, I excused myself.

Coming up the stairs, I stared at my desk. I closed my door, grabbed my computer and sat at the smooth, shiny wooden surface. My fingers shook as I opened the drawer and took out the pieces of folded paper I'd tried to block out of my mind. Smoothing them out on the desktop, I traced over the looping slant of her writing and opened up the hidden folder where I'd had the emails sent.

She hadn't stopped sending them. I covered my mouth with my hand to choke back the rising emotion in my throat. Her monthly messages for me sat waiting on my screen. I clicked on the most recent one. The screen blurred as even more tears joined the ones I'd only stopped shed-ding. She was blowing out candles on her birthday cake. I glanced at the date. Less than two weeks ago. *How had I forgotten that?* It was like I'd made myself forget. Pretended until I hadn't needed to pretend anymore.

She was surrounded by friends. There was a healthy glow to her cheeks and a twinkle in her eye that I'd never remembered being there before. And a sadness too. That I'd remembered well. I closed that one and went back to the first unread email she'd sent after I'd called off our meeting.

There was always at least one picture inside. Her own photographic journal or testament to the fact that she was in a better place. That she was a different person than the one I might remember. The numbness seeped out of my fingers, and I rested them on the keyboard.

If there was anything this week had shown me, it was that we could never predict the future. There were things that happened in life that blindsided us in any number of ways. The only thing we could do was try to live our lives so that our future selves would be robbed of the chance to what-if anything. A life without what-ifs.

That didn't mean pain and heartache didn't go hand in hand, but I wasn't sorry I'd raced after Heath when he'd shown up at my classroom, and I sure as hell wasn't sorry that I'd been there for him when he needed it. That what-if was taken care of, and my flayed wounds would heal.

Angie was another what-if. If something happened to her or hell, something happened to me... Preston's death had shown me that age didn't make anyone immune from the grip of death. This was something I needed to do to wipe away those doubts, those questions, and words I'd kept locked away for years.

The words appeared on the screen as my fingers danced

across the keys, typing out all the things I needed to say. I needed to know that if we met, she'd know what I needed from her. What I deserved from her before we could start anything new. My finger hovered over the enter key. I closed my eyes and stared up at the ceiling and the constellations that came to life in the dim light of my room.

Heath...my heart ached thinking about him. I couldn't process it. His retreating figure. The finality of his words.

I tapped send and closed everything down. Crawling into bed, I gave myself a pass. Tomorrow, I'd I started making plans for the rest of my life. It would be one without a single what-if. But for now, I buried my face in my pillow and cried until my breath was ragged and my throat was raw. Crying tears for the guy who'd helped me see who I really was and what I could become and then left me behind.

The skating didn't work. I could barely feel my legs, but it didn't help. Exhaustion didn't do anything to blank my mind. My hands were shaking so hard I could barely unlock my car door. I wasn't okay. Not even a little bit.

My phone vibrated across the dashboard. Declan. Again. His worry was the only thing that compelled me to answer. That cold tendril of fear that snaked itself around your neck when someone you cared about went missing wasn't anything I'd inflict on anyone.

"Hey."

"Jesus, Heath. Where the hell have you been?" The worry in his voice sent another barb into my stomach.

"I'm at the rink."

"Still? I checked there first."

I'd figured he would, so I'd stayed away for a while to make sure I didn't run into him.

"I drove around for a little bit first."

"Are you coming back to the house?"

"I—I'm going to go for a drive."

"I don't think you should be driving, man."

"I need to clear my head."

"We have a game tomorrow."

"I know. I'll be there. The bus doesn't leave until noon. I'll be there and ready."

"You sure you don't want me to meet you wherever you are?"

Mak's low voice murmured in the background. I'm sure she thought I was the biggest douche to walk the planet after what I'd done to Kara.

"Nah, it's fine. I need to handle this on my own."

"Do you want to talk about Kara?"

"No." I ended the call and threw the car into reverse. The headlights washing over me got fewer and farther between as the hours ticked by. Refilling my tank in the middle of the night, I drove with no place in mind. Only away. Running away from the raw ache that threatened to crack my chest wide open.

And then I was at the spot I should have known I'd come to. A place I hadn't been in a long time. *The beach.* The last time I'd seen the crashing waves and heard seagulls cawing, it had been clear across the country. A night where I'd curled up in a ball on the sand and prayed my mom and I would survive. I hadn't been to the Jersey Shore, ever. I'd been close a few times, but usually the drive was enough to ward off whatever demons were chasing me. The respite of the wide-open space and nature's soundtrack hadn't been needed once we moved. The memories were too strong there, but now I needed something strong enough to push away the fresh ones. The ones where I'd repeated the same mistakes all over again and hurt the one person I was supposed to protect.

Shifting gears, I let the hum of the engine create the

soundtrack of white noise I needed to block everything else out. Across the Ben Franklin Bridge, I kept going, needing the rolling waves to calm me. The signs for Shore Points was usually where I turned around going back home, but I couldn't this time. I needed to lose myself in the oblivion of something far larger than me.

I don't know how long it took me to get there, but I got there, and sitting on the hood of my car, I leaned back against the thin, warm metal. The crashing waves over the dunes brought me back to California. When I hadn't been at the rink, I'd been at the beach. Anything to get out of the house. Whether it was a board or ice under my feet, I could race toward the waves or the net and feel like I was safe.

Moving across the country meant I'd left the beach behind. That was where I'd gone in the middle of the night when the yelling and shouting got to be too much. When I was seven, I'd climb out my bedroom window, take my bike and ride to the beach. Sitting out there as the waves crashed, I'd watched the sun rise more times than I could count.

Tugging my shoes and socks off, I set them on the hood of the car beside me and rolled up my pants. Kara's face when I'd told her it was over would be etched into my brain forever. The sand came right up to the edge of the street, and I hesitated before taking that next step. The small, coarse texture scraped against my feet. I walked the path leading over the dune to the water.

Coming back to the water was different than stepping onto the rink. The beach had been where I went when things went bad. When things were fucked and I'd needed to clear my head. When I'd needed to yell at the top of my lungs because the pain was so sharp and all-consuming that I couldn't hold it in anymore.

I hadn't felt this bad in years.

Every light in the surrounding houses around me was out. The streets had been empty as I'd driven through the quiet shore town. It was still off season. Still too cold for anyone to entertain sitting out in the water and soaking up some rays. Not that anyone would be out late at night either.

Walking to the water's edge, I braced myself against the freezing water. The waves rolled up onto the sand, sending the icy biting salt water hit rushing against my skin. The sand was dragged out from around my feet, and it felt like it might drag me away too.

This wasn't how the night was supposed to go. The memory of the sting of hurt in Kara's eyes made me double over. I rested my hands on my knees and stared out at the water.

Why couldn't she see how bad things could get for her? That she'd be throwing away everything trying to give me what I needed. Things had been scary for a while. It was harder to keep a handle on the anger, and it was burning even hotter with Preston gone. The flames were stoked even higher. The way she had to put her hand on my arm to hold me back from the guy who'd threatened her. She knew what I might have done. She'd seen it and yet couldn't see why I needed to step away. That fear still lurked in me. That there was a switch that could flip one day and I'd find myself becoming a person like *him*.

Leaning back, I stared straight up at the pitch-black sky. Everything I'd bottled up for years came pouring out. My yell sliced through the still night air. The waves did little to drown them out as I clenched my fists and let out everything I'd bottled up.

Every flare-up. Every time I'd shoved the boiling back down and clamped the lid on tight ripped out of my chest so fast and ragged that I was left panting with my hands on my knees, watching the waves crash into my legs.

I squeezed my eyes shut tight against the visions racing through my mind. The way the tears had pooled in her eyes. She'd blinked them back because that's who she was. Her strength and independence had drawn me to her. Walking in that bar door, she'd hesitated. Assessed the situation and said fuck it. Pushed ahead even when she was unsure. She deserved the life she'd envisioned for herself before I'd shown up.

Backing away from the water, I collapsed into the sand, falling flat on my ass. Dragged my knees up, I rested my arms on them and tried to get a hold on my world.

With a raw throat and choppy breaths, I stared up into the ink-black sky and wondered if this wasn't for the best. Kara could wreck me with a look. Topple every bit of restraint I'd had to protect her. The walls I'd put up when my mom and I had made that car ride across country, still beaten and bruised, came tumbling down when I was near Kara. And it scared the shit out of me.

31

KARA

Sending the e-mail off to Stevenson should have been scary. It should have made me want to hide under the sheets for the rest of the weekend, but that would have only left me dwelling on how I hadn't heard a peep from Heath. Our next meeting was tomorrow.

Mak had seemed so sure that once he had some time to process everything, he'd call me. He hadn't. My phone was collecting cobwebs. Despite myself, I'd checked on the scores of his team. Since the day after the memorial, they'd been on fire. Won every game since then—and not messy wins; decisive and overwhelming victories.

Seeing pictures of Heath online hurt. I'd finally stopped looking at the articles and stuck to the stats. They'd made it into the playoffs. Our other sessions had been canceled because he was traveling for games. My stomach was an absolute mess in anticipation of tomorrow. Would he even show up? What would he say when I told him I'd quit the PhD program?

I'd already put in a few applications to some writing fellowships and programs. This late into the academic year, most of the deadlines had passed, but there were a few still open. I'd scoured every program to see which might be the best fit. No one had ever seen my writing. The thought was equally exhilarating and nauseating.

It had been long nights taking old composition books, rereading what I'd written, and submitting the best samples. Then there had been the job applications and apartment hunting. The savings I'd had since high school were finally coming in handy. I figured it was time for me to really leave the nest. Stop worrying that if I wasn't home anymore, I'd no longer be a part of the family.

Making all these plans still felt like I was making plans for a different person. I moved through the motions, but it was still someone else's life.

"Who'd have guessed Miss Perfect herself would end up fucking one of her students?" Jason leaned against the doorjamb of the office with his arms crossed over his chest like the smug asshole he was.

I gritted my teeth.

"Who'd have guessed someone with a nose as brown as yours would be threatened by someone who actually knows their shit and does their job?" I closed my laptop. This place was officially on my do-not-study list. I might not be going into the PhD program, but I sure as hell wasn't going to finish on a bad note. It wasn't in my nature.

He scoffed and stepped into the office. "If you think I'm going to let you waltz in here and take a prize that belongs to me, you're out of your mind."

"I didn't waltz into anywhere! All I've done since freshman year is work my ass off and do everything I can to get where I am now. You mean to tell me there weren't any donations in your name to get you your spots?" I shoved back from the desk, and my chair smacked against the wall.

"You've always thought you're better than everyone else, but I saw through you from the beginning. You're trash and always will be."

The loud, sharp laugh shot straight out of my mouth before I could stop it, not that I would have wanted to. A month ago that might have stung. It might have been enough to send me into an impostor syndrome-spiral, trying to figure out how he'd seen through me, but now I saw it for what it really was. The flailing of a pathetic guy who needed to belittle other people to try to make himself feel better.

"I was comforting a friend after his good friend died. He happens to be a student, but I would never let that kindness affect the way I grade. A grade, I might add, that doesn't even really matter for him. He's finishing out the season and going on to the NHL. How much do you think walking across the stage and getting that piece of paper matters to him?" I crossed my arms over my chest.

Jason's nostril's flared, and he looked like a cartoon villain. The only thing he was missing was mustache twirling.

"It's still inappropriate." He jabbed an angry finger at me.

"Maybe it was, and maybe I am trash like you said. But I know what I'm not, and I'm not a pretentious asshole who gets his rocks off on being a dick because I feel inadequate in every way possible."

I let my gaze drop to his crotch to really hammer it home.

His face turned a nice bright shade of red. If he said anything, he could get Heath's grade voided and then the team would be screwed.

I crossed my arms. "How about I give you what you want?"

His eyebrows scrunched down, and his gaze traveled to my breasts. Of course that would be what he'd want. I was vile and trash unless I was willing to spread my legs for him.

"I'll withdraw from the running for the fellowship. Isn't that what you want?"

"Not that you would have won anyway," he sneered with his haughty I'm-better-than-you-because-I-was-born-into-a-family-with-money look.

"Maybe I would, maybe I wouldn't, but now there's no question. I'm out. You're in. We're done."

And he stormed out. I probably shouldn't have poked the bear. I shouldn't have let myself revel in making him feel like shit like he'd tried to do with me. If he said something to Stevenson or anyone else about me and Heath, I had some plausible deniability. Going with him to the memorial wouldn't constitute a breach anyone would hold over me. Extenuating circumstances were always considered, and since Heath had left me standing in the middle of the brick walkway crossing campus, we weren't anything more than TA and student. Had we been more than that? There wasn't a label on what we'd been doing.

We'd had a few dates and had some awesome sex. *Was it more than that?* It had been to me. The way he'd made my body sing, made me laugh, and how he'd taken care of me even when he was hurting. It wasn't something casual. A shiver shot through my body as I imagined we were back in the shower and his fingers were sinking into my scalp. I'd bit back a moan because it hadn't felt appropriate then. But his firm yet gentle touch and the way he'd worshipped my body on more than one occasion meant it was beyond anything I'd experienced before. He'd helped me discover some things about myself that I'd tried to hide from for as long as I could remember.

32

HEATH

The teeth-shaking blare of the horn signaling yet another goal filled the stadium. I skated past our bench and climbed into our team box. Sweat poured down my back, and I stared out at the ice as the guys changed positions and foraged forward, keeping the momentum going.

Glancing up at the scoreboard, I gritted my teeth. 3-3 and there were only forty-five seconds left in the game. My blood pounded in my veins. With my fingers gripping my stick so hard I thought I might snap it, I stood as one of the juniors on the team made a breakaway. His jersey flapped in the wind created by his speed, and he shifted the puck back and forth with his stick before faking out the goalie and sinking it cleanly into the back of the net.

Our bench exploded, and the guys grabbed each other, shaking the nearest person like they were trying to choke them out. Sticks and pads flew everywhere.

We'd done it.

We'd made it to the final four. I wrapped my fingers around the ledge of our box and ducked my head.

Only four games sat between us and the championship. The one we'd been a lock for at the beginning of the season. The one we'd decided to win to show Preston we could still kick ass even if he was laid up, and now the one we needed to win to put this team back together.

Everyone around me shouted with excitement and relief. We'd done the impossible and come back from the cusp of disaster. Somehow it all felt foreign and hollow. The gnawing pit in my stomach hadn't let up since I'd turned my back on Kara. Walking away from her was the hardest thing I'd ever done. Sometimes when I was on the ice, I'd go blank and I was right back outside watching the tears glitter in her eyes. A hurt so bad I'd double over and have to take a knee until the wave of guilt and pain ebbed away enough for me to suck the air back into my lungs.

I had a singular focus: Win these games. It helped keep the dreams at bay, stopped the thoughts of what I'd walked away from crushing me under the universe's boot.

I'd been so stupid; if that asshole said anything the class was voided, our wins for the semester wouldn't count, and Kara would be in deep shit. Everything we'd accomplished would be washed away in the snap of a finger.

I should have thought about that before I went to her. I should have thought about that before I let her kiss the numbness away and turned my heart over to her. Tomorrow we'd see each other for the first time in a long time. I didn't even know how I was supposed to sit in that room with her breathing the same air, watching her lips move and hearing her words.

Declan's hands landed on my shoulders, not to hold me back but with an excitement that vibrated off him. I couldn't hold back my own smile at his pure joy.

"We did it!" he screamed in my ear.

I threw my arms around him, and he thumped me on the back. "Preston would be proud, man. He'd be so fucking proud." Declan's hands fisted my jersey. The rest of the guys piled in around us, and we were under the crush.

But I knew he wouldn't be proud.

I'd crossed the line I'd said I wouldn't. Done the thing he'd warned me about, and tomorrow I'd have to sit across from a woman I'd torn down with my selfish need a little over a week ago. The guys deserved this chance, and I may have jeopardized everything.

We filed out of the stadium and onto the bus. Water dripped from my hair and down the back of my shirt. I couldn't get tomorrow out of my mind. I needed to stop myself from doing what I truly wanted. What I'd wanted to do since the moment I'd told her it was over between us.

Everyone was wiped on the bus. It was so much more subdued than you'd think coming off a win like that, but it was a long drive back to campus, and we still had two more games to make this season count.

With my head pressed against the bus window, I shoved my earphones in and turned up the volume. The thumping beats of the music warred with the pounding in my head. Tomorrow I'd see her. Tomorrow I'd sit in front of her and hope she didn't see that my heart broke a little more every second I made myself stay away. But I owed it to the guys to not implode the season. I owed it to her to not ruin her life, and I owed it to myself to never hold someone else's fate in my hands and make it turn to ash.

"Mom, I got the onions. They had to go into the back to get enough." I flopped the sack on the table. The letter I'd snagged from the mailbox was burning a hole in my back pocket.

"So you're not avoiding me anymore." She came into the room and hesitated.

I squeezed my eyes shut. I'd been avoiding her since the memorial. I didn't want to see the disappointment in her eyes at what she'd almost witnessed.

Her arms wrapped around mine. "Why've you been running, sweetheart?" The sadness in her voice made my throat tighten.

I opened my eyes. "I'm screwing everything up."

She let me go and tugged me down into one of the chairs at the kitchen table.

"What's going on? I saw what happened at the service."

"I don't know what got into me. He was saying that stuff about Kara, and I lost it. I snapped." My mouth opened and closed as I tried to find the words.

"I'm not talking about that."

My head snapped up. "I almost hit her, Mom. I nearly hit her."

"It was an accident." She cupped my cheek. "Accidents happen."

"Not like that. I know all about the accidents you had and I'll never have that kind of accident."

"Oh, honey." She squeezed me to her. "There are so many things I regret, but one of the biggest is that you'd ever think you're capable of doing what your father did." Letting go, she looked up at me with so much caring it made it hard to swallow.

"I was so angry." I fisted my hands in my lap, tears welled in my eyes.

"You don't think I get angry? You don't think sometimes I want to break something? That doesn't mean you're an abuser, Heath. If you don't let it out, if you try to bottle it all up inside it's going to come out in ways you can't predict. Explode out of you when you can't contain it anymore."

I nodded.

She put her fingers on my chin and made me meet her eye. "Is that why you walked away from Kara?"

"One of the reasons." I dragged my fingers through my hair.

"What is going on? You used you tell me everything."

That was all it took for me to spill everything.

Mom covered my hand with hers. "Wow, that's a lot you've got going on."

I hung my head. "I've always got to go after the women I have no business being near."

"Heath, stop. I know you, probably better than anyone, and I know what's in your heart." She pressed her hand against my chest. Tears welled in my eyes.

"Remember those seashells you used to bring me? You'd always look for the biggest and most colorful ones to try to get me to smile. There isn't a doubt in my mind that you won't figure out a way to get through this. You're strong. So much stronger than you should have had to be at your age."

"Mom, there's something else I need to tell you." I slipped the letter from the parole board out of my back pocket. "I took it a few weeks ago. I didn't want you to worry."

Her eyes got wide and she took it from my hand, reading it over.

"We'll deal with this later. Don't worry. I love you, and you are my joy." She pressed her lips to the top of my head. "Now, be a dear and help me cut these onions."

I wiped my nose with the back of my hand. "I guess I'll be crying for real in a little bit."

"You're strong, honey. You can handle it."

I left my mom's house and drove back to campus. Sitting in my car, I stared at everyone walking around in their backpacks, going about their lives. The weight of the secrets I'd been keeping from my mom were lifted, but the rest of it was still there, sitting like a stone on my chest, making it hard to breathe.

Less than ten minutes until I met Kara. I climbed out of the car and walked into the last of the unrenovated buildings on campus.

I leaned against the wall outside the door to the office. It was a place that had been equal parts torture chamber and retreat over the semester; now it was something worse. The email I'd sent asking if we were still on had gone unanswered. Not that she owed me one. I was the one who'd walked away.

Sliding my phone out of my jeans, I checked the time. Ten after. So it wasn't my mind playing tricks on me, skewing time. I shoved my phone back in my pocket and adjusted the strap to my backpack. My foot was propped up against the wall, and my sneaker squeaked off the tile in the deserted hallway.

I pushed off the wall, trying to figure out how to get her to talk to me. I needed to finish the semester. I didn't care if she gave me a D, but we'd have to talk eventually. I needed to see her so badly the pain woke me up at night.

Fixing things was all I seemed to be doing lately. Hockey was the only place that worked. Even then that had a hell of a lot more to do with the guys than it did with me. My shoes scuffed the tile as I rounded the corner and smacked right into the woman who occupied so much of my mind it was hard to remember to eat.

The books in her arms went flying, and I reached out

to steady her. Her eyes were wide until she knew she wasn't going to bite it on the floor, and then her eyes narrowed and she stepped back, shaking off my hand. I expected nothing less, but that didn't mean it didn't still hurt.

"Sorry," I mumbled, squeezing the back of my neck.

She tilted her head and peered up at me. The emotions swimming in her eyes made me wish for so many different things, but most of all that I'd kept her out of my grief. When you're drowning, it's hard not to cling to the person who you haven't been able to get out of your head when they are holding out their hand to you with love in their eyes.

The hurt you gave was the hurt you got. I fisted my hands at my sides to resist the urge to do anything that might hurt her any more. She crouched to pick up her things scattered on the floor at the same time I did, and we narrowly avoided smacking our heads together.

My hand brushed against one of her notebooks before she whipped it away and added it to the stack balanced on her bent legs.

"I didn't think you'd come." She stood straight and breezed past me. The cinnamon-and-sugar smell was like it always was and made me think of cinnamon rolls on a cold winter's day. Her black waves were tucked up on top of her head, and her jeans hugged her hips, making my fingers itch to touch her.

"I was thinking the same thing."

She jammed her key into the lock like it had wronged her. The door opened, and she stepped inside.

I followed behind her. After this semester was over, she could pretend she'd never met me and continue the life she'd been on the path to. A master's, PhD, professorship and one that wasn't wrapped up in my ability to screw over the people I cared about.

She stood behind the desk, using it like a shield with her arms over her chest.

"You didn't answer my emails. I wasn't sure how we should do this."

"I'm not going to fail you if that's what you're worried about."

A fraction of my worry lightened, but the biting edge to her tone made the blood pound in my veins. "I never thought for a second you'd do that. I know you're not like that."

"And you think you know me well enough to make that decision? You think that after a few months, you know who I am? I don't even know who I am." She lifted her eyebrow.

"I know you're not someone who'd be vindictive because you can." I stood in front of the desk with the edge digging into my thighs.

"Maybe I should be." She sat on her seat and opened her bag, dragging a few folders out. "But you're right, and I'm not. You've pretty much finished your project, and I read over your final write-up. I'm going to get one of the other professors in the department to read it over and give me their recommendation. While I like to think I can be completely impartial, who the hell knows." She threw her hands up and slid the stack across the table to me.

My gaze darted from her to the paper.

"Read it. This will be the last time we meet."

My head snapped up. "There are still three weeks left in the semester."

"This was all about it being flexible for you, right? I'm sure you're busy with the championship coming up. We can finish anything else by email." Her eyes were shuttered and guarded.

"Kara...can we talk about this?"

Her eyes dropped, and she squeezed them shut.

My lips parted, but the words died in my throat when her eyes snapped back up to mine.

"Talk about what, Heath? How you broke the little cold war we had going on and then threw me away once you'd made it past your time of need?"

"Is that what you think? That I don't still need you? That I don't still crave you so badly it makes it hard for me to think of anything else. That your heart wasn't the only one broken and held together with shitty glue and tape?"

"You're the one who did it. You left me standing there and ran away from me." The accusation in her voice lashed at my soul.

"Because I could have hit you! Your asshole colleague saw us, and I was trying to protect you and the career you have ahead of you." There were so many reasons I'd left. It should have been simple and easy, but nothing in my life seemed to be going that way lately.

"I didn't ask for your protection! I didn't ask for you to fall on any swords for me." She shot up out of her chair and pressed her hands into the top of the desk. "I'm an adult. I'm fully aware of my decisions and what kind of result they can have, even if it's a shitty one. I was there for you because I wanted to be. It was a choice I made!"

"And it was a stupid one. I shouldn't have gone to you that night, and I shouldn't have had you by my side at Preston's memorial."

Her head snapped back like I'd slapped her, but I continued.

"I'm not going to be the reason you don't get to have your

dream. I'm not going to be the person who stopped you from getting your PhD and teaching."

"No, you're not. I am. I quit the program."

My eyes got wide, and I recovered from that kick to the stomach. "What?"

"I sent in my letter withdrawing from the program earlier this week. I'm not continuing on to get my PhD."

"Why would you do that?"

"Because I didn't want it anymore. And it wasn't until I met you that I realized how much I didn't want it."

My chest was tighter than the last time I'd had the wind knocked out of me on the ice.

"But that was your dream." I couldn't be responsible for this, for taking away something that meant this much to her.

"Dreams change, Heath. They change all the time. First it was a PhD and teaching." She swallowed and stared at me. "Then it was you." Her voice cracked.

I took a step toward her, and she bolted. She snatched her bag off the desk, and the door slammed between us. The silence of the room pressed in on me. I needed to go after her, but my legs wouldn't work. She'd given up on getting her PhD and teaching for me? I was her dream turned into a nightmare. She deserved someone better than a ticking time bomb. She'd been mine since the second I'd laid eyes on her, and I'd broken her heart.

33

KARA

Two weeks later, I cracked open my eyes and stared up at the ceiling. The summer breeze flowed through my open window. The nighttime sounds of crickets and an occasional car were all I could hear. Somehow I'd made it through. Somehow I'd managed not to crack and ball my eyes out in front of him. I'd saved that for when I got home. How did I look the guy who'd stolen way more than a piece of my heart in the eye and tell him he was my dream, and all he could think about was how the one thing I'd done for us to be together was a mistake?

I hadn't heard from Heath in nearly a week, not even a missed message. The team was doing better. I'd followed the stats. They'd won the last three games, and he hadn't gotten a penalty since. The championship game was tonight.

Pride warred with the raw ache deep in the center of my chest. I'd been the one to walk away this time. It hadn't felt any better. Hadn't healed the ragged wounds that were still there. Making plans for the future had helped me cope, but it was all I could do to get out of bed.

This was a rollercoaster I needed to get off. Figure things

out for myself. I couldn't help piece him back together when I was broken. I would never regret being there for him when everything happened with Preston, but I needed to be my own life preserver.

Writing had been my respite. The files on my computer multiplied daily and on the days when the words didn't come, I took my old words and typed them until my fingers ached. The clarity was coming, slowly. I knew what I didn't want: The life I'd pretended would make everything perfect when the truth had been staring me in the face all this time.

I shifted from foot to foot in the doorway of the living room. Mom and Dad were curled up together on the couch watching TV. The interview I'd gone on earlier today cemented the decision in my mind, and there was no going back now.

Taking a deep breath, I stepped into the room.

"Hey, sweetie. Do you want some popcorn?" Mom held out the bowl to me, shaking the buttery mixture under my nose.

My stomach clenched tight, and I shook my head. "No, I'm good."

"Oh wow, she's got her serious face on." Dad sat up straight, and Mom put both her feet on the floor.

Bile shot up my throat, and I clamped my lips together. Keeping my eyes down, I sat on the coffee table in front of them. My fingers were numb and shook as the nervous energy shot through me and made me light-headed. I clasped my hands together.

"You're starting to scare us, Kara. Get it all out there and tell us what's going on." Mom stared at me with worry in her eyes.

"I—" I cleared my throat against the tightening fist wrapped around it. I was about to shatter their dreams for me, and deeply disappoint them. I swallowed again. "I've decided I'm not going to continue on with the PhD program."

They stared at me with wide eyes for a few beats, and then they both nearly blinded me with their smiles.

"I'm so happy for you!" Mom hopped up from the couch and hugged me.

This definitely hadn't been the response I expected.

"You're not upset?"

She dropped her arms and sat beside Dad.

"No, honey. Your mom and I have both gone through advanced degrees, and we know the pressure it puts on you if you're not one hundred percent committed to it, if you don't live and love whatever you're studying. We've seen so many unhappy people push through for the sake of finishing. They are the most unhappy. A total mess and feel trapped. If you're feeling like it's not for you, then it's better to know now rather than later." Dad's eyes were filled with sincerity and so much love.

How could I have ever doubted how this would go? That they'd disown me or kick me out because I didn't want to follow in their footsteps. Guilt burned in my gut. That wasn't who they were. It wasn't the type of person they'd raised me to be.

And there was another thing. I dropped my gaze and picked at my hands. "Angie contacted me."

"Oh." The small noise came from Mom.

"I'm thinking about meeting up with her. She said she's clean and sober and she has been for a few years and she wanted to speak to me." I peered up at them.

"You've been holding onto a lot, huh?" Dad chuckled, and that retying knot in my stomach eased.

"I have. I didn't know how to bring it up to you. I wasn't

sure what I wanted to do, and I didn't want to say anything until I'd made my decision. It wasn't something I came to lightly, but I'd like to talk to her. The last time wasn't exactly a memory I'd like to be my last of her."

"You don't owe us an explanation, Kara." Dad took my hand. His warm grasp and weathered skin from countless times of scrubbing in comforted me.

"You're an adult, and she is your mother. We aren't offended or sad that you want to see her. It's natural that you'd want to, especially if she's sober like you said she is." Mom's eyes seemed to reflect the same hope in my heart. That it was true.

"I think I'm going to do it."

"Whatever you need to do. Do you want us to be there? Do you want to meet her here?" Dad squeezed my hand.

I shook my head vigorously. "No, I'm not sure yet." I bit my lip. "I will figure it out soon, but I wanted to let you know." Standing up, I was immediately enveloped in my parents' arms. The ones that had calmed a scared preteen wondering what her place was in the world provided the same comfort to a scared twenty-something trying to figure out where that might still be.

"I love you guys."

"We love you too."

Climbing the steps to my room, I glanced at my phone. Message after message from Heath. The ones I'd hoped for a couple few days ago, hell maybe even a few hours ago were rolling in, but I didn't want to talk to him. I couldn't talk to him until I knew I was fully immunized from the feelings he evoked in me even. I probably only needed another few decades to figure out how to stop them. Seemed like as good a time as any to reply. I set a reminder for 2058 and sat at my desk.

My fingers flew across the keys, and I poured even more of my thoughts and emotions out onto the keyboard, and the words formed in front of my face. That's one thing I'd say for having your heart ripped out. It made those words flow quicker than I could type them. Recovery by opening those wounds and pouring as much salt into them as possible. Salting them like you salted the fields soothing could grow there anymore, and eventually the hurt would stop.

34

HEATH

I sat in the Dean's office, not the regular dean's, but the big dean with a capital D, Dean. My leg bounced up and down. My fingers dug into my thigh, and my sneakers squeaked on the tile floor. I felt like I'd been sent to the principal's office, only worse. I'd expected the whole team to be called in to meet with him since it was game day, but it was just me.

We'd made it to the championship with almost no help from me. Coach called me off—well, shouted louder than I've ever heard him shout—to get me off the ice. My speed was crap. My passing was abysmal, and my shots on goal were shit. It was like I'd been replaced by someone who'd barely played.

Only a few more hours until I'd have to skate to center ice and try not to skate like it was my first time around the rink.

"Mr. Taylor, Dean Morrison will see you now." The older secretary startled me, and I shot up out of the chair and followed her down the hall.

"We are all rooting for you. We've been following you all

this entire season. I'm so proud of you boys." Her kind words didn't do much to calm me down.

"Ah, Mr. Taylor." The Dean stood from behind his desk and walked around the front, shaking my hand in a firm grip.

"I wanted to congratulate you on a riveting season, especially with everything that happened in the New Year."

My throat tightened, and I nodded. Riveting was not how I'd describe it. Soul crushing. Blindingly painful so you'd shoot up out of bed in the middle of the night clutching your side. Those were more fitting descriptions. His voice melded words together into a blanket that threatened to sedate me in the chair.

"I was especially surprised that you were taking extra courses this semester with everything that was going on."

My ears perked up at that, and my eyebrows scrunched down. "Extra courses?"

"Your independent study. Well, I guess it could be any of your courses."

"I don't understand. We need to take five courses to be considered full-time."

"Not for second semester seniors. Didn't your advisor go over all this with you?" He clicked his pen and made a note on the file on his desk. There was a crack in the window. The window overlooking the sunny, flower-filled meadow with a distant figure with her back to me and wind blowing through her hair.

My heart pounded so loud I thought he'd glance up from what he was writing to see if someone was beating a drum.

"No, he didn't. I don't need five courses to graduate? To be eligible to play this semester?" I leaned forward in my seat. The arms of the chair groaned under my grip.

He glanced up and smiled. "No, not at all. Second semester seniors are only required to take two classes to stay enrolled and graduate on time as long as all the other graduation requirements have been met."

And that window turned into a door that had been kicked wide open.

"I need to drop a class." The words erupted from my mouth so fast and forceful, the Dean jerked back.

"The withdrawal period ended a few weeks ago, Mr. Taylor." He furrowed his eyebrows.

If I dropped the course, it could never come back to bite her, and my eligibility for the semester would never be under scrutiny. They couldn't retroactively take away our wins, and she'd be able to stay in the program. Even if she said she didn't want it anymore, there was a difference between voluntarily leaving something behind and never being able to go back to it.

"If there is anything you can do, I know it would help take some of the pressure off for the championship game tonight. I'm begging you here, sir."

I'd get down on my knees if I needed to.

Jumping in my car after my meeting in the Dean's office, I peeled out of my parking spot making a beeline for the only place I needed to be. It had been a week since I'd seen her. Too long. Way too long.

I parked my car on the street. The houses were all bright and cheerful with red doors and colorful shutters. It might have looked unassuming, but this place was swimming in money. Walking up the pristinely paved sidewalk, I stepped onto the flagstone walkway leading up to the front door.

After searching through the student directory, I'd found Kara's address. With communication effectively cut off, I'd had to go to desperate measures to finally talk to her. I wiped my sweaty palms on my jeans. The drive over had been a white-knuckle ride where I'd nearly talked myself out of it at least five times. *What if I show up and she slams the door in my face? Should I wait? Isn't this kind of impulsiveness what got me into trouble in the first place?*

Despite what everyone thought, patience wasn't my strong suit. Not when I needed something, when that need rode me so hard I couldn't think straight. I'd never experienced anything like this before. She was long drives, sitting on the beach, and skating on the ice all wrapped up in one. None of those things would ever make me happy again if I wasn't with her.

Kara was all that mattered. I needed to see her. Needed to touch her and tell her all the things I'd tried to say over the phone and with messages. It didn't do it justice. I couldn't show her what she meant to me without looking into her eyes so she'd see I was completely serious.

I'd lifted my hand to knock on the bright red door when it flew open. A willowy teenager with dark brown coily curls piled up high on her head like Kara always wore it and chestnut skin stared back at me.

"Can I help you?" She had a big smile on her face and leaned against the door.

I leaned back, checking the house number again. *Definitely the right address.*

"Is Kara here?" *Had she moved and not updated it in the online system?*

"Kara! Your boyfriend's here!" she yelled toward the stairs. The gleeful grin on her face was one only a younger sibling could give. I'd seen it a hundred times on Olivia, Colm's sister, and Grant, Ford's brother.

There was a *thud* of a door opening, followed by footsteps. All the words I'd repeated in my head fled as she appeared at the top of the staircase. My pulse picked up the pace as she froze on the first step with her eyes wide. Rushing down the steps, Kara shook her head at the girl, who had to be her sister, and stepped outside.

"I'm going for a walk."

I backed up, and she closed the door before her sister could say anything. Shoving my hands into my pockets, I followed behind her as she stormed down the walkway. I picked up the pace and stepped in line with her.

"What are you doing here, Heath?" She had her arms wrapped around her waist as she walked.

I caught myself staring at her. Watching the way she nibbled on her lip as she walked down the tree-lined sidewalk, I wanted to touch her. Wrap my arms around her and somehow get her to believe it would all be okay.

Our eyes locked and it, snapped me out of the spell she'd woven over me with every breath she took.

"I dropped the class," I blurted out.

"What? Why?" She looked at me like I'd lost my mind.

"I talked to Dean Morrison. Turns out, I didn't need the class to begin with and my dean is a moron."

"But the class was finished. You got your grade."

"Wiped from the records."

"Why?" She stared at me like I'd lost my mind.

"Because I don't want it to be something looming over your head. Now no one can ever say you weren't impartial or that you violated any rules. The class, my grade, it's all gone. You can still do your PhD."

"Heath." She shook her head and started walking.

"And I came to apologize."

"Isn't the championship tonight?" Her purple and pink top showcased her smooth skin.

"In about an hour."

Her eyes got wide. "What the hell are you doing here? You've got to get there."

"The guys can do it without me. Hell, they've pretty much been doing it without me for the past couple of months anyway. This is more important."

"You've worked too hard for this, Heath. Go, just go, and we can talk about this later."

"I'm not leaving before we talk."

"No, you need to go. I'm serious." She tried to push me toward my car.

I captured her hands against my chest, letting her feel my racing heart.

"So you finally understand." I stared down at her.

"Understand what?" Her eyes were clouded with confusion.

"The need to put what you want aside to protect someone you care about. The feeling of saying screw it and pushing that person toward something you feel they have to do for their own happiness."

"But I didn't just do it for me. I did it for you. For you to have your season and play your games, which is why you need to go." She tried to turn me again.

I reached across my chest to cover her hand with mine.

"I can't tell you how it's eaten me up inside to think that I'd killed something you loved. That you felt you had to choose between this career you'd worked hard for and being with me."

She was shaking her head before I finished my sentence. "It had always been something in the back of my head. A little voice telling me this wasn't the path for me and I wouldn't be happy going in that direction, but I'd wanted to be like my parents, make them proud. Being with you made me brave enough to do what I wanted to do. It made me brave enough to face down the doubts I'd had about who I wanted to be."

I lifted my hand slowly, giving her all the time she needed to step away, but she didn't. I ran my knuckles over her jaw and rested my forehead against hers.

"I never want you to feel like you have to be anyone other than who you are around me. You being true to yourself is all I ever need from you."

She fisted her hand in my shirt. "You said we were over and walked away. Do you have any idea how much that hurt?"

"I know and I hate that I hurt you like that. Hurt myself like that. Thought I was protecting you. But I'm making you a promise."

She stared up at me with glistening eyes.

"I will never do anything like that again. I'll never make that choice for us, even if it kills me."

Dropping my hold on her hand, I sank my fingers into her hair and held her close. Our lips whispered against each other.

"Can you find it in your heart to forgive me? I've screwed this up left and right, and I'd like to stop doing that now. I'd like to be everything you need me to be, and I'm not getting in the way of us anymore."

She nodded, and my heart soared. "I need you to be you. And I need you to love me."

I sank deeper into our kiss as the words barely made their way out of her mouth. I pushed my own love and devotion into the dance of our tongues and the press of our lips.

"More than anything, I love you. You're the first woman I've ever said that to. I love you more than you can ever know, and it might even be verging on scary, so you're in trouble now because I'm sticking to you like a barnacle."

Her laughter against my lips was music to my ears and fed my soul. She snapped her eyes wide open and grabbed on to my shirt.

"What the hell are we still doing here? You've got a game. You've got to get back to campus." She tried to push me away again.

"Only if you come with me."

She bit her lip and nodded when she saw I meant it.

"Okay, let's go. Let's go!"

We climbed into the car, and I held her hand all the way to the stadium, fighting traffic the entire way. An hour until game time. It was the championship we'd fought for all year and it was time to show everyone what we were made of.

35

KARA

Sitting in the bustling row, I was decked out in my Knights gear head to toe. Championship banners hung all over the stadium. The care package had been delivered to my seat with a note tucked inside.

Wear it for me.

-Heath

I was ready to stand and cheer the whole time, even if I didn't have any idea what was going on. Finding Makenna in the seat beside mine had been a pleasant surprise.

"Hey! Kara? What are you doing here?"

"Heath invited me."

She'd smiled wide.

"I told you he'd come to his senses." She'd been a hell of a lot more confident than I was.

We chatted while the place filled to the brim. Some of the guys were out on the ice warming up.

"I'm guessing this means it's official. You're Heath's girl-friend," she said it in a singsongy way and bumped against my shoulder.

I couldn't hold back my smile. "I guess." I shrugged; we

hadn't gotten into the nitty gritty. There was still a lot we needed to talk about, but for now I was here to enjoy the game and support him.

"I'm glad you're back, Kara. It was rough for a while. And I know how hard things were on him. He was a mess." She nodded toward the ice.

"It wasn't just hard on him."

She slipped her hand into mine and squeezed my fingers. "I know. It's still crazy to think I've known them since high school."

"Were you dating Declan then?" Seeing the two of them together, it was like they'd been together forever. Comfortable and silly.

She let out a sharp laugh, shaking her head. "No. Definitely no. High school was...interesting for us. A lot of animosity over stupid stuff. Wait until you have your first outing with all the Kings."

"The Kings? I thought the team was the Knights." I glanced down at the jersey Heath had given me.

"That's what they call themselves. It was a bunch of the guys from the bar that night you met Heath." She rolled her eyes. "That was the name of our high school team. The Kings. Quite a demotion for Heath and Declan to be Knights now."

"It sounds interesting." It seemed like I was missing a lot. I'd get all the dirt later.

"You have no idea." Mak bumped her shoulder into mine. "They've worked hard to get here. From the way things were looking in January, I didn't think they'd make it to the Championship. But they did it."

"They sure did. I'm sure Preston would have been proud."

"Yeah, he would have been." Her bottom lip quivered.

Everyone got to their feet as the buzzer signaling the end of warm ups sounded.

She jumped up beside me. "Game time!"

While I didn't know much about the game other than reading the scores I'd seen online, Makenna filled me in on anything I didn't understand. I couldn't believe she'd only been to her first game a few months earlier. She was every bit the brainiac everyone said she was. Watching Heath out on the ice, I saw exactly why he looked the way he did. Every muscle I'd explored on his body was out there put to full use.

It was tied up 1-1 and neither team gave an inch. Heath whipped past the glass. His skills were equal parts graceful and power. When a guy from the other team grabbed him by the jersey and punched him in the head, I was a second from climbing out onto the rink myself. Declan skated up, and Makenna wrapped her hand around my arm, her eyes glued to the guys on the ice. Her fingers bit into me a little as Declan threw himself between Heath and his opponent.

Heath kept his cool, and the guy was thrown into the Sin Bin. With a man down on the ice and only thirty seconds left in the period, everyone was on their feet. My heart hammered in my chest, and I held my breath as the other team took a last-minute shot at the goal.

Declan got the puck and passed it to Heath who made a breakaway, flying past the other team. He drew back his stick and released, making contact with the puck. Adrenaline pounded in my veins and the place went absolutely silent as everyone watched the small black disc fly across the ice.

The goalie lunged for it with his glove, but the net behind him billowed and and the puck dropped to the ice inside the net. Half the stadium erupted into cheers. I threw my hands up into the air, and Mak let her monster whistle loose.

The final buzzer sounded, and Makenna and I linked arms, jumping up and down as the guys piled on one another out on the ice. Popcorn flew everywhere as people hugged each other and high-fived.

"Come on." Mak grabbed my hand and tugged me down toward the ice. I raced down the stairs behind her as people poured out into the aisles. We ducked and dodged the hordes of people flooding the space around the ice. "Follow me." She tightened her grip, and we skirted past one of the security guys with a nod from Mak.

We ended up in the mouth of the tunnel that led to the locker rooms, judging from the smell wafting down the hall. The place roared with the cheers and chants of the crowd. People rolled out a carpet onto the ice, and a group of guys pushed out a mini stage. The Knights' Coach stood in front of them in the box, giving out hugs, and the guys had huge smiles on their faces. Heath searched the stands where we had been before, his head dipping and ducking over the high fives from his team-mates. There was no way to get his attention in all that commotion.

Mak let out her whistle, nearly deafening me in the semi-enclosed tunnel, and Heath and Declan whipped around. Tracing a heart on the glass, Heath held up his finger for me to wait while the guys grabbed him and pulled him out onto the ice.

"They have to do the award ceremony and everything first, but we can stand here until they are finished."

I pointed down at the ground, letting him know I wasn't moving from that spot. The place vibrated with celebratory energy. The entire team whipped off their jerseys and slid another one on. It wasn't until they turned to walk out that I saw why.

Preston Elliott was stitched on the back of their jerseys. There was barely a dry eye in the place as the team stood up there with a gap in their line for their teammate. A lone woman walked out on the ice on the carpet they'd laid out there.

"Imo," Mak said it so quietly.

My throat tightened up. "They invited her out."

"I guess so. She...she's really great."

They hoisted the trophy over their heads and held up their fingers pointing to his retired jersey hanging in the rafters. One of the guys lifted Imo so her hand stayed on it.

My heart ached for her. I couldn't imagine what she was going through. Her teary smile had me brushing away a trail of wetness cresting down my cheek.

Heath squeezed her in a big hug and glanced up at me. He'd worked so hard for this, they all had and they got to give their messages to Preston. Although he wasn't here, he'd helped the team get to where they were, and no one would forget it. I hadn't met him for long, but even I'd felt his impact.

They all filed off the ice after everyone got their pictures and video footage. Heath gave me a quick peck on the lips as he passed by into the locker room. He was out in record time looking smooth as hell in a nice button-down shirt and pants that hugged him in all the right places.

"Wow, look at you."

He spun in the tunnel walking toward me. "I figured I should spiff up a little bit for tonight."

"You spiffed up so much you're almost too bright and shiny to look at." I shielded my eyes. Heath strode up to me, tangled his hands in my hair. I let out a short gasp and he delved into my mouth. My stomach fluttered.

"I've got a surprise for you."

"Are we going to the party?"

"Not that party, something I wanted to do for you." He rested his forehead against mine.

I looped my arms around his neck and swayed with him as we moved to music no one could hear. His hands pressed against my back with his thumbs skimming along the top of my ass. I couldn't hold back my grin. It burst out of me whenever he was around like I was a high schooler getting asked to the dance by her crush.

"Okay."

We said bye to Mak, and Heath got me into his car.

A short drive later, I stared up at the glass and metal structure I remembered so well. A sizzle skimmed across my skin. "The greenhouse?"

"Yeah, let's go." Threading his fingers through mine, he pulled me through the double doors. The heat smacked me right in the face. It was like walking from the fridge into a sauna.

There was a large almost overgrowth of green shrubs right at the front. Lots of green and not much else. Rounding that living dividing wall in the front, I gasped. We walked past rows of flowering plants, neatly lined along the walls and in rows in the center of the wide partitioned building. Automatic sprayers misted some of the plants as we passed. There were vibrant blues and purples everywhere. Red flowers I'd never seen before, and yellows so bright they mimicked the sun. Every plant gave off its own scent, filling the air with a mixture that screamed *life*.

"It's beautiful." So different from the last time we'd been there.

The path to the darkened area in the back of the green-house was piled high with empty pots. They were stacked haphazardly all over the floor, some teetering almost on the edge of a crash. The dark, earthy smell of soil was a sharp contrast to the lightness of the plants, but this was what they all needed to grow.

"What are we doing here?" I glanced around at the ceiling, praying there weren't any spider webs. I did not want to have to go all girlie girl in here.

"I wanted you to be here for this." He flicked on the lights in the dark room, and the entire room lit up with a gentle glow. Strings of white lights dangled and draped from the ceiling, and there was a small table for two set in the middle of the floor and a small potted plant sat in the center.

Taking my arm, he turned me toward the table and stood behind me. His hands crisscrossed my front, and he told me what he'd done to prepare for this. Each syllable skimmed across my skin as his mouth got closer to my neck. The clenching in my stomach traveled south as his chest pressed against my back. He walked me closer to the table, and I spotted the food containers sitting on top of the plates.

"How did you pull this off?"

"I've got a good friend who's looking for lifetime season tickets once I go pro."

I stared at the leaves and the flower, racking my brain for its significance, and then it hit me. My mind cleared for long enough to put together a coherent thought. His research paper. Getting the two plants to cross-pollinate had been the biggest hurdle he'd faced when it came to the project.

"Is this it? The one you figured out?" I reached out to the beautiful purple and pink flower, nearly touching the petals before I snatched my hand back. "Sorry." My cheeks heated.

I'd karate chop someone in the throat if they thought about touching one of my experiments, especially one I needed for my research. But none of mine were anywhere as stunning as this.

"Don't worry. I know all about wanting to touch things that you shouldn't. Things that are so fucking beautiful it hurts to look at them."

My body hummed pressed up so close to his. Every shift of our bodies together reminded me of how good they felt when we didn't have anything between us.

My head whipped up to meet his gaze, and he stared down at me.

The playfulness and excitement of this visit to the greenhouse shifted. Heath's goofy demeanor changed, and his eyes were filled with more than happiness over his plant. My blood pounded, and it all centered right on the one spot crying out for his attention.

"I named it *Alyogyne huegelii karaus.*"

The burning desire in his eyes nearly made my knees buckle. He growled against my cheek. His hot breath skimmed across my skin, and my stomach clenched as he slid his hand around my waist.

My words didn't even make sense and came out all choppy. My need for him riding me hard. Running his hands through my hair, he kept my head turned as he dipped his head and my lips parted. No hesitation at all. I was ready for Heath.

Our tongues danced together with the promise of more to come. I wanted to turn around and tug down his jeans and let him fuck me on the work bench.

But he had other ideas. He slid his hand under the waistband of my pants and down toward my throbbing core. A mewling sound burst free from my lips the second his fingers tapped on my clit. My knees buckled, but he held me up, pinned between him and the smooth topsoil-coated table.

"Are you ready for me?"

I nodded, not trusting my own voice. There were no sounds in the room except for the automatic misters going over the plants outside the potting room, but it was shortly accompanied by the evidence he was looking for. His fingers pushed inside me, straining against the waistband of my pants as the fabric bit into my waist.

"You're so wet. I can't wait to taste you," he rasped against the side of my face.

My eyes shot to the wide-open greenhouse outside of our little alcove in the back.

"Don't worry. No one will come, except you."

A laugh escaped, but it was quickly cut off as he dragged my jeans over my ass and sank to his knees behind me. My moans caught in my throat at the first swipe of his tongue along my molten-hot core, and I knew I'd never look at gardening the same way again.

36

HEATH

I brushed some of the potting soil off Kara's ass and gripped the top of her jeans, tugging them up and buttoning them. She held on to me, her fingers sinking into my skin as she leaned in. Her smell, mixed with the earthy scent around us, enveloped me.

The greenhouse had never been more beautiful than when she was leaning into me after her screams had rattled the glass. I looped some of her hair around my finger, letting it glide through them as she took a deep breath and stepped away.

Shaking her head, she threw her well and truly sexed-up hair into a ponytail. A smile tugged at my lips. Sex hair looked extra hot on her, especially when I knew it was me who'd been running my hands through it.

"I can't believe we did that." She laughed and slid her shirt over her head. The foliage surrounding the greenhouse and distance from other buildings on campus meant the odds of someone seeing us were slim. Throw in a hockey national championship and everyone was out partying.

The disappearance of her breasts back under the

Knights jersey almost made me as hard as when I'd had them cupped in my hands. Knowing what was under there was pure torture. Bending over, she picked up her bag off the floor, dusting the dirt on it.

A rag from the workbench smacked me right in the face. I caught it and threw it back at her.

"Stop looking at me like that. You were inside me like five minutes ago."

"I can't help it. It's not my fault you give off a need-to-touch-you pheromone." I grinned at her, and she rolled her eyes.

I caged her between my arms. "And I can't help it that I love you more with every second I'm near you."

She traced her fingers along my chest. The feather light touches sent sparks of electric pleasure throughout my body. It alternated between the pads of her fingers and a gentle scrape of her nails across my flesh. It wasn't a random pattern. I peered down.

"What are you doing?"

Her eyes were locked onto my skin.

"Committing this to memory, so I'll be able to remember it always. Starting our story with a new line, right here." She tapped her finger above my heart where her spiraling and tracing ended.

I covered her hand with mine and let her feel my racing pulse. "I hope this new story has a happy ending."

Her eyes, framed by her thick eyelashes, pulled me into their chocolaty fullness.

"I hope so too." She bit her bottom lip.

I ran my fingers under her chin and lifted it up, capturing her lips again.

"I know so." I skimmed my thumb across her full bottom lip.

"There's something I need you to do for me. Something I decided while we were apart." Her fingers dug a little into my waist where she'd wrapped them around me.

"Tell me. Whatever it is, we're in it together."

The worried corners of her lips turned up.

37

KARA

I ran my hand down the side of my pressed cream-colored pants. Heath slid his hand into mine and ran his thumb along my palm. We'd been in his car outside of the coffee shop for ten minutes. Neutral ground. A coffee shop didn't have the same expectations of a restaurant. A bar certainly wasn't appropriate. Meeting at my house was out of the question.

Mak had recommended the quiet coffee shop as a place we could sit for as long as we needed to without being bothered. I was already five minutes late for the meeting.

My parents had asked if I wanted them to come. I wanted them to stand by my side like they had since the second I'd arrived at their house, but I didn't want anything that happened at the meeting to hurt them. I needed to figure out what I was going to do first and then let them know. I knew they'd support me in whatever I did, but my struggles were hard for them to see.

"You don't have to do this. We can turn around and go." His eyes were filled with so much love it almost hurt.

Our road to this today hadn't been easy, but we were here and I needed to do this.

"No, I'm ready." I threw the door open and slid out before I lost my nerve. Smoothing my hands down the crisp navy, cap-sleeved top, I stepped in front of the door to the shop. My reflection stared back at me as Heath stood beside me. He brushed his thumb along the inside of my wrist.

"Relax." His soothing voice rolled over me, and my shoulders inched back down.

My pulse jumped under his fingertips.

Heath opened the door, and I stepped inside. My small kitten heels clicked on the polished floor of the coffee shop/bookstore. I tightened my grip on his hand as I spotted Angie in the far corner near the back.

Our eyes met, and she stood up. With her hands clasped in front of her, she didn't move. Probably afraid if she took a step, I might turn right back around and run out. I wasn't one hundred percent sure that wouldn't happen. My stomach was a knotted mess, and my heart pounded so hard I swore everyone around me could hear it.

She looked great. The best I'd ever seen her. The floral print sundress highlighted how young she was. Not even forty yet. When she was my age, I was already seven. Her skin had a healthy glow, and her hair was shiny and smooth. If I hadn't known who she was, she'd look like any thirty-something woman going out for a coffee on a bright and sunny day.

A simple silver bracelet was wrapped around her wrist. Jewelry was never something I'd seen her wear. Maybe she'd had some at some point, but by the time I came around, everything of value was usually sold as quickly as it arrived.

We stood in silence in front of one another. My fingers

were laced so tightly around Heath's that he must have felt like he'd stuck his hand into a bear trap.

"Hi, Kara."

"Hi." It had been so long since I'd seen her, I didn't even know what to call her. Angie. Mom.

"I'm really glad you decided to come. Thank you." Her voice caught on the last word, and she put her hand to her lips. Her eyes glistened as the tears welled in her eyes.

And like that the hold I had on myself dissolved. The dam burst, and I was an ugly-crying, snotty mess in seconds. It was like a decade of worry and the desperate need to forget were ripped from my chest.

It was the splinter that had settled in my soul for so long I'd almost forgotten it was there unless I nudged it. This was way past nudging. This was taking a baseball bat to it. Heath wrapped his arms around me, his strength giving me something to hold onto as the world seemed to tip on its axis.

We'd barely said two words to each other. How was I going to make it through this?

I glanced up, and my mom had crossed the space between us. She clutched her hands to her chest with tears pouring down her cheeks. Her gaze shot to Heath's arms enfolding me, and what she wanted was clear as day.

I nodded and she lunged forward, her arms wrapping so tightly around me my chest ached. Heath gingerly dropped his, so it was only me and her left. She rocked us, gently swaying on our feet. Her hand stroked my back like she'd used to when I was little. I was transported to those tender times when she wasn't completely bombed. When she'd keep me home from school and I'd sit on the couch and watch daytime TV with her.

Those happy memories I'd buried deep down. It was much easier to only remember the bad. To cling to them and hold them tight, wrapping the pain around me like a warm blanket of distance and anger. If I only remembered those times, it was easy to not miss her.

But here, with my arms wrapped around her when she smelled so clean and light, it made it impossible not to have those memories bombard me.

Heath stepped away, probably to tell the people working there that we weren't two women having a nervous breakdown. Well, maybe we were.

After those minutes stretched on, we finally broke apart. We dropped our arms, and my mom grabbed on to my hand. She guided me toward the seat beside her, and I sat in the oversize chair. The kind you could curl up in with a good book and sit in for hours.

Her lips were pursed together, and a fresh sheen of tears was in her eyes. "I never thought I'd get a chance to see you again. To hold you in my arms." Her voice cracked, and my throat tightened. "I'm so happy we're finally getting to do this."

I ducked my head and tried to clear the tightness in my throat. "I'm sorry about before and what happened with your letters."

She was shaking her head before I'd even finished speaking. "Don't be sorry. I can't even imagine what I put you through over the years. It hurts my heart too much to know that I hurt you while I was so screwed up. You have every right to protect yourself. I do hope one day you'll be able to forgive me."

Heath stood behind the chairs across from us. He was looking to me. Stay or go. I tilted my head, and he sat on the other side of the small table in front of us.

"I know it came as a shock to you when I contacted you, and I thought about it for months, probably years, before I did it. Every day I had to prove to myself that I was not going to put you through anything like I'd put you through before."

She squeezed my hand, and we spent hours talking. Heath was our server, running to get us another drink or some food. The entire thing was surreal. It was like I was looking in from the outside watching this conversation happening. The one I'd had in my head a million times over the years. The one I'd hoped I'd be able to have some day.

A part of me had steeled myself for the phone call I might get one day to come identify her body. But this was harder. A hell of a lot harder. That was final; this was something else. Something I'd have to process and we'd have to work through if a relationship with her was what I wanted.

With her arms wrapped around me and a teary goodbye, we made plans to see each other in a few weeks. The emotional toll was high, and I needed to talk to my parents and figure out what I wanted out of all this. At least now I knew. She was alive and well. Thriving after getting her degree and a job as a caseworker helping kids out who'd been like me. I guess it was her way of atoning and trying to be the light in the lives of other people going through so much.

Heath and I sat in the car for a long time outside Heath's house. I hadn't wanted to go home yet. There was already so much I had inside, trying to talk to Mom and Dad about it would only have piled it on even higher. Heath's hand never left mine for the entire drive.

I stared down at our interlaced hands, and I knew without him this day wouldn't have come. As much as I'd told myself I'd do it later and I would talk to her, there was no way I would have. Not if I hadn't met Heath. Hadn't had a mirror held up to my life and seen everything I was missing.

He glanced over at me. The bright blue of his eyes was like a bright summer day, cloudless and perfect.

"Thank you." I gave him a tight-lipped smile to hold back the emotion choking me. There had been enough tears today already.

"There's nothing to thank me for. I'm glad even with my bumbling and a complete and total fuckup, I could help even a little. What do you want to do?"

"Let's go inside. Watch a movie or something."

"My mom sent over some chicken parm this morning."

My mouth watered. His mother's cooking was outstanding. I could already smell the chicken, breadcrumb, and cheese combo from out here. "Why the hell didn't you say so earlier? We've been wasting all this time." I threw open the door and slammed it shut.

Heath laughed over the roof of the car and waited for me as we climbed the steps. The early evening, warm breeze, and quiet street were a reminder of everything going on even when our lives felt like they'd been turned upside down. It was reassuring to know that the world hadn't stopped spinning because of one day I'd never forget.

Opening his front door, Heath stopped short in the doorway. I bumped into his back and looked around him. We both burst out into laughter so loud the two heads of the chicken parm thieves whipped up.

Declan and Mak had a fork each, bent over heaping plates of food, shoveling it into their mouths wearing nothing but their underwear. Their cheeks were filled like chipmunks who'd been caught at a bird feeder. And I'm pretty sure there were pasta sauce splotches all over Mak's shoulders and chest.

A giant swirl of spaghetti fell off Mak's fork before she

yelped, her cheeks going bright red. Dropping the fork onto her plate, she jumped behind Declan.

"We got a little hungry," Declan said through what must have been a half pound of pasta and chicken. His eyes were wide, and he shoved the last bite on his fork into his mouth.

There were tears pouring out of my eyes now and there was a pain in my chest, but it was because of how hard we were laughing. I struggled to catch my breath as we all stood —well, Heath and I were doubled over at the scene in front of us.

Heath wiped the tears from his eyes. "Looks like you guys found the food."

"Yeah, sorry about that. We got a little hungry and carried away," Declan said as he swallowed.

"I can't believe you would desecrate my mother's cooking like this." Heath's big grin didn't hide an ounce of his amusement.

Mak's hands appeared on the top of Declan's shoulders, using him to obscure the view of her nearly-naked body. "We're really sorry. My stomach was growling, and Declan was trying to get some food into me before..." Her voice trailed off, and she buried her head in his back. "I'm going to go outside now and jump off the roof."

"Why don't you two go get some clothes on, and we can eat the food like we didn't walk out of a cave. Did you heat up the garlic bread?"

Both their heads whipped toward the fridge. "There's garlic bread?" They said it at the same time, and I had to squeeze my side at the stitch that formed there.

"Go get dressed. I'll heat it all up and we can have a real dinner, if you two can keep your hands off each other for two minutes."

"Look who's talking," Declan joked, walking sideways across the kitchen with Mak clinging to his back like a koala.

"Touché. We will turn our backs so you two can go upstairs, and then I'll start heating up the food. I take it from what you said about the garlic bread, that means you didn't find the brownies either."

We jumped out of the way and turned toward the living room wall as the two of them darted past us and upstairs. Heath took my hand, and his shoulders shook from laughter. After the weight of the world on my shoulders this morning, it was good to laugh and be around friends.

"You coming?" He tilted his head toward the kitchen as the bumping and thudding of Declan and Mak sounded overhead. The things people would do for Heath's mom's cooking.

We shoved a military battalion-sized worth of food into the oven and ate to our heart's content. The four of us rolled our way to the living room and turned on the TV to ride out our food coma.

I was curled into Heath's side when my phone went crazy on the living room table. We exchanged glances, and I picked it up. I'd already talked to my parents while the food was heating up about the meeting and how it went. They were over the moon and wanted to talk more when I got home.

The messages were rolling in so fast I could barely keep up.

Sam: Congrats!!

Anne: OMG! Congratulations!!

Charles: You did it! Wooohoo

I shrugged at Heath and replied.

Me: What the hell are you guys talking about?

Sam: OMFG Have you been living under a rock?! How did you miss the announcement?

Me: ???

Charles: You got the Stansfield Fellowship

I reread the message about ten times.

Me: No, I didn't. I told Stevenson to pull my application.

Anne: Well I guess she forgot.

I turned to Heath. "They said I got the fellowship."

Sam: Probably had her mouth too full of weasel dick

Me: WTF?!

Heath brightened and sat up, leaning over closer to my screen. I tried to scroll to the top of the messages when a phone call came in. It was Sam. I put it on speaker.

"You're on speaker. What is going on?"

"Where the hell have you been? Major craziness went down. Jason and Prof. Stevenson were having an affair. Her husband showed up at the school and also e-mailed all these texts and pictures they'd been exchanging to everyone in the program. Holy shit, it was so juicy. So she's on, like, a forced sabbatical, and they are going back through everything of Jason's she ever graded. He's not in the running for the fellowship, and yours was the best. They announced it by e-mail earlier today."

"Holy shit!" Heath jumped up and laughed even more. Declan and Mak stared at us both with their eyebrows furrowed.

"I'm not finishing the program."

Their shocked outbursts exploded from the phone.

"Kara, are you sure?" Heath's hand wrapped around my arm.

"I'm a hundred percent sure. Even more now. The fellowship isn't what I want anymore. I don't know if I ever wanted it in the first place. It was another way to prove that I was good enough, but I don't need that anymore." I trailed my fingers along the side of his face and tugged on his hair.

I took my phone off speaker. "You guys up for a drink?" I pulled the phone back at the high-pitched hell yeses from the other end.

I raked my fingers through my hair in a daze. "Wow," I said to no one since Declan and Mak were engrossed in Heath's dramatic retelling of the story of us.

"Yeah, wow, congrats, Kara!" Mak gave me a woohoo.

"I'm not taking it, though."

"Still, I say we celebrate." Heath jumped up from the couch. "You two up for a drink?"

I grinned at Heath. "The Bramble?"

"Of course!" they chorused.

He picked me up as I ended the call and spun me around.

"Let's go!" We all jumped up and grabbed a cab on our way to the place where it all began.

We showed up on the balmy June afternoon to meet Declan and Mak after the Rittenhouse Prep graduation. Mak wanted to show her support to Avery and Avery's little sister, Alyson, and where Mak went, Declan followed.

Kara fidgeted with her dress.

"Are you sure?"

"Of course. You've met everyone before." I tugged her in closer to me and ran my finger along her jaw.

"Not under the most ideal circumstances. This seems like a friends-and-family type of thing."

"And who do you think you are? You'd better get used to this motley crew because we're going to be seeing a lot of them. And they'll love you because I love you."

"Can I hear that one more time?" She looked up at me, her deep chestnut eyes making me forget what I was going to say.

"That they love you?"

She bumped against my shoulder. "You know what I want

to hear." Her fingers tickled the hair at the base of my neck, and I was tempted to find an abandoned classroom in the school to teach her a lesson about the unfairness of teasing me in public.

Pressing her against a tree that lined the sidewalk of the school, I buried my face in the nape of her neck.

"I love you," I repeated the words as I peppered her face with kisses.

She laughed and pushed me away as someone cleared their throat behind us.

"Looks like you two are cutting straight to the after-party." Colm laughed.

Kara's cheeks turned rosy red as she saw the entire Kings crew assembled beside us. She'd better get used to it. I couldn't keep my hands off her.

We walked in together so we could all sit together. It was strange being back at our old stomping grounds. Everything looked smaller and a little bit off how I'd pictured it in my mind.

Unlike Ford, I hadn't had a reason to come back since we'd thrown our hats up in the air in the air-conditioned auditorium four years ago. Showing our support for the next generation was what we did. We were a big family. Screwed up. Too loud and full of a shit ton of love.

A bunch of us had driven up to Boston to see Liv graduate as well. It was crazy to believe that Alyson, Grant, and Olivia would be starting college in a few months. Hell, I couldn't believe I'd graduated college and was officially a professional hockey player.

Olivia still had some local friends she kept in touch with, so she'd wanted to visit. We'd all be heading down to the shore after for a summer of sun before we kicked off the most grueling training of our lives.

"Does Emmett know we're returning his money for the shore house?"

"I don't know, but I'm sure he'll be pissed when he figures it out."

Emmett walked out on the stage with the rest of the board members of the school. He took his seat beside his parents, who were also members. His family had been big donors to the school since it opened over a hundred and fifty years ago. This would probably be the first time he'd been in a room with Avery in four years. At least a room he or she didn't immediately exit.

It wasn't until his eyes traveled down the line of people in our row that the thought kicked me in the back of the head.

"Did anyone tell him we were sitting with Avery?"

"I thought you did," Declan whispered back to me. Mak leaned over with an eyebrow raised.

"Shit."

Kara glanced over at me, and I took her hand and gave her a reassuring smile. This was not going to be good.

We all saw the second his eyes landed on Avery. She was at the end of the row with her graduation program folded on her lap. Emmett's back went ramrod straight, and he looked at us with his eyes wide with betrayal.

I mouthed *sorry*. With him on the West Coast, Avery had kind of become an occasional member of the group the last few months. We'd been pretty good about keeping them far apart, but a clash was bound to happen eventually.

The discomfort only got worse when Alyson stepped up to the podium as the valedictorian to give her speech.

"And there is one person I know I couldn't have done it without. My big sister, Avery. She's been there for me every step of the way from homework at the kitchen table to making sure I've got extra sunscreen on shore cleanup day. I love you, Ave."

Everyone in the auditorium clapped. The muscles in Emmett's neck strained as Alyson waxed poetic about what an amazing big sister she had. Avery wiped at the corners of her eyes and smiled so wide her cheeks had to hurt. None of us really knew what had happened that night in high school to split Emmett and Avery apart. Mak swore up and down that it wasn't what anyone thought, but she clammed up beyond that, saying it wasn't her place.

As the last of the students walked across the stage, my phone buzzed in my pocket. Everyone stood up and the place was abuzz with excitement for the new graduates.

Emmett: Can't make it to the shore. I hope you all have a great time.

Colm: Are you seriously going to bail on our first summer where we can all hang out in forever?

Ford: ...

Declan: Dude, get your head out of your ass, you're coming

Heath: Chill out and don't make us come get you

"Emmett!" Declan shouted, but his voice was drowned out over the enthusiastic, milling crowd leaving the graduation and snapping pictures. Ford, Colm, and Liv wove through the other people around us to get to me and Declan. Kara's gaze bounced between all of us.

I slid my hand into hers. "Don't worry, I'll explain it all later."

"I swear, this group has more drama..." She laughed.

Emmett: My parents invited me along for a vacation, so I'm going.

All of our heads whipped around. That was new. What the hell?

The level of BS in that statement was staggering.

Colm: Seriously?

Ford: What?

Obviously, I wasn't the only one surprised. We shrugged, not even sure of a comeback for that one. Absentee didn't even begin to describe Emmett's parents. They were more like ghosts. How else could we have had such awesome parties back in high school?

Emmett stared over our heads at Mak and Avery disappearing into the crowd with Alyson to get some pics. He spun on his heel and left the stage with his parents. Maybe it wasn't a bullshit excuse.

I shook my head, and Declan let out a frustrated sigh.

"We're going to lose him if they don't get this Avery thing figured out."

"Lose who?" Olivia poked her head into the mini huddle we'd created.

"Olive, let the grown-ups speak." Colm squeezed her out of our circle.

"I'll show you grown-up," Liv mumbled under her breath.

Colm snapped his lips in a tight line and turned back to me.

Emmett: I'm not coming.

Declan: She's not even going to be there. She's going to be around, Em. Maybe you two finally need to have that talk

Emmett: I'm not coming.

We spotted Mak, Avery, and Alyson outside. I kept my hand tight around Kara's, not wanting to lose her in the crowd.

Declan threw his arm around Mak and kissed her on the side of her head. "Emmett's not coming."

Mak gave him a sad smile. "I know you wanted him to be

there." Pressing her hand against his chest, she kissed him. We finally got outside in the bright, summer sun.

Avery hugged Alyson. They let go and Alyson climbed into a car with her friends. Grant did the same, hopping into his car with some other guys. With warnings from their older siblings to be safe and not get too crazy, Avery and Ford waved bye to them as they pulled out into the line of cars exiting the jam-packed parking lot.

We'd parked on the street a few blocks away since they'd reserved parking for students and some of the VIPs. Mak and Declan followed behind us as we rounded the corner.

"I'm hungry. You guys wants to get some food?" Everyone turned to the normally silent Ford. "What? I'm just saying, I could eat."

I laughed. "Definitely. Let's get some food. We'll need to find a place that's not packed with the post-graduation crowds."

"Avery is going to join us wherever we decide to eat," Mak said from under Declan's arm. Good thing Emmett hadn't decided to come with us.

After checking in on eight restaurants, we found one that could seat us.

Avery walked up to our group like she was approaching a den of vipers, but visibly relaxed when she saw there wasn't a certain King there with us. We went inside and ordered drinks.

"Wow, I can't believe they're off to school already." Avery read over her menu.

"Not yet, they still have the summer," Colm said, breaking off from his little spat with Olivia. She glared back at him and crossed her arms over her chest.

"Not for Alyson, she's got a college enrichment program. She leaves tomorrow. I won't see her until I show up for

Family Day at the beginning of the school year. I don't even know what to do with myself. The house is going to feel so empty." She stuck the program into her bag.

"Why don't you come to the shore with us?" Mak blurted out.

Our entire group froze.

"Uhh, I don't think that would be a good idea," Declan said beside her.

"Why not?"

"Mak, no. Don't be silly. I'd have to take off work, and it's short notice, and I've been saving up for school. I don't have money to chip in, and I'm not going mooch off you guys. Don't worry about it." Avery glanced between all of us. She'd been one of us when she was with Emmett. Since they had been joined at the hip, where he went, she went, and that was usually with us—until it all fell apart.

"Don't worry about it, Avery. You should come," Colm said without looking up from his menu.

All our eyes shot to him.

"Really, it's not that big of a deal, I wasn't saying anything to get you guys to feel sorry for me. I know things are weird for all of us now. I'm not trying to make waves." Avery fidgeted in her seat.

Kara's eyebrows wrinkled.

Declan, Ford, and I exchanged glances. "Avery, seriously. We'd like you to come. It will be fun, and I know Mak, Liv, and Kara would appreciate a little more estrogen to balance the scales. And, Emmett's not going to be there." I addressed the elephant in the room, smiled at her, and her shoulders relaxed.

Avery bit her bottom lip. "I'll see what I can do work-wise. Maybe come down for a week or maybe a weekend."

"Whatever works for you." Mak practically bounced in

her seat.

And Avery did come down. She made it a week after we arrived. The house was amazing, as expected from Emmett. It was a six-bedroom wonder right on the beach with wrap around balconies and everything we would need for an unforgettable summer.

"Avery! You made it." Mak tipsily hugged her as we finished up our game of beer pong.

Kara sank the last ball into the red plastic cup on the other side of the table. She wrapped her arms around me, and I swung her around.

"Reigning champions!" She kissed along my neck. There were no more worries about public displays of affection between us. We were completely and totally open with each other and everyone else.

Mak showed Avery to the single empty bedroom on the first floor. Avery dropped off her things and came back out to join the party. Music from high school spilled out of the speakers, bringing back intense nostalgia.

The girls all disappeared into the kitchen laughing and determined to make up a new shot for everyone to try. Olivia was allowed to join under the threat of torture by Colm if she didn't stick to the root beer.

"I bet you twenty bucks whatever shot they come out here with is going to be pink," Ford said, looking up from his beer.

"I'll take that bet. Kara's a straight up vodka drinker. She'll be able to persuade them." I hopped off the stool and threw down the money.

"We've got another ten weeks in this house. Please let's try to keep this place in good shape," Colm said, sternly.

"Thanks, Dad. Have you met us? We never once trashed

Emmett's place, and it was like a museum in there." I took a sip of my beer.

"Speaking of. Has anyone heard from Emmett?" Declan glanced between all of us.

"Nope." Ford picked up a ping pong ball and bounced it on his palm.

We all shook our heads.

The front door swung open, and we all turned to see who it was. Emmett.

He dropped his bag by the front door. "I told my parents no way was I missing out on our epic last summer together, so here I am." He stood with his arms wide open and a huge smile on his face.

The ping pong ball Ford had been bouncing clattered to the floor.

"Don't all look so happy to see me." Emmett dropped his arms and strode closer to our party set up.

"Okay guys, I think you're going to love these. We were going for a cotton candy flavor." Mak came out first and skidded to a halt when she saw our new arrival.

It caused a pile up and Avery shouted, "Jesus Mak, you almost made me drop the tray." Avery stepped out from behind Mak and stopped dead in her tracks.

Emmett's gaze snapped to hers.

"What the hell are *you* doing here?" They both shouted at the same time, staring wide eyed at one another.

"Oh shit." Ford muttered.

Kara stepped up from behind Mak and Avery. "Okay, *now* will someone explain this history to me? I've been dying to know what the hell is going on!"

～

Thank you for reading RECKLESS KING! I hope you loved Heath and Kara!

If you haven't had enough of Heath and Kara, check out there extended epilogue HERE!

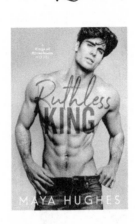

My dick never got me in half as much trouble as my heart...

We were high school sweethearts. I was head over heels for her and no one could tell me we weren't going to last forever. College? Going pro? My family's money? None of it mattered. She was all I needed.

Then she ripped my heart out. But I'm not going to let that happen again.

She's back. Invading my life and acting like she was the wronged one. The pain is still there, but I can't keep my eyes off her. I can't stop thinking about her and how much was left unsaid between us. Being this close is making me question everything I thought I knew about her.

This time everything will be on my terms. Everything...

Emmett and Avery's story is here and ready to bring all the feels! Grab your copy or read it for FREE in KU!

Looking for another sweet and steamy sports romance read?

The Perfect First - Reece + Seph

The Second We Met - Nix + Elle

AUTHOR'S NOTE

Thank you so much for taking the time to read Reckless King! Heath and Kara's story was special to me for so many reasons and I hope you enjoyed their journey.

This series is really personal to me because of all the changes in my life in the past year. August 19th is the one year anniversary of my mother's death and my writing has helped me get through this difficult time.

Love and loss are such important parts of live and that can present itself in many different ways.

To answer some of the questions I've gotten about the Kings and this book in particular:

1) Imogen will get her own book :)

2) Emmett and Avery's story, an enemies-to-lovers, second chance romance is here - Ruthless King!

3) Ford and Liv's story unfolds in Fearless King

4) Colm's book is also in the works - Heartless King ;)

Thank you again for reading and I hope you'll follow the Kings on the rest of their journeys.

<3

Maya xx

ACKNOWLEDGMENTS

It seems that the more books I release, the list of people I need to thank gets even longer. To amazing friends I've gained in the community, I don't even have words. You've helped talk me off a ledge so many times, held my hand through plotting and releases and been a shoulder I can lean on whenever I need it

To my editors, Lea Schaffer, Tamara Mataya and Anka. I couldn't imagine publishing a book without you even if I have to read your comments through my fingers sometimes.

To every awesome blogger, bookstagrammer and reader who helped spread the word about this book and made me cry with their kind words and shouting from the rooftops about Reckless King!!

And to *you* reading this, thank you so much. Every one of these stories means the world to me and I am always amazed at how welcoming everyone is to my characters. Thank you a million times and I can't wait for you to meet the rest of the Kings!!

<3
~Maya

ALSO BY MAYA HUGHES

Kings of Rittenhouse

Kings of Rittenhouse - FREE

Shameless King - Enemies to Lovers

Reckless King - Off Limits Lover

Ruthless King - Second Chance Romance

Fearless King - Brother's Best Friend

Manhattan Misters

All His Secrets - Single Dad Romance

All His Lies - Revenge Romance

All His Regrets - Second Chance Romance

Under His Series

Under His Ink - Second Chance Romance

Breaking Free Series

Blinded - Second Chance Secret Baby Romance

Mixed - Enemies to Lovers Romance

Served - Enemies to Lovers Romance

Rocked - Rockstar Romance

Standalone

Passion on the Pitch - Sports Romance